ROBERT WILSON
AND THE
INVASION FROM WITHIN

D0062810

SCOTT RUESTERHOLZ

PERMUTED
PRESS

A PERMUTED PRESS BOOK
ISBN: 978-1-64293-928-6
ISBN (eBook): 978-1-64293-929-3

Cover art by Cody Corcoran

PERMUTED
PRESS

Permuted Press, LLC
New York • Nashville
permutedpress.com

Published in the United States of America
1 2 3 4 5 6 7 8 9 10
Printed in Canada

For Katie, my sister and best friend.

CHAPTER 1

The Ice Planet Killjorn
Earth Year 2014

In the far reaches of the Milky Way galaxy, the planet Killjorn sits isolated, making its lonely loops around its distant white dwarf sun. Formerly a trading outpost, Killjorn is now home to an elite training program for advance infiltration agents of the League of Planets. Formed over two hundred Earth years ago, the League was intended to be a cooperative among several planets where intelligent life had developed hyperdrive via the construction of traversable wormholes, permitting speedy interplanetary travel. However, as time passed and ambitions grew, the quest for absolute power proved unquenchable, despite the spillage of untold blood and fortune.

While much history has been lost or erased—leaving only half-forgotten memories and legend—in recent decades, the League has been nothing more than an ever-expanding empire. Sitting atop the throne is Supreme General of the

League Council Anton Frozos. First serving as a leading military commander at the age of twenty on the Eastern Frontier, amassing significant territory and natural resources to feed the League's ever-growing need for nuclear fuel and food, Frozos would leverage his popularity among the troops to take control of the Council by force at the age of twenty-five, nearly fifteen years ago.

At six foot five inches, his pale blue-skinned frame, fiery red eyes, and short white hair casts a dominating figure that combines with a deep, booming voice to instill drive in his soldiers and terror in political opponents. Today, he enjoys total political power, with the Council serving only ceremonial purpose. The combination of an ever-expanding planet count, providing with it a fresh supply of slave labor and heavy surveillance has brought stability. For now, a consistent supply of food has been worth the price of lost freedom for most of his subjects. Significant rebel activity hasn't been spotted for years, leaving the discontent to wonder if the rebel cause was little more than legend anymore.

Today, Frozos is visiting the Planet Killjorn to pick one pupil for a critical mission in the expansion of the League. Students have been subjected to intense training, physical and mental, to be a new breed of soldiers beyond the front lines as Frozos seeks to expand his intergalactic power. They will be sent to the far reaches of the universe to nascent intelligent civilizations, laying the groundwork for a planned invasion, perhaps in months, perhaps in years. Lying in wait, and with knowledge of far advanced technology, finance, and military strategy, these soldiers should be positioned to quickly climb social, economic, and political ladders, weakening institutions from within and priming the planet for easy conquest.

Frozos stands in a spartan cafeteria where graduating students, ranging from fifteen to twenty-five years of age, have eaten every meal for at least three years. There are ten such facilities on Killjorn. While it will be a long day of ceremony, Frozos enjoys this annual tradition, for he suspects his eventual successor would be a graduate of this scouting program. To minimize the risk of being discovered on their future planet, no two students from the same class are sent to the same planet, and there is absolutely no interaction between facilities. Each are to act as individual scouts, unless and until the League gives orders otherwise.

This gray-tiled room has been repurposed for today's ceremony with the twenty-five graduates standing at attention in blue coveralls in front of a modestly raised stage. For each of these groups of graduates, approximately eight prospects failed. To ensure the absolute secrecy of the program, those who fail out are sentenced to a quick and unappealable death sentence. Standing to each side of Frozos are half a dozen instructors—stern-faced men and women of varying species—who have overseen these young spies' development. On his left, there is a desk topped with envelopes.

Taking to the lectern, Frozos offers brief remarks: "Congratulations on reaching this point—a pinnacle of achievement most can only dream of. You will now play a critical role in ensuring the safety and security of this great League of Planets, home to more than 1.25 trillion souls. While our security services maintain peace and order, it is up to you to scout for sources of food, resources, fuel, and paths of transport. We can ensure peace and security today, but it is your sacred duty to lay the groundwork for our future peace and security.

"You will be entering societies that may feel foreign or backwards, but be comforted by the fact we will be coming to bring you home and pull the poor, feeble residents of your planet into the future at a pace they could not otherwise achieve. It will be your job to facilitate their entrance into the League as smoothly as is possible. I know you will succeed."

Frozos now steps aside from the lectern, allowing the Director, a pudgy, balding humanoid, to take his place. The Director begins calling the names of the graduates one-by-one, from last to first in the class. They walk on stage, shake General Frozos's hand, take their envelope, and walk out to their room where they will open the letter and discover their assignment.

The final student, the valedictorian, thanks to unparalleled technology scores as well as a high emotional quotient, and despite only median military strategy scores, is seventeen Earth years and is now standing alone. Born of the planet Nayan, Marcus Natent is virtually identical to humans on the outside, except that his life expectancy is closer to 150 Earth years. Given the rugged life on this mining planet, Nayans also have rapidly coagulating blood, healing skin, and a second heart behind the lower abdomen. He stands five foot nine inches tall, with short but messy black hair, and thoughtful brown eyes. He stands, jaw clenched, firmly at attention.

Frozos walks off stage to him, as he did for each valedictorian. Extending his hand, he says, "Congratulations, son. Come with me, and let's discuss your future."

"Thank you, Supreme General; it would be an honor."

Together, they make the short walk to a small adjoining room, taking seats at a small wooden table. To enjoy such an intimate audience with Frozos would be the ultimate honor for any military recruit.

"You know, Marcus, of course, that you are the first Nayan to graduate this program. We are fortunate Admiral Tyrone Tiberius saw your potential and pulled you up from a life working the Nayan mines."

Marcus concurs, "Yes, I saw firsthand how years of toiling at that mine crushed my father's will. I am fortunate the League opened such opportunity to me. I look forward to gifting the same opportunity to a new planet."

Handing Marcus the envelope, the general said, "Good. In there, you'll find the details of your assignment. Given your unique skillset, we are giving you a long-term mission. You will be heading to Earth, a planet we anticipate reaching in fifteen of what you will soon know as 'years.' Earth is critical to the next phase of our development. In addition to significant natural resource potential and an innovative, albeit backwards and tribal population, Earth sits near the linchpin of our transportation strategy. Within three to five years, we will have saturated this portion of the galaxy. To meet the needs of our growing population, we must be able to travel quickly and safely to the far end of this galaxy, which is ruled by a collection of small-minded despots. We are in early stages of building a large-scale web of speedways where we can quickly move tankers of troops to expand outward and secure sup-ply-lines. In every design, our engineers map out Earth as the central point of this wormhole system. We must control Earth to protect troops in passage and eventually secure food and supply lines back home from rebels and pirates."

"I see, sir. It is an honor to be assigned to such a critical planet to our expansion plans."

"It is. Earth is our longest-range project in this program. With your skills, you should be able to gradually attain sig-nificant power. When we make contact with Earth, you can use that power to persuade the human race to quickly and peacefully join the League. From there, with our superhigh-way complete, the universe will be in the palm of our hands. Do not fail us. Do not fail me."

And with that, Frozos stands up, gives Marcus a pat on the back, and leaves him alone to read the details of his assign-ment. Details he will memorize during his ten month jour-ney to Earth.

Marcus opens the envelope to see what his new name will be: "Robert Wilson." Taking a red pen out of his pocket, Marcus writes next to his new name:

REMEMBER THE MINE

Putting the paper back in the envelope, Marcus gets up and walks out of the room to begin his new life.

CHAPTER 2

Jersey City, New Jersey
November 15, 2028

obert Wilson stares out of his office window. Today is a momentous day, an unveiling of his masterpiece, a new headquarters for his company, Arbor Ridge. Standing tall in Jersey City, New Jersey, the sleek silver structure holds seventy stories of offices. On the northeast corner, extending from the ground level, is a purple spire that reaches 125 stories into the sky.

To build this one structure in eighteen months would have been impressive, but this was a project on a global scale with buildings constructed around the world, just outside the major cities of Los Angeles; Vancouver, Canada; São Paulo, Brazil; Bogota, Colombia; London, England; Moscow, Russia; Cape Town, South Africa; Dubai; Sydney, Australia; Hanoi, Vietnam; and Tokyo, Japan. Together these twelve buildings, costing a combined $20 billion, will be the work home to over

130,000 employees and serve as a command hub for regional operations. While each building's habitable space ranged from forty to seventy stories, depending on regional needs, all have the same 125-story purple spire—a universal corporate emblem of sorts.

Staring out at the Manhattan skyline, Robert can't help but feel satisfied with proving the naysayers wrong and finishing this project on time. With these towers, Arbor Ridge is staking its claim as a global behemoth—the largest and most powerful company on the planet, worth over $11 trillion, and he owns 80 percent of it. It has been a long, exciting thirteen years on Earth, but Robert is finally positioned as necessary and is prepared for the looming inevitability.

Arriving on Earth in 2015, Marcus assumed the identity of Robert Wilson, created in advance by Frozos's army of cyber hackers. Records showed he was homeschooled by reclusive parents in rural Wyoming, and he had been accepted into the incoming freshman class at Yale University. His parents were "killed" in a staged car accident on his way to Yale. Free of potential complications, it was from here that Robert began his mission.

Given his advanced technological knowledge, Robert saw this as his clearest path to power. He partnered with two students he befriended at Yale: Chris Bailey, who showed a gift for financial matters, and Mark Morrison, who would aid in marketing given Robert's lack of knowledge about America's culture, which was excusable given his supposedly cloistered upbringing. Chris and Mark remain alongside Robert to this day at Arbor Ridge, each owning about 5 percent of the shares. While Robert has never disclosed his secret to them, neither man is a fool, and they recognize something beyond their grasp is at work.

Beginning in mobile games, Robert had "created" several viral apps (in reality, they were just adapted versions of games that had proven popular in the League of Planets) by December of 2015, making him one of the youngest billionaires on the planet. Dropping out of school after their first semester, building the business became the full-time focus of these three friends. Again focusing on inventing things that had already been invented a galaxy away, Robert pivoted his focus to defense contract work, showing the American government satellite and missile defense technology that was decades beyond what existing companies could offer.

Robert has carefully established his public image over the years, cultivated by a burgeoning gaming and consumer electronics empire, unparalleled technology, and help from select members of Congress, namely a young, ambitious congressman from the state of Florida: Nick Neverian. While there was initial difficulty in convincing the U.S. government to sign multiyear defense contracts worth billions with someone who still couldn't legally purchase a beer, his stature as boy-genius eventually made Arbor Ridge the top defense contractor for the Air Force as well as America's military allies. From 2015 to 2022, the focus remained exclusively on consumer electronics, gaming, and a near monopoly in virtual reality technology, anchored by the *Galactic Flyer* gaming franchise, as well as the defense business, which was rapidly expanding into Space. Arbor Ridge was the country's most valuable company, enjoying steady, unprecedented profit growth, and Robert's innovations were credited with spurring a productivity revolution, greatly accelerating economic growth.

But in 2022, Robert abruptly shifted Arbor Ridge's strategy, greatly widening the focus of the company. Inventing massive industrial batteries and transmission systems that could power cities for days, Arbor Ridge began acquiring electric utility companies, long seen as boring, stodgy businesses. Expanding further afield in ensuing years, Arbor Ridge began acquiring global food and beverage companies, deep sea drilling firms, a wireless telecommunications company, and transportation companies, from railroads to air cargo companies.

By the end of 2026, Arbor Ridge was a verifiable conglomerate, the leading company on the planet in defense, consumer electronics, virtual reality gaming, food, electricity generation, and transportation. The company even operated a research base on the moon. Even if there were a logic behind the seemingly random pattern of purchases, it was not apparent to the outside world. That said, there was a clear pattern of behavior post purchase: increase research and development investment, fire the CEO and much of senior management, and give rank and file employees 5 to 15 percent raises to improve morale, boost profit sharing, and lower turnover. Robert focused his energy on managing the operations, but it was Chris's job to manage the finances and essentially keep Robert from buying too many businesses. As it was, internal business investment was running so high on undisclosed long-term projects that Robert turned down his dividends to fund this investment,

ROBERT WILSON AND THE INVASION FROM WITHIN

for he was wary of borrowing money and wanted to ensure dividend payments to the 10 percent of the company owned by the public, including his nearly seven million employees, would be uninterrupted. While many questioned the tens of billions being invested each quarter, there was little pushback since it was essentially his money.

Meanwhile, Mark, whose job had always focused on maintaining Arbor Ridge's brand, was increasingly focused on strengthening relationships with government regulators who worried over how much power Arbor Ridge was amassing across multiple industries. His efforts were aided by the public's strongly favorable view towards the company, thanks to its cutting edge technology and gaming business, well-publicized pro-employee pay practices, and the fact that the economy was booming past any previous projections, a boom often credited to the leap forward in technology Arbor Ridge had brought. The American economy was poised to pass $55 trillion, growing a previously unthinkable 8 percent per year, and with an estimated one in seven American households reliant on Arbor Ridge for their income—either because someone worked for the company or one of its suppliers—the boom times were being widely enjoyed.

Since the end of 2026, Robert has essentially stopped his acquisition spree, apart from buying an American 24/7 news channel, *Headlines Now*, in early 2028, focusing instead on fully integrating all the new businesses, boosting internal business investment, and launching his great towers project. Now, in November 2028, the projects are done, and it is time to show them to the world.

15

Mark and Chris walk into Robert's office on the seventieth floor. The space is sleek and relatively modest, with grey carpets and a glass desk with three steel-framed chairs. On one wall hang several TVs showing various news channels, and behind the desk stands a bookcase, where several photos of key moments over the past thirteen years are scattered.

Robert turns to greet them, happy to see his friends and partners. "Morning, guys. Mark, is everything all set downstairs?"

Mark responds, "Yes, boss. We're ready whenever you are, but I think Chris has some finance stuff for you to go over—"

Chris quickly chimes in, "Yeah, nothing major—it can wait until after the events this morning, but there are some questions over the material costs for the buildings."

With a knowing hand gesture and unable to conceal a subtle smile, Robert can't help but ask, "Let me guess. It looks like we bought more steel and concrete than needed to build structures as tall as these?"

Chris says, "Yep, and beyond the excess billing we'd expect from the construction industry, given their standard graft."

Robert nods. "Okay. Let's talk about it this afternoon. It seems you, like just about everybody, are too focused on how tall they are and not what's underneath them. Frankly, I'm a bit disappointed it took you this long to question the numbers. You're getting a bit lazy, Chris!"

All three knew of course that Chris had a sense the numbers didn't quite add up for some time, but these towers were funded by the dividend payments Robert declined, and Chris never worried as much about that spending. As far as he's concerned, it's Robert's money anyway, and if he wants to waste it or keep its purpose secret, that's his business.

Together, the three founders take the elevator back down to the lobby. Robert checks his appearance in the mirrored walls. He's wearing a slightly different outfit to Mark and Chris, who wear suits with no ties. In the early days of the company, Mark suggested to Robert that he use his wardrobe to develop a personal brand, pointing out how other visionaries like Steve Jobs, with his trademark black turtleneck, could better ingrain themselves in the public consciousness this way. And so, as with every major product launch and company announcement, Robert is wearing a white t-shirt, black suit jacket with an American flag lapel pin, and dark jeans. Even though at first he'd found the whole show annoying, Robert has come to recognize the performance art necessary in his role and appreciates the wisdom of Mark's advice, even if he has grown weary of the t-shirts. He's now thirty-one, and his frame has filled out since leaving Killjorn. His hair a bit tamer and trimmer, and his eyes betray a man contemplating deep thoughts, even if few of those thoughts are ever revealed beyond his close inner circle.

The lobby, as in each building, is a grand five-story atrium, mostly open to the public with the latest games and consumer products on display for test trials. And at the center stands a magnificent oak tree, basking in the natural light from the surrounding window facades.

Robert is scheduled to begin this morning with an interview on the leading business channel. He's prepared for a wide array of topics, from the purpose of these buildings, to last week's Presidential Election.

Congressman Nick Neverian has taken the political world by storm, bringing the opposition back into power. While his victory seemed likely in the closing stretch of the campaign, his forty-state romping with nearly 60 percent of the vote surprised nearly everyone. While Neverian helped Arbor Ridge secure its first government contracts over a decade ago, he had campaigned on cutting defense spending, given a world at peace, and made implicit criticisms of the company's growing size. Arbor Ridge shares are down around 7 percent in the past week, wiping out nearly $900 billion in value. It has been an interesting time.

With Mark and Chris in the background to cheer him on, Robert takes his seat under the hot, shining lights across from morning anchor Jim Storks, a fair interviewer Robert had spoken with countless times before. After a handshake and quick hellos, the red light flips on; they are live.

Right on cue, Storks speaks into the camera. "Good morning from 111 Park Plaza in Jersey City—Arbor Ridge's new global headquarters. We are lucky to have on with us today Robert Wilson. Morning, Robert. We've been touring around the building earlier, and I must say, it's magnificent."

"Thanks, Jim. It's a pleasure to have you and your crew here this morning as we formally open this global headquarters and eleven regional ones."

"Now, Robert, I know you've addressed the issue quite often during construction, but now that this project is complete. What does it show? Was it worth the twenty, twenty-something—"

"Twenty billion dollars, not twenty-something. Just twenty billion," Robert interjected.

"Sure, Okay. Twenty billion dollars. On budget and on time, we know! But was this an investment worth making?" Storks asks.

"Absolutely, Jim. A luxury of being such a closely held company is that we can think for the long term, a luxury most public companies lack. And we've shown to be good long-term planners. The mere existence of these buildings, frankly, with their stunning purple spires, will lift the Arbor Ridge brand, particularly overseas where we are still less well known. In a sense, part of the expense can be justified from a marketing perspective. More importantly, we are centralizing operations across departments to create a cross-fertilization of ideas. Most of management will work in these buildings, which we hope will become innovation centers. Lastly, from each building, employees can easily travel to key manufacturing facilities. In fact, this building has two key factories within five miles. You'll see operating performance improve; I guarantee it."

In the background, Robert sees Chris cringe; he was never supposed to promise or "guarantee" better financial results, but he can never do these interviews without annoying Chris, if only for the fun of it. And as he sees it, most of his promises were later proven right. After several more business questions, the interview shifts towards politics.

Storks asks, "So, Robert, I have to ask about last week's Presidential Election. As has been your norm, you stayed silent on the election. Given the beating your stock has taken, was that a mistake? Are you worried about President Neverian's impact on Arbor Ridge?"

"Jim, everyone makes mistakes, and unfortunately for the people who sold Arbor Ridge's stock post-election, they did just that—"

Storks interrupts, "So you think the eight percent drop isn't warranted, despite Neverian talking about opening up the defense bidding process to diversify contracting work at the Pentagon?"

"Yes, I feel as optimistic about my company's potential as I did two weeks ago. We have the greatest employees on the planet, so we'll continue to win day in and day out. Listen, I'm not going to get into politics. That isn't my job, and I don't want to mix any personal views with my professional responsibilities to my shareholders and to my employees. Here's what I will say. We got a foothold in defense contracts for two reasons. First, we had the best technology. Second, there was a competitive process, thanks to pushes from members of Congress like the President-Elect, to pick the best products, even if they came from small companies. I want today's entrepreneurs to have a fair shot, which I think is what's being proposed. There won't be a diversity of suppliers for the sake of it, and I'm happy to have a competitive bidding process because frankly, we still have the best products and most innovative technology. Our work in defense shields, on the moon, and in space travel are without parallel."

"But is that still true?" Storks asks. "Some competitors are trying to increase the use of drones and pilot-free fighter aircrafts while you still require pilots. Are you missing something?"

"No. We think computer-operated crafts can handle logistical work and other tasks, but in combat, I firmly believe in the human element. Because computer programs will always choose the optimal choice, they actually can be predictable. The unpredictability of the human element, the occasional misstep, can actually be an asset in battle. I want our future to be in the hands of trained Americans, not a computer company, and I'm prepared to bet our combat aircraft program on that belief," Robert says.

"Okay. Speaking of human pilots, I'm told you have an announcement for us?"

"Umm, yes, we do. As you know, *Galactic Flyer* is the most popular VR game in history with over 250 million active users, and our most recent adaption, *Invasion*, released in August, offered a competition. The ten best players of ages eighteen to twenty-five, who could lead their squadrons in our multiplayer universe, would get a one-year paid internship here at Arbor Ridge. I'm happy to introduce you to our winners, who come from all around the world."

Robert gets out of his chair, with the camera panning as he walks over to greet the ten winners—six men and four women. Within the group, there are four Americans, Mike Murphy, Anna Small, Jerome Smith, and Angela Perez; one Englishman, Adrian Murray; a Russian, Dmitry Ivanov; a Brazilian, Paulo Cruz; an Australian, Samantha Sharp; a South Korean, Kim Ji-Yoo; and a German, Karl Muller. Each is introduced on camera, with their proud, beaming families behind them.

Returning to the interview, Storks continues, "Very cool moment, indeed. I'm sure they are very excited to begin their internship here. Finally, Robert—one last question. There's been a lot of attention paid to your acquisition of *Headlines Now* earlier this year, particularly given your stated apolitical nature. Why'd you buy it if not to drive a political narrative?"

Shrugging, Roberts replies, "Jim, don't be silly. The news operation is run entirely separately, and we play no role in its coverage. Why'd I buy it, apart from its nice profits? Well, I was told billionaires are supposed to buy newspapers and sports teams, and so I bowed to the social convention, assuming the same was true of trillionaires, and figured why not buy a news channel? But don't worry, Jim, you'll still get exclusive interviews!"

And with a quick handshake, Robert is off-camera. Tailed by Mark and Chris, Robert begins greeting all of the Arbor Ridge employees arriving for their first day in the new headquarters. Shaking hands, taking photos, and making small talk—this is among Robert's favorite parts of his job. After nearly an hour of this, it is time to get on with the day and finally address Chris's questions.

CHAPTER 3

Jersey City, NJ
November 15, 2028

Robert, Mark, and Chris walk back into his office. Before settling into his chair, Robert pours himself a glass of water, offering the same to his friends with Chris accepting. Chris takes a big gulp before settling into his seat. Clearly uncomfortable, Robert notices him shooting Mark a nervous look. Undoubtedly, they had been gaming out this conversation for days. Even though they've known each other for over a decade, Chris hates asking pointed questions. Robert never liked being backed into a corner, and they've grown accustomed to his secrecy. At the very least, they wouldn't have to lie if they didn't know all the real answers, and problems always seemed to find a way of working themselves out in the end for Robert, at least so far.

Chris begins, or really, stammers, "So, Robert, these per unit numbers don't make sense."

Robert interjects, "Let me interrupt, Chris. We used at least a third more concrete than was needed, twenty-five percent more steel, twenty percent more of other products, and that isn't even accounting for some confusing figures around the cost of the spires."

Chris says, "Well, yes that all sounds roughly correct. The reason we are raising this is…"

Seeing his opportunity to focus the conversation, Mark jumps in, "Listen, Robert. Neither Chris nor I care about the exact particulars. We are just making sure that project costs aren't being spread across different projects. Neverian has made clear he plans on cracking down on defense contracts, looking to see if excess cost is being added to baselines to boost profits. Because defense still provides the base cash flow for our operating budget, we just want to be sure we aren't exposing ourselves here to other accounting issues and contract repricing."

Robert gets out of his chair to look out his window where he has a spectacular view of Lower Manhattan, contemplating how he should respond.

Chris adds, "The other thing is that Neverian's likeliest nominees to the SEC and Department of Justice have talked about accounting scrutiny. I think this is code for digging into our massive capital expenditures and whether we need to write down the value of our assets, given it's unclear if they are generating any new cash flow. There will be questions about 'Project Ridley.'"

Project Ridley had been a secret investment program under Robert's exclusive purview. It had been up and running for five years and consumed most of Robert's time the past two years, coinciding with the end of his acquisition spree of other companies. Over the past five years, over $750 billion had been spent on the project with spending continuing to accelerate. Aside from $20 billion on the buildings, Chris and Mark didn't know what Ridley was about. In fact, Robert didn't think Chris or Mark had ever even mentioned it by name to him before.

Turning with a wry smile, Robert deadpans, "If you wanted to know what Project Ridley was, you could have just asked."

"Well, we're asking now. And come January twentieth, which is the President's Inauguration Day, we won't be the only ones," Mark says.

"I know," responds Robert, who then pulls the book *Great Expectations* off his bookshelf behind the desk and presses a button behind it. The bookshelf opens like a door, revealing an elevator. "Come, I think you'll find an accounting probe is really the least of our problems."

The three men get into the elevator and Robert presses the button marked "Basement 12."

Chris says dryly, "These buildings are only supposed to have seven basement floors. I guess we know where the extra concrete went."

"Well, Chris, you're not as dumb as you look," jokes Mark, to which Robert chimes in, "It's not as if you figured it out either, Mark."

Finally, the elevator doors open—they've reached Basement 12, more than 150 feet below ground level. They walk onto a cavernous, buzzing factory floor. Mark and Chris recognize the basic layout as similar to that of the fighter jet factories. There are four assembly lines, each with several planes in varying stages of production. The planes must look oddly familiar, though Mark and Chris wouldn't quite be able to place them as being a known product. Their wingspan must be thirty-five to forty feet long, with what appears to be a single seat and a single engine. The planes look to be entirely black except for two gold stripes down the end of each wing.

The factory is buzzing with robots and human labor alike, there are at least a hundred workers in navy-blue jumpsuits—how they got here is a mystery to Mark and Chris. As they continue across the factory floor, two long tunnels laid with railway track come into view. As they walk, the workers continue about their jobs, which strikes the two co-founders as surprising. Normally, Robert's presence ground a factory floor to a halt as workers tried to talk to him. It is clear to them that his presence is routine around here.

They've now reached the end of the line, standing next to a nearly completed plane. Robert turns to them and says, "So now you can see where those extra building materials went. Money well spent I think."

"I'm guessing we built twelve of these, didn't we?" asks Chris.

"Oh at least. There's one under every new tower, perhaps a handful scattered elsewhere."

"And those tunnels," Mark points.

"Well, how do you think we get the men and supplies down here each day? As you know, I made sure every tower we built wasn't just near a major city but also within a few miles of existing factories. That way we can funnel the product through those factories and down here. Everyone at the factories just thinks there's a separate project going on, there's no need for them to know the extent of it," Robert responds.

"Okay, so I see the money we spent on steel and concrete went to use, but what about all the money building the planes? What are we getting for that?" Mark asks.

"I was waiting for you to ask. Come." With that, Robert gestures to an open elevator bay that a finished plane is being rolled onto. They hop on alongside it, and the elevator begins to lower.

A puzzled Chris can't help himself. "The only thing I don't get is how you built these while building the towers and no one noticed."

"That's simple, Chris," a beaming Robert boasts. "This was all built before the towers, and we just put the towers right on top of them with only a single elevator bay connecting them, from my private office in each building. Much more discreet that way, don't you think?"

Mark and Chris can't help but chuckle to themselves. Having travelled at least another thirty feet underground, Robert is pleased to see the stunned looks on their faces as they see dozens, maybe even a hundred completed planes.

Knowing what they were about to ask, Robert jumps in, "So there are seven storage floors, each housing 108 units. We have just stocked up five floors. That's 540 jets. Across the twelve towers, we should be nearing 6,500 with a smattering elsewhere. We're on track to complete this stage of the program by March first, 2029, just in time, I'm hoping."

"For what?" asks Chris.

"Come, let's go into my office. No one on the floor here knows the purpose of their work, but it's time to let some friends in on it."

Robert slides a card through a scanner, then does a palm and a retina scan. The doors open, and they enter his office. It's not really an office so much as another steel room, windowless with no decorations. It could easily be confused with a jail cell, except in the back is a black metallic sphere, perhaps with a twenty-five-foot diameter. There are wires coming out of it, attached to what appeared to be a giant mainframe and several large computer monitors. Robert is sure Mark and Chris will recognize some of the programs from the space communications systems the company sells, but the language on the screen will be unrecognizable. It appears to also be tracking other communications with red dots percolating in several regions. On a table lie notes with "BEIJING" and "WASHINGTON" written in block letters across the top.

"Take a seat, we may be here awhile." Robert gestures towards three folding chairs. Luxury is in short supply down here. The three men settle into their chairs.

"So, I bet you're wondering why I'm building an Air Force. Well, it's not quite that, but we'll get there. Just remember, more than anything else, I need you to trust me right now. I need your trust." With a reassuring nod from his two true friends on this planet, Robert resumes: "Let's start at the beginning—actually more from the middle. You see, I'm not exactly from Wyoming…"

CHAPTER 4

The White House
March 30, 2029

President Nick Neverian is nearing the end of his first hundred days in office. The first hundred days are critical to setting the stage for the success or failure of a Presidency, as they often prove to be among the most productive. Having won a surprisingly large victory in 2028, Neverian has continued to build upon his popularity, sporting an over 70 percent approval rating among the American people who have rallied behind his anti-corruption message.

His Attorney General, Brian Braddock, has been leading this effort. A stout man of five foot ten inches, he is relentless and pugnacious. He spent much of his career in business, ascending to the top of one of the world's largest food and beverage companies. Just over three years ago, Robert Wilson took over Braddock's company in an ugly affair that culminated in Braddock's ousting. There was no love lost between the two men. It was clear to the world why Braddock had been given the Attorney General job.

Neverian had given Braddock broad discretion to oversee probes into Corporate America, and Braddock, in just three months, had certainly uncovered significant wrongdoing. Nearly every large government contractor, particularly those in the defense sector, was found to have grown a bit lackadaisical in their accounting, and it seemed like every error cost taxpayers more and goosed the bottom line. Thus far, he had reached settlements with dozens of companies, netting the government over $40 billion and the Neverian Administration more goodwill from the American public.

Arbor Ridge was the one company whose billing practices were found to be entirely accurate, with not one penny of cost wrongly attributed to a government contract. While the details of Project Ridley remained a mystery to them, it was increasingly clear that none of its cost had been misappropriated. And so was the great irony. Neverian's quest to undermine Robert had instead boosted him in the public's eye further, as one of the few truly honest business titans. Robert further capitalized on this by making the popular virtual reality game *Galactic Flyer: Invasion* free the very day Braddock was confirmed as Attorney General (a shrewd marketing gambit from Mark). At the same time, his Administration's successes uncovering fraud elsewhere boosted his own popularity, making both men's popularity rise in tandem. The symbiotic relationship between the two men that began when Neverian was a minor congressman, backing Robert's startup ventures for defense contracts seemed to be continuing, even if their intentions had apparently diverged.

This is a source of great exasperation to the President, who is currently staring out the window of the Oval Office. Braddock is seated in a chair in front of a massive oak desk, trying to explain away the unproductive nature of the Arbor Ridge probe with his successes in other matters, though both men knew the outcome was unsatisfactory. The magnitude of the office and the tasks that he faces has begun to weigh on Neverian, who at forty-one is ten years elder to Robert. His perfectly coiffed blonde hair is showing more than a few grays, though he remains militant in his exercise regime. With a chiseled jawline, strong smile, not to mention his loving wife and three young children, Hollywood producers couldn't have cast a more perfect First Family to reside in the White House.

While Braddock had been focusing on corporate corruption, Neverian has been devoting his time to international relations, in particular forging closer ties with the People's Republic of China. His shuttle diplomacy, including two trips to Beijing to meet with President Li Macous, and once hosting Li in Washington D.C., had proven fruitful.

Like Neverian, Li was a fast riser. He had assumed control of the Party six years prior as a forty-four-year-old. He had developed a reputation as a reformer in the Western provinces, modernizing rural parts of the nation that had been left behind during the nation's economic boom. The son of a farmer, he leveraged his emotional connection with less politically active working people into tremendous political power. As President these six years, he had been steadily consolidating control with a booming economy buoying high personal favorability. He is entering his second term with few serious domestic political rivals. Unlike Neverian, he did not cut as idyllic a picture on the world stage for he was bespectacled, balding, and portly.

In early March, Li and Neverian had announced an agreement to reduce nuclear weapons and military spending with a formal signing to be held in two weeks. Even with these apparent successes, Neverian looks troubled as he stares out across the South Lawn, tuning out Braddock's protestations.

Finally, he turns and sits behind his desk. "Brian, enough. We were running against the clock, and we've lost. Time isn't on our side. The activity behind Jupiter continues to accelerate; it's all the Joint Chiefs are focused on. I've got another briefing in the Situation Room in a few minutes to go over the latest development."

"So are the rumors true, Mister President? About contact?" Braddock asks.

"Cut the crap. You know as well as I what is coming. Our agenda is over; the crisis is coming. Fortunately, I've made inroads with world leaders, and hopefully I'll have their buy-in. Let's just hope he's on our side. I'm not sure anymore."

Braddock nods along; both men know the "he" to be Robert Wilson, but some things are best left unsaid. "What about the Vice President? How involved is she?"

Running alongside Neverian in the Presidential campaign was the Governor of Minnesota, Victoria Larom. Larom was chosen due to her reputation for competent leadership, not to mention Neverian's goal of winning states in the Upper Midwest. The fact she would be the first female Vice President provided a tantalizing historical allure that Neverian couldn't pass up. Once in office, he relegated Larom to mostly ceremonial duties and sought little input from her on his key agenda items. Their relationship was cordial at best.

"No, I've kept her out of it. She's been a good soldier; who knows for sure if we'd be sitting here without her, though I think we would. And I'll ensure she is rewarded for that, but we can't have more wildcards at a time like this. One is enough."

Several hours later, Neverian is in the Situation Room, being briefed on what may have seemed like fantasy just a few decades prior. Any day now, the public will be made aware of a fact that would change Planet Earth forever.

CHAPTER 5

The Sky Above Earth
April 2, 2029

I t's 2:59 PM in Jersey City, and Robert Wilson has just returned to his office from his personal elevator. He's been preparing most of his life for this very moment, but the last three hours have been draining: emotionally, mentally, and physically. Mark Morrison and Chris Bailey are with him. They've had far fewer months to prepare for this inevitability, and frankly, even though they'd been told to expect it, this moment is as surreal for them as for the other seven billion people on the planet. And now like everyone else, they sit and turn their television on because just hours before....

It's a beautiful day in Midtown Manhattan. The weather is unseasonably warm, pushing above seventy degrees. The trees are nearing bloom, the sky is bright blue, and there's just enough of a breeze to keep the air fresh. It's lunchtime, and it's the sort of day where everyone goes outside to grab lunch, just to enjoy a few minutes of fresh air before resuming the workday.

Outside the United Nations overlooking the East River, streets are abuzz with locals and workers enjoying the sun. Representatives from all around the world congregate in the tall glass structure, a key landmark of Midtown East. As with business people and residents, many officials are out walking, enjoying a beautiful day, oblivious as to what's about to transpire.

Church bells ring to signify 12:00, high noon, in the capital of the world. Suddenly, a darkness falls across several streets out of nowhere. Some look up to see if there's a single cloud in the sky that has blocked out the sun. Instead, there are looks of befuddlement, screams of panic, until all of Manhattan grinds to a halt as everyone looks to the sky above.

Perfectly situated between the UN building and sun, casting a long shadow across this symbol of the international world, is a spacecraft of some sort. It resembles a flying oil tanker. Even though the science is foreign to everyone on the ground, the hulking structure clearly looks like a transport vehicle of some sort. Up in the sky, it's impossible to judge its size, but it seems massive, larger by an order of magnitude than any flying machine man is known to produce. The oblong white body is set atop two red semi-spheres. Perhaps these helped to power the great ship?

Within minutes, images of the spacecraft hovering over Manhattan are being broadcast over every channel from Paris to Tokyo to Los Angeles. At first, some can't help but wonder if this is the mother of all April Fools' jokes. But that hope is dashed as governments closed financial markets and schools, urging everyone to return home in an orderly fashion.

Back in Washington D.C., President Neverian is taken into a secure bunker underneath the White House. The room is filled with a frenetic panic with generals, advisors, and staffers holding phone calls, gathering info, and making contingency plans. All major world leaders agree they will address their respective nations at 3:00 PM Eastern time, coordinating information so as to ensure a smooth conveying of knowledge to the world's seven billion people. It's 1:30 PM already, and the alien spacecraft continues to hover over Manhattan. The U.S. Air Force has begun reconnaissance flights, keeping enough distance so as not to inadvertently cause hostilities. They estimate the ship remains about 150 miles above the Earth's surface. Given its size in the sky, it's likely at least two miles long and half a mile wide. No one knows what's inside, but it could hold tens of thousands of soldiers.

Throughout the last ninety minutes, Neverian has been a source of stability for his government as well as his global counterparts, never raising his voice or projecting anything other than calm, deliberate steadiness. Given the activity behind Jupiter, military officials and political leaders have been gaming out scenarios. Thus far, the alien ship has not made its intentions known to the world, but as Neverian counsels, the very fact they have waited ninety minutes without making a move is encouraging. They had an opportunity to attack when the planet was entirely defenseless; instead, they permitted time for militaries to scramble and nations coordinate. Perhaps resistance would be futile, but the longer they wait, the greater the hope of peaceful intentions, or so Neverian advised.

For the past forty-five minutes, the Pentagon—working with the militaries and intelligence agencies of other nations—has been pinging the ship across every known frequency, trying to communicate across multiple languages and through arithmetic puzzles, but it has been to no avail. The radio silence from the craft is convincing the world's intelligence agencies that the ship wanted to wait for the Earth's leaders to speak first, gauging the official response, before conveying their own message. This made it of the utmost importance for all world leaders to offer the same message to their people. Seeing the wisdom of this approach, Neverian walked into a video conference room with fellow leaders to draft a joint statement that each leader would read to their own nation in their own native tongue.

It's 2:15 PM in Jersey City. Robert, Mark, and Chris are perhaps the only individuals on the planet worried more about what's happening below ground than what's hovering over it. Two hours earlier from his office overlooking Manhattan, Robert saw the ship arrive. He immediately telephoned his two friends to come to his office. Within minutes, they were back in Robert's subterranean office. Robert was videoconferencing the managers of each tower's Project Ridley production facility. The Jersey City facility had completed its final plane last week. In storage, there were now seven floors of planes, 108 per floor, or 756 planes. In recent days, each other factory completed its allotment, essentially on schedule for a fleet of roughly 10,000, more than the entire U.S. Air Force.

But Robert knows this already. Today's call focuses on phase two of his production plan. Robert knows the next two weeks will be crazy and potentially dangerous, and getting to the other side is critical to achieve victory. The men and women at these factories have developed unparalleled expertise in building these aircrafts, but Robert fears substantially more will be necessary. And so, he has converted the production floor of these facilities into tent cities for workers and their immediate families to live.

Doing this is highly contentious. Mark objects that bringing families would endanger the secrecy of the project while Chris fears that these select employees are being treated better than Arbor Ridge's other employees. Ultimately, they acquiesce. Each factory employs about 1,000 workers with 1,500 family members also present. Space is cramped, though they can utilize the railway tunnels, as the shuttling of production materials has been completed and the tunnels closed.

The next debate is whether to alert the workers as to what exactly was going on. For morale, it's agreed something should be said. All concurred to keep televisions on, and as anywhere else, workers and their families are gathering around TVs to get a glimpse of the ship. However, Robert deems it important to offer a few words himself as they'd undoubtedly question their connection to this. At the least, it would be a good test for what was to come, he felt. And so using the closed loop system, he speaks to his employees from a folding chair in his signature white t-shirt, black jacket, lapel pin, and dark jeans. While he looks calm, the bags under his eyes betray his lack of sleep over the past week.

"Good afternoon to you, my colleagues, and to your families. I am glad you are all safe. You did not know this, but your factory was one of fifteen. Twelve under each of our towers, and three smaller ones in separate locations." He speaks in a reassuring way, as if he was talking right to each person watching, alone at their fireside.

"As you are seeing, an alien ship has arrived on Earth. There have been signs this day was coming for some time now. That's what Project Ridley was all about—preparing us for this moment. I know the next few days being cooped up in these factories will be difficult. But keep your spirits up. What you have done is critical to ensuring we rise to the occasion and remain secure. I am deeply proud of what you have done, and I know that your families are as well. We will speak again soon."

Robert checks his watch—it's getting near 3:00 PM, and he needs to get upstairs to hear what the President has to say, as well as prepare communications for the rest of Arbor Ridge's employees. As he, Mark, and Chris walk past what was once the production floor and is now a tent city, there's a deafening ovation. The roar energizes Robert, and those bags under his eyes melt away. With a boost to his step, Mark and Chris can barely keep pace as they near the elevator.

At 3:00 PM in Washington D.C., President Neverian is sitting behind his desk in the Oval Office, looking across at a dozen cameras. His remarks will be brief—he doesn't love that. But they still haven't heard anything from the ship, so there really isn't much to say. Getting a single text to which all leaders could agree proved to be difficult, but Neverian leveraged his close relationship to get Chinese President Li on board, and soon other leaders had stepped into line. Neverian is wearing a navy-blue suit, crisp white shirt, and deep-red tie. This is among the most momentous times in history, and he wanted to be sure he looked the part. He takes a deep breath, and when the camera light flips red, signaling he is speaking to the nation, he begins.

"My fellow Americans, today, April second, 2020 is a day for the ages. We have apparent confirmation of intelligent life outside Earth. I have been in consultation with leaders across the world, and we have agreed to speak with one voice, for this is a moment that transcends national boundary.

"At noon today, a spaceship entered the upper atmosphere and has hovered over Midtown Manhattan, specifically the United Nations building. We take this to mean that whoever is in that spacecraft is familiar with our planet and wants to interact with us on a global basis. We are prepared to do that. We have attempted contact repeatedly but have heard nothing. We wish to be clear that above all else humanity seeks peace for itself and in its relations with others. Out of an abundance of caution, military alerts have been raised, but we aim to make no provocative actions.

"Tonight, there will be an 8:00 PM curfew nationally. Schools and all but essential businesses are closed for the duration of the week out of an abundance of caution. Looting, violence, and any criminal behavior will not be tolerated. Rest assured, all governments are working closely together, and so we expect you, our citizenry to be calm and act accordingly. I know we can rise to this challenge. Americans always have.

"To our alien friends who I am sure are listening, every nation has asked our news networks to leave the 6 to 6:30 PM Eastern time slot open, so you can speak to the world if you so wish. From there, we hope to engage constructively with you. God bless the United States of America."

The camera flips off, and President Neverian sighs a breath of relief. He delivered the remarks flawlessly; hopefully, he has reassured the public to remain calm, at least until 6:00 PM. His advisors give him thumbs up, and there is scattered applause. His wife and three children who were listening in the adjoining room burst in, and he crouches down to give his kids a big bear hug.

"Want some ice cream?" he asks his kids.

"Yes! Please!"

"Alright, let's get out of here."

Neverian knows family time will be hard to come by in the next few days, but the next few hours should be quiet, so he's looking forward to at least an hour with his kids before he'll be back at work in the Situation Room, waiting alongside humanity for someone on the spacecraft to speak.

Nearly every world leader reads these same words as they address their people. The only exception is Russian President

Mikhail Malvodov, an authoritarian nationalistic strongman, who includes a final concluding sentence in his remarks: "Let me assure you that only a Russian will ever rule over the Russian people." Malvodov is a pariah on the world stage, generally contemptuous of international norms and politically oppressive to his own people. Little is known of his background other than that he has worked in various intelligence agencies. He stands at around five foot eight inches, stout, and has combed-back fluffy white hair, with cutting blue eyes that never betray an emotion. He has been ruler of Russia for over thirteen years, and while Russia was nominally a "democracy," it's well known that the elections were rigged, which is ironic because Malvodov is likely sufficiently popular to win fair elections anyway. Even though he brutally cracks down on political dissidents, Russia's economy has boomed in recent years due to Arctic mining, buoying his popularity and funding a military modernization effort. Despite his uncouthness, his fellow leaders recognize his cunningness and shrewdness in international affairs. Undoubtedly, his off-script remarks will be the subject of much chatter overnight in diplomatic circles.

It's barely 3:30 PM, less than twenty minutes from the conclusion of the leaders' remarks, but it feels like hours to all of humanity. Time has slowed to an interminable crawl as they wait for the clock to strike 6:00 PM. Most major cities have become ghost towns. Streets are empty, bars and restaurants closed. Everyone is home with their families.

Robert is still in his office with Mark and Chris, the closest thing he has to family. The TV is still on in the background with pundits discussing the speech and unified global response. The reviews are glowing, and their idle speculation as to what the aliens may or may not say fills the empty time. Arbor Ridge has just sent a company-wide email, giving all but a few "essential" employees the rest of the week off from work, as per the President's orders.

"He's sure a smooth operator. I would've been shaking. Heck, I'm just watching and I'm shaking," Chris says, betraying his trademark nervousness.

"And that was a smart move, having every world leader speak together, though of course Malvodov was going to do his own thing," Mark chimes in.

"But was he wrong?" Robert asks.

"What do you mean, Robert? There's no need to be provocative."

"I mean we all know he's a tyrant, and no one should 'rule over' the Russian people, they should govern over themselves. But he's got a point. We seek peace, but not in exchange for servitude. Some things are worth fighting for," Robert pointedly responds.

"Sure, but I don't think Neverian was suggesting *that*," Chris jumps in.

"I hope you're right Chris. I really do. I just, I'm just not sure..." Robert trails off as he stares off into the distance. Mark and Chris know this look. The gears are turning; he's pondering over something, a thought that has been nagging at him for some time is resurfacing.

"Okay, I have some things to do. Go, get out here, go to your families. You've been neglecting them too much the last few weeks as it is."

Just as they get up to leave, his desk phone rings. Chris and Mark only hear half of the conversation.

"Hello?"

"Mister President, those were wonderful remarks. True leadership. How can I help?"

"I see."

"Absolutely, you can count on me. I'll be there."

Robert hangs up, leans back in his chair, and brings his clasped hands to his face.

After about a thirty-second silence weighs on the room, Chris asks, "Well? What did he want?"

"You know, I haven't talked with him since the day I called him after he won his election to congratulate him. I forgot how winning his personality is," Robert gleefully non-answers, happy to string along his friends.

"And he called because…?" Chris tries again.

"Well, there's that big spaceship in the sky behind us," Robert points out the window.

"Yes, we're aware, why specifically did he call though?" Chris tries again.

Having enjoyed himself as spectator to these shenanigans, Mark decides to help his friend out, "Where is it you said you'll be?"

"Oh, that. He invited me to the White House tomorrow. Apparently, he's hosting a bunch of corporate and social leaders to discuss our response to whatever it is the aliens say tonight."

"He's got a good PR mind," marvels Mark. "He's got world leaders on board, speaking from the same script. Now, he'll get non-government voices to join the chorus."

"True. Okay, I've got work to do, get out of here and to your families."

With that, Chris and Mark walk out, Robert takes his elevator back down to Project Ridley, and walks into his office, determined to find an answer to a question he has been wrestling over for months. With a few keystrokes on a computer, a hole forms in the black sphere, and a ramp pulls out. Robert walks up the ramp and goes into the sphere.

Finally, it's 6:00 PM on the East Coast. Robert is back in his office with the TV on, perhaps the only man above ground in the Jersey City tower.

President Neverian is back in the White House bunker. He's seated at the head of the table, surrounded by generals and advisors. There are two TV screens on the far wall. One is linking him to a bunker in West Virginia where Vice President Victoria Larom has been taken. For government continuity purposes, they are to remain in different places, at least for today. Neverian is happy to have it this way, never viewing her as a close advisor in the first place. Like all of humanity, a news channel is broadcast on the second screen.

Every news channel is just showing a blank, black screen. No transmission yet. 6:01, nothing. 6:02, nothing. Then with a screech, the screen goes white, and a figure appears.

Supreme General of the League Council Anton Frozos is now sixty years old. His red eyes are as fiery as ever, but his frame seems a bit slighter than Robert remembers it. Rather than his customary brown military tunic, he is wearing a white button-down shirt, likely an effort to humanize himself, Robert assumes. Most strikingly, a deep scar runs from the outside of his left eye nearly to the edge of his lip. Robert can only wonder who or what caused it.

"Greetings, Earth. My name is Anton Frozos. I am the Supreme General of the League Council. This council governs the League of Planets: a galaxy wide federation. Today, 478 planets make up the League, and we hope to make your Earth number 479.

"We come from a more ancient, distant part of the universe. Our technology is far more advanced than yours; that's how I am able to speak to each of you in your native tongue: English, French, Chinese, and so on. We have developed speedways—imagine them as shortcuts—folding spacetime and allowing us to travel great distances that would have taken decades in mere minutes. The transport destroyer above your United Nations building hopped through these speedways to reach your planet. I am speaking to you through this ship, but it is commanded by Admiral Tyrone Tiberius who is my representative on this mission.

"Earth's location in the universe will be a critical junction in our network of speedways as we seek travel to the far distances of this galaxy. That is why we offer you ascension into the League. Merge into our federation and coexist with our government structure. We seek peace and deal fairly with

those whom deal fairly with us. We can share our technologies and advance your civilization generations forward in
mere days.

"But know that if you resist this offer, Admiral Tiberius
has my full authority to act as necessary to convince you to
change your mind. His ship carries fifty-seven thousand crew,
hundreds of space fighters, landing vehicles, and planetary
weapons you have yet to imagine. And his ship is but one of
hundreds in our military.

"There is but one logical choice. Join us. And if you do,
we expect unanimity. This is a planetary decision, and I do
not tolerate rebels and saboteurs. You have seventy-two hours
to provide Tiberius with your answer. That is 6:00 PM New
York time, April fifth."

Seventy-two hours, Robert thinks to himself. He has been preparing himself for this very day for the majority of his life, and
the next three days need to go perfectly to have any chance of
success. And even then, it would be a long shot.

CHAPTER 6

The White House
April 3, 2029

Robert Wilson takes his seat at a long table in the Cabinet Room of the White House. There's a giant rectangular table, with perhaps twenty seats on each side and two at each end. President Nick Neverian will be sitting at the center, his back to the windows. Robert is on the other side and about five chairs off-center. He is still wearing a black suit jacket and American flag lapel pin, but he's traded the t-shirt for a white button-down shirt and a blue-and-yellow striped tie. Now is not a time to be a corporate mascot.

It's 9:00 AM, and he's tired. With the total lockdown on air travel, he drove instead, leaving at 4:00 AM, not that he would have been able to sleep anyway. The roads were empty. Fortunately, for the moment, people are calm, or at least shell-shocked, to be more accurate. There has not been significant civil unrest, looting, or panic, though Robert noticed a much larger police presence on Washington D.C.'s streets.

As well as Robert, there are numerous dignitaries in the room: leaders of international institutions like the World Bank and UNESCO, organizations like the Chamber of Commerce, Unions, major charities, a movie star, the Archbishop of Washington, a musician, the Speaker of the House of Representatives, and several other business leaders. Robert is set to be seated next to Attorney General Brian Braddock, who fortunately is yet to arrive. Much of the crowd is mingling, but Robert sits at his seat, takes out his phone, and plays one of the first viral apps he "invented"—a Tetris-like block game. He swipes away news alerts of troops amassing on the Russia-China border; those rumors have been flying around for several hours now, ever since President Malvodov went off-script in his remarks.

Finally, Braddock sits down. "Morning, Robert how are you?" he asks, extending his hand.

Robert shakes it. "I'm just relieved you have something else to do than investigate me for a change," he says with a smile.

"It must awkward for you to be here."

"Why?" Robert asks, feigning ignorance.

"I think six of the attendees used to run companies you acquired." He points them out. "Myself, Johnson who the President put at the World Bank, Clemons at Commerce, Sayers our Ambassador to the UN, Stewartson, and Paulson."

"It's seven—you forgot Bill Williamson. Understandable— he's a forgettable man. But I don't see why it'd be awkward for me."

"Well, taking over people's companies and firing them isn't all that endearing."

"That's not how I see it, Brian. I made you all rich buying your companies, and now you've all got jobs where you get to spend time with the President of the United States. Seems like you should be thanking me."

Braddock's smile disappears, and Robert gets back to his game.

Finally, the President walks in. The murmurs of the crowd fall silent as everyone settles into their seat. Robert slips his phone into his pocket. Walking in with the President are China's Ambassador to the United States, a moderately obese man of about fifty-five, and the Secretary-General of the United Nations, the former President of Chile, a woman of sixty-five, who are seated to either side of Neverian.

Neverian, as ever, looks the part of President with a well-tailored black suit and a blue-and-red striped tie, but he looks tired. Undoubtedly, it was a night of numerous phone calls and little sleep. He has some prepared remarks laid out in front of them, but doesn't really rely on them. It is in settings like these where Neverian really shines.

"Thank you all for coming; the media will be here in a few minutes. You don't have to say anything in this room, though I'm sure they will ask you for comment later if you're inclined. Your presence here is critical as we must show a united front to rally the support of our people. I've asked the Chinese ambassador and Secretary-General here, because President Li and I have rallied the world's governments to a consensus. The UN Security Council—that's the U.S., Russia, China, France, and the United Kingdom—and several rotating members will pass a resolution today accepting entrance into the League but requesting that we manage our internal planetary affairs. It is our best option to preserve life. It's critical everyone here support this message."

The heaviness of those words hangs over the room, but several individuals start voicing support.

"Thank you," the President continues. "So, we will bring in the press, I'll basically repeat that, everyone will be on camera, so look resolute, and we'll march on."

"I'm sorry, I have to ask," Robert jumps in, eliciting glares from all over the room.

Braddock pushes his chair away as though his proximity could suggest approval.

"Yes, Mister Wilson?"

"How do we know—even if they say yes—they'll let us govern ourselves autonomously as we do now?"

"We can't for sure, but Frozos in his remarks last night didn't signal intent in ruling over internal affairs."

"I just don't think we can hand over the keys to the kingdom on a promise from an individual we know nothing about," Robert retorts.

"Their technology is clearly superior; it'd be a massacre. I'm trying to save lives."

"At what cost? Is trading in a free life for one in servitude a wise decision? Is nothing worth dying for? Sure, we'd be underdogs, but some fights need to be fought, despite the odds. That's how he thought." Robert points to a painting on the wall behind Neverian—it's a portrait of George Washington.

"Well, Washington may have been outnumbered, but the British only had guns. Who knows what weapons they have? I hear you; these decisions are not ideal, but here we are. I was elected to make tough decisions. So I need you to get on board, like everyone else."

Robert gives a slight nod, so Neverian nods back and signals to his aides to bring the press in.

A rush of cameramen and reporters swarm in to the room—at least two dozen people and six cameras. They are standing at Robert's back so they have a clear shot of the President, who proceeds to give a similar brief statement that he had just outlined to the key leaders in the room. When he's finished, China's ambassador briefly speaks, echoing Neverian's remarks and signaling his nation's support for the proposal. The Secretary-General then speaks to outline the process. Reporters start shouting questions, which Neverian ignores as his aides attempt to shuffle them out of the room. The photo op is over.

Sensing the moment slipping away, Robert jumps in, "That's a good question, did you hear that Mister President?"

"I'm sorry?" Neverian inquires as he glares an annoyed look at Robert.

"The reporter, over there, I think she asked about Russia and China?" Robert points to her, by the far head of the table.

"Thank you, Mister Wilson," the reporter says. "Yes, Mister President, there are press reports of troops amassing on the border of Russia and China. I was wondering if you or the ambassador have a comment on that situation?"

"Well, I think it's important for us to put aside our squabbles, not fight amongst ourselves, or be aggressors. And I would condemn and will not tolerate any destabilizing or military actions. Okay?" Neverian says.

"I'm relieved to hear you say that, Mister President," Robert says, leaning forward in his chair to insert himself into the conversation. "I'm not a diplomat, but it sounds to me like we believe all international borders should be respected?"

"That's one hundred percent what I'm saying, Robert."

"I think that's comforting to hear for many, no, all of us. I know you're not a man of idle threats, so I assume it's safe to say the United States would stand with a nation who was attacked and provide military support? As you know, Arbor Ridge maintains a large inventory of arms, and if a nation came under attack during this time, we'd gladly provide supplies for free. I agree with you, it's a time for solidarity."

Backed into a corner, Neverian has no choice but to agree. "You're right. I'm not a man who bluffs. National borders will be respected, I can assure you and the American people."

"And I'm sure the ambassador agrees?" Robert asks.

"Of course," he says.

With that, the meeting is over. The press is escorted out. Many of the members of the room engage in casual conversation, but Robert makes a beeline for the exit, walking with the Secret Service out of the building. Outside the White House, Robert is struck by the silence. It's a beautiful April day. The sun is shining; it's almost eighty degrees. He expected to see tourists, walkers, and locals enjoying the day. But the streets and lawns are empty. As he walks down the driveway, many of the same members of the White House Press Corps who were in the Cabinet Room are assembling to get some footage or comments from the attendees. Robert is, as was his plan, the first one out.

"Mister Wilson, do you have a comment on the President's remarks?" a reporter shouts.

Robert walks over. "Yes. I was very heartened to hear the President forcefully and unequivocally promise to the American people he would not let any country take advantage of the present situation by invading another. I stand ready, as do all the employees of Arbor Ridge, to help in those efforts, should that prove necessary."

"Yes, but what about the President's approach to the Aliens and his peace plan?" asks the same reporter who Robert just helped ask the President a question.

Robert bites his lower lip, leans back on his heels, putting his hands in his pockets. He takes a look up at the sun, thinking for a few seconds. Having collected his thoughts, he says, "Well, to be honest, I disagree with every last word the President said. I'm just one person and I may not be privy to all he knows. But it sounded to me like a surrender plan, not a peace plan. I've never thought of America as a nation that can be knocked out with one punch, let alone a nation that waves the white flag before a punch is even thrown. I think we can be capable of great things if we just endeavor to try."

"But is it just a suicide mission?" an incredulous reporter asks.

"No, I really don't think so. I don't know what that ship up there is capable of; they haven't shown us anything other than the ability to travel great distances in little time. And we have tremendously bright people, and we have much more to fight for than they do. But if I am wrong, ask yourself, wouldn't you rather die a free man than live a slave?"

Having made his point, Robert walks away, down the driveway, off the White House grounds, and into the rear passenger seat of the black SUV that was waiting for him. As his driver pulls away, he loosens his tie a bit and unbuttons his top shirt button. He turns on a TV embedded in the back of the seat in front of him and starts flicking through channels, most of whom are carrying his remarks. The talking heads seem generally positively inclined toward his statement. His phone keeps vibrating with emails from employees, saying variations of "good job" or "proud to be an Arbor Ridge employee." Robert keeps the TV on, but turns the volume down to a whisper, laying his head back, trying to get at least a little sleep on the drive back.

Back in the White House Situation Room, Neverian is livid. His carefully laid plan is getting blown up. Russia has been withdrawing its troops from its eastern border. Neverian and President Li had been leveraging China's troop presence to compel Malvodov to vote with them at the Security Council later this afternoon. After Neverian's comments on the matter, apparently Malvodov felt the odds of invasion were low, leaving him comfortable to remove his troops. It seems likely he will veto the measure this afternoon.

Neverian felt a Russian veto could be explained away, but now the French have signaled they may veto as well. His coalition is collapsing, and he is now berating his top diplomat, Secretary of State Alexander Monroe, a man of about sixty-five who has worked in the State Department his entire career. He is mostly bald with a valiant, but ultimately futile, combover and a bushy mustache. He is not a partisan man, but is one who had forged deep relationships with foreign leaders over his long career in international relations.

"If you don't get the French back in line, you better not show your face around here again. We can't have some unelected plutocrat kill two billion people," Neverian booms.

"Well, sir, you're the one who invited him to the meeting in the first place." It's Vice President Larom, speaking from one of the telescreens in the Situation Room. She remains in West Virginia but is videoconferencing into the meeting. She's had misgivings about Neverian's strategy but has largely been sidelined as a peripheral figure, included in these meetings as a formality. But it seems she's had enough.

"Victoria, now's not the time for second-guessing and snarky remarks," the President condescends.

"I agree, but it's better to pause and find the right answer than continue with the wrong one. As President of the Senate, I'm compelled to suggest we consult with Congress. All three branches of our government should be united on this."

"We've been over this already," Braddock, the Attorney General, chimes in. "In a crisis like this, the President has legal authority to act unilaterally."

"What are you still doing here?" the President snaps at Monroe. "Shouldn't you be off calling the French?"

As Monroe gets up and gathers his papers to leave, the President turns to his intelligence chiefs. "We need to start tracking Wilson and what's going on at Arbor Ridge. Now. He's up to something."

There's a loud ringing. It startles Robert awake; he must have dozed off a bit. They are on the New Jersey turnpike, he should be back in the office in about twenty-five minutes. Shaking himself awake, he sees that Mark Morrison is video calling him. He picks up and sees Mark and Chris sitting in Mark's office. Both men are sporting their usual suits with no ties. Creatures of habit, all of them.

"Hey boss, how's it going?" Mark asks, in clearly a jovial spirit.

"To be honest, you woke me up from a bit of a nap."

"Ah that explains it, Chris, why don't you tell him?"

"Sure thing. So you'll see the email, but in the past hour, we've gotten phone calls from four plant managers in the defense business. Massachusetts—they make lasers; Chicago—that's fighter jets of course; Nevada—defense shields; and Alabama—communications and satellite equipment. It seems that the factory workers reached out to know why they haven't been classified essential workers. They want to get back to work. I liked this quote from one of them: 'Now isn't the time to furlough democracy's arsenal.' So they want to reopen. Seems your comments convinced a couple of people."

"Well, sounds good. I look forward to having them back at work tomorrow." Robert smiles, feeling a bit more validation about his faith in humanity.

"Not quite, you see. They're already back on the job. The emails were more of a heads-up than a request."

"That's wonderful news, Chris. Seems like I should spend more time out of the office and let you two run things! I should be back in a few minutes."

"Sounds good," Mark says. "I forwarded you a press release we want to put out announcing our factories' operations."

"Thanks, Mark, I'll give it a read, but I'm sure it's fine."

Robert disconnects from the call, and looks out the window. It's still a beautiful day. He sees that damn transport destroyer up in the sky, but he feels optimistic, increasingly confident that his faith was well-placed.

"You know, sir…" a voice says. It's Robert's driver, a man whom he hadn't met before.

"Yes?"

"I was just going to say—and this may not be my place, but please permit me a minute."

"Of course." Robert leans forward in his seat, giving the driver his full attention.

"You see, when I was a child, my uncle had been unemployed for quite some time, gave up hope, and committed suicide. I'll never forget my father telling me, 'People are brave, but sometimes they needed to be reminded of that.' No one reminded my uncle. So please sir, remember that, and don't let us forget it either."

"Thank you. I really appreciate you telling me that story," and Robert means that. As he gained wealth and fame, he had found people treated him differently, acting more formal, awkward even. So when he could have a real conversation with someone, even if it was just a few words, he treasured it.

As they near the Arbor Ridge tower, the scene is chaotic. Cameramen and journalists are everywhere. And the streets are filled, not with rioters, but peaceful marchers, waving American flags, and makeshift signs saying "*freedom*" or "*no surrender*." Robert is struck by the diversity of the crowd, from toddlers to ninety-year-olds, of all races and backgrounds, at least several hundred. It's not easy, but Robert's driver is able to get near the entrance of the building, which has been blocked off by police. Robert fixes his shirt button and tie, and tells the driver, "Well done, my friend."

As he closes the door, he hears the driver say, "God bless you."

Seeing Robert get out of the car, reporters and their cameramen rush towards him, as do nearby marchers.

Robert walks up to the metal fence barricade. "Excuse me, officer, who's in charge here?"

The policeman is a young man who couldn't be out of the police academy more than two years, if even that long. He's clearly overwhelmed by this entire situation. Stumbling over himself, the officer says, "Um, the chief should be around here somewhere, I'm not sure where exactly, sir. I can try and find him."

Robert sees the officer's silver name tag of "Johnson." He points down along the metal fence. "That's okay, Officer

Johnson, what's this metal fence doing here? The atrium of the building is open to the public. Here, help me move this." Robert grabs the metal fence to open it.

"Sir, you shouldn't be doing that. They're worried about the building."

"Listen, officer, it's my building. I didn't ask for you to block it off, and I don't want it blocked off. So if your chief has a problem with that, tell him to take it up with me."

And so Robert makes an opening through the barricade and lets some of the marchers through. As he nears the entrance himself, several members of the media catch up to him.

"Mister Wilson, there are reports that the President's motion could fail at the UN tonight. Any comments?"

"I think you know how I feel already about that," he answers. "But, I do have something to say. And I believe we've just released or are about to release a press release with all the details. Only essential employees are at work today. So for us at Arbor Ridge, that means necessary crews at our power plants to keep your electricity running, maintenance techs for our wireless networks so that your phones and internet work and so forth. We did not include any of our manufacturing workers. However, workers at four of our defense plants showed up unsolicited after talking amongst themselves and told management, myself included, they were working whether we liked it or not. Inspiring stuff.

"So I just want to say two things. First, the choice we make regarding Frozos's offer; I'm just one person, one voice, I can't make nor do I want to make it. But know that whatever we decide, this company will do everything it can to ensure we are adequately resourced in the coming days, weeks, and months.

"Second, and you'll see this in the press release, an employee told us something along the lines of, 'Now isn't the time to furlough democracy's arsenal.' I appreciate that sentiment, but don't quite agree. Bullets or planes aren't our greatest weapons; they're mere tools. Our courage, grit, determination, and willingness to do what's right, no matter the cost, is our strongest weapon. And today, I've been reminded over and over again that that force can never be furloughed. Thanks."

Robert walks inside, through his atrium, crowded with people, and up the elevator to his office.

CHAPTER 7

The United Nations
April 3, 2029

The Chamber of the United Nations Security Council is a great cavernous room where many a momentous debate about peace and war have taken place, but perhaps, there was never a more consequential debate than tonight's. At the base of the room is a large, semi-circular table with a representative from each nation that sits on the council. Five nations—the United States, China, Russia, the United Kingdom, and France—are permanent members who can veto any measure. Then there are another ten rotating members. Behind the semi-circular desk, there is a great mural of a phoenix rising from its ashes, just as the world rose from the horrors of World War II.

It is 7:00 PM, and there has been extended debate over President Nick Neverian's peace plan. Tensions have grown heated inside the chamber after a two-hour debate that has been at times vitriolic and personal. But tempers are flaring outside as well. Across world capitals from Paris to Seoul there have been protestors on both sides of the issue. There have been increased reports of looting, and several nations have been forced to deploy their military domestically to supplement the police, restore order, and enforce curfews. The shell-shocked calm of last night is increasingly transitioning to panic and chaos.

Now, nearly twenty-five hours into the seventy-two-hour window of decisions, the United Nations Security Council is voting. First, the ten rotating nations vote on Neverian's resolution:

Ghana: No
Liberia: Yes
Saudi Arabia: Yes
Thailand: Yes
Japan: No
Estonia: Yes
Ukraine: No
Mexico: Yes
Argentina: No
Australia: No

The ten rotating members deadlock five against five. If any of the five permanent members oppose the plan, it loses even if wins a majority.

The United States: Yes
The United Kingdom: No
The People's Republic of China: Yes

Russia: No

France: No

The motion fails seven to eight with three vetoes—a stunning loss for Neverian, and one which he could not have fathomed even ten hours ago. There is no joy in the Security Council Chamber. The world appears hopelessly divided as to its next steps. While eight nations voted against Neverian's proposal, they actually have no affirmative proposal of their own. This realization hangs over the room. Meanwhile, the clock continues to tick—twenty-five hours seemingly wasted—what to do in the next forty-seven?

Robert Wilson is in the makeshift tent camp of Project Ridley. He sees reports of the vote failing at the Security Council. He's relieved that's the case, but also feels there's little more for him to do. Ultimately, the world has to decide for itself what it wants to do. For now, he's focused on keeping morale high, talking with workers and their families, playing catch with kids, trying to keep his mind off of matters as much as he is trying to entertain others.

Inside the White House, Neverian is enraged. He is sitting in the Situation Room as advisors debate next steps. Military officials are increasingly pushing Neverian to increase preparations, but he continues to resist, saying he does not want to antagonize the aliens.

It's 7:35 PM Eastern time. Suddenly, televisions globally cut out, no matter the channel, in a flash of white. On the screen, there is a figure. He has the shape of a human, but the skin of a reptile. Perhaps on his planet, a lizard-like creature had evolved into the dominant species rather than a descendant of apes. His coloring is dark green, and viewers on Earth are undoubtedly relieved much of his body is covered by a blue military uniform, emblazoned with metals and pins, signifying his rank as Admiral. He has beady yellow eyes off towards the corner of his head with open nostrils that converge like a snout into his mouth. As he speaks, his jagged yellow teeth are apparent. From Tokyo to Cape Town, viewers must be wondering how many species make up this League of Planets. What are these distant worlds like? Behind him are windows showing outer space, and Earth can be seen among the stars.

"Greetings, my name is Admiral Tyrone Tiberius. Supreme General Anton Frozos spoke to you just over one day ago. You have nearly two more days to reach a verdict that is to be the unanimous decision of your planet. Some bickering is to be expected, and rest assured, it will not impact your treatment should you accept our most generous offer within the allotted time.

In times of indecisiveness, I have found an event can help crystallize choices, make tangible worries that would otherwise be theoretical. We follow your press closely, and there have been questions about our military power. I believe a display of power may hasten your decision. Given the discretion General Frozos has left me, I have decided to take a symbolic action. This ship is equipped with a laser cannon that will disintegrate the moon.

We've realized that all of our actions have been occurring over New York, so we have decided to take this action at 12:00 PM tomorrow New York time, when the moon is visible across most of Asia. Your decision will still be due at 6:00 PM April fifth, New York time, or thirty-six hours after the destruction of your moon. Choose wisely."

In reality, the destruction of the moon would be far more than a symbolic gesture, but one with profound consequences, altering human life as it is known. As every body of mass does, the moon exerts gravitational force upon the Earth. Consequently, the moon is responsible for the tides of the ocean, which in turn helps to regulate the amount of time it takes for the Earth to rotate on its axis—the twenty-four hours in a day. Without the moon, the magnitude of high and low tides would likely be lower, and the speed of the Earth's rotation would hasten, perhaps to a mere twelve hours.

These are the long-term changes if the moon were to disappear. Immediately after its disintegration, the resulting loss of gravitational force on the oceans could cause immense tidal waves across the world, perhaps wiping out entire coastal cities like New York, New Orleans, Bangkok, and Hong Kong.

Shortly after Tiberius's remarks, scientists on television begin relaying these basic facts, and panic begins to ensue. Across the world, citizens ignore governmental curfew policies to get into their cars and out of coastal areas, filling up roads, many without cars even take to walking, as public transportation has been closed for the curfews.

In Washington D.C., President Neverian is being walked with his family onto a helicopter, Marine One on the South Lawn, for a short ride before getting on a plane, Air Force One, ironically to join the Vice President in West Virginia. There is a chance that Washington D.C. could be impacted by the tsunami, and so he is being moved to higher ground as a precaution, along with other key members of his Administration.

Now on the plane, he is sitting in an office with Attorney General Brian Braddock and a smattering of other advisors. An intelligence official hands him a document.

Reading it over, his face fills with disgust. "Jesus, the man is insane," he says, tossing the paper onto the desk.

"What is it?" Braddock asks, reaching for it.

"Remember how I said to keep an eye on Wilson? That's an email Wilson sent to his employees working in his new office towers, telling them to stay calm, it's a bluff, and if they are worried, they can come with immediate families to seek shelter in the buildings, which are, what's the quote? 'Indestructible'?"

"Wow," is all a puzzled Braddock can muster, leaning back in his chair, face in his palm, exhaling a long breath.

"And this man's antics are responsible for this," Neverian bellows. "I tell you what we are going to do. Leak it at 11:45 tomorrow morning. We'll make sure the world sees how dangerous he is, and then rational heads will prevail."

"I tell you, Mister President. It's almost as if he acting so irrational as to undermine the legitimacy of those who want to wage war," Braddock offers.

"Hmmm, now, that is interesting," Neverian says.

Meanwhile, back in Jersey City, it's about midnight, and Robert is feeling calm, better than he has in weeks, convinced he is set to accomplish his mission. Based on key card data, about two-thirds of employees have come to the office. Fortunately, several floors in this and most other towers aren't fully occupied, as he built the towers to have capacity for Arbor Ridge to continue to grow, and there is also plenty of common space. It may not be comfortable, but there's room for everyone who came.

Mark Morrison and Chris Bailey walk into his office. They've traded their trademark suits for untucked polos and jeans, or as Robert calls it, "the disheveled-woken-up-in-the-middle-of-the-night dad look."

"So, I know we used excess concrete in these buildings, but I don't think they were built to survive a tsunami?" Chris asks.

"Well, Chris, you know me well enough that I always keep an ace up my sleeve," Robert says with a sheepish grin as he gets up out of his chair to open his secret elevator.

"You know, you could have told us about this part of the plan," Mark says, more than a little peeved.

"Sorry, I had to keep this one close to the chest. You never know who's listening." Robert concedes as they get into the elevator to descend into Project Ridley.

"You know," Chris says, "all these trips in a secret elevator behind a bookshelf to an underground lair has me feeling like we're a bunch of superheroes."

"I just hope we don't end up being a bunch of supervillains," Mark counters.

"Well, it's all a matter of perspective, I suppose," Robert says, as the elevators open and they head to his underground office.

CHAPTER 8

Jersey City
April 4, 2029

I t's 11:50 AM on the East Coast. Robert Wilson's email to Arbor Ridge employees has indeed been leaked by President Nick Neverian's Administration, and Robert is being blasted across cable news channels and social media as a megalomaniacal fool. How quickly public perception can turn! But Robert isn't watching TV. He's been working all night on the large computers connected to the black sphere in his underground office. Mark Morrison and Chris Bailey have gone back upstairs to be with their families; it's not as though they could be of any use anyway. At 11:54 AM, Roberts emphatically bangs the "ENTER" key.

"Done." And now, like everyone else, he waits.

Overnight, the spacecraft that had haunted Manhattan departed to make its way toward the moon. The moon lies nearly 250,000 miles from Earth, so the ship is no longer visible to the naked eye, having come to a rest about 1,000 miles from its target. But thanks to advancements in satellite and camera technology "invented" (on Earth at least) by Robert, ironically enough, humans are able to see a close up of the ship and the moon, though many in Asia have congregated outside to marvel at the moon one final time with the naked eye.

President Nick Neverian is watching from a control center in West Virginia. The layout is similar to his Situation Room in the now vacant White House, and he is seated at the head of a table watching a television. Only for the first time in this crisis, Vice President Victoria Larom is seated next to him. Neverian is exhausted, powered only by coffee and adrenaline. He's even let his tie go crooked—unusual for a man so meticulously focused on his appearance.

All night, there have been conference calls with world leaders. He and Chinese President Li Macous have remained steadfast allies and have been pushing their fellow leaders to adopt their peace plan to stop the damage. With the exception of Russian President Mikhail Malvodov, most have become supportive of their plan. Given the deadline was not for thirty-six hours, and with so many leaders facing mass curfew violations and panic in coastal areas, they have decided to hold off on making any announcements until that evening so governments could first focus on keeping the domestic peace and controlling their populations.

In the minutes before the attack, the transport destroyer lines up at the moon. Its position between the Earth and the moon will ensure any debris, or in the very unlikely event of a miss, the laser blast itself will not directly harm the planet. An opening appears on one of the red spheres on which the ship appears to sit, and a long tube, at least fifty feet long, extends out. This must be the laser cannon that Admiral Tiberius had mentioned. Humanity can only wonder how this laser is powered.

It's 11:59. Robert is still in his underground office. He is watching a live feed from the Arbor Ridge research facility on the moon. It is home to 847 employees right now. His leg is shaking rapidly; his arms are crossed and he's biting his finger-nails. "Can't it be 12:01 already?" he thinks to himself as time slows to a crawl.

Then, it's 12:00 PM in New York, and it's 12:00 AM in Beijing, where a burst of yellow light across the night sky is visible. Then the entire sky turns brighter than day. There are shrill screams of panic. As the sky darkens, it becomes appar-ent—the moon is still there! First, there is confusion, but then cheers of joy.

In his makeshift control center, President Neverian and his advisors are equally baffled. What happened? Was it a bluff? Was there a malfunction, or did they miss? Would they try again? Hosts of the news channel on the TV are asking the same questions. Finally, they bring back the footage, using the satellite cameras, and slowing down the tape. First, viewers see the ship's cannon emit a yellow ball of energy spiraling at the moon. But then about fifty miles above the moon's surface, there is an explosion as it collides with something unseen by the naked human eye. The yellow ball of energy breaks up, sliding around the moon and disappearing into nothing.

At 12:10 PM, there is another flash of light across the night sky, but once again, the moon is still there. Again at 12:20, and once more at 12:30. Four tries, but the moon is still there. What was intended to display the League of Planets's military supremacy instead proves to be a comical display of impotence. But how is the moon still there? All of humanity is wondering—or almost all.

Back in Jersey City, it's nearly 1:00 PM, and Robert is relieved. His gamble has paid off. He'd been confident in his invention, but it had never been tested to this extent before. On one of his monitors, the livecam from Arbor Ridge's moon base still plays. Robert notices that the transport destroyer is moving out of view. It has given up on trying to destroy the moon, likely set to re-enter Earth's atmosphere. With a frenetic energy but unwavering confidence, he starts typing away and after about thirty seconds, one again emphatically hits the "ENTER" key.

As he leans back in his chair, there is great rumbling throughout the basement floors and up through the entire tower. Employees and their families who had taken refuge in the tower hug each other tight, wondering if the building or the planet is under attack. Then the shaking stops. Those workers who are near the northeast corner point out the window at a sight that is a marvel to behold. The purple spire that extends 125 stories into the heavens is lit up and from the top a purple light shoots up into the sky. After a few moments, individuals throughout the building notice that wherever they look outside, there is just the slightest of purple tints, as though a veil has been draped over the building and to the ground.

Little do they know, but the same scene is playing out at each of the twelve towers Robert has built near Los Angeles; Vancouver, Canada; São Paulo, Brazil; Bogota, Colombia; London, England; Moscow, Russia; Cape Town, South Africa; Dubai; Sydney, Australia; Hanoi, Vietnam; and Tokyo, Japan. From each of them, a great purple light extended into the skies. It isn't long before news channels in the United States and around the world are showing images of these buildings. Speculation is rampant as to what these buildings are doing, but there is no doubt that it has something to do with why the moon is still there and why the alien spaceship has yet to return to Midtown Manhattan.

In Neverian's West Virginia compound, the room is as filled with speculation about Robert's towers as is every living room in the country. It's now nearly 2:30 PM; the towers have been shining for nearly ninety minutes, and there is still no definitive answer. Phone calls to Robert's office have gone unanswered, and the President was not used to having his calls ignored. He has just gotten off the phone with his French counterpart who was pressing him for details. Was the U.S. government aware of what these towers could do? What exactly could they do?

Neverian answered quite honestly that he had no idea, but there was some skepticism among fellow world leaders that was actually the case. How could America's leading defense contractor have developed what appears to be a weapon and not tell its government about it? Neverian had promised to get answers and to get them quickly. After all, the seventy-two-hour deadline continued to tick ever closer. In fact, a little over half an hour ago he had ordered the military to raid the Jersey City headquarters, get a hold of Robert, and figure out what exactly was going on.

The television in the Situation Room shows a live feed coming from Army Jeeps headed to the Arbor Ridge tower, which have just entered Jersey City. Neverian is at the head of the table, Vice President Larom is to one side and Attorney General Braddock on his other. Elsewhere at the table are an array of advisors. The military officials are manning the phones in constant contact with the convoy and supervising over the mission. The jeeps are three blocks from the tower's entrance.

"Get your popcorn ready," Neverian tells Braddock. And then one block from the towers, the jeeps crash to halt, slowing from thirty-five miles per hour to a stop in an instant. The feed shakes wildly as the suddenness of the stop causes the camera to move. Soldiers are thrown from the jeeps.

"What happened? Why did they stop?" bellows a confused, exasperated Neverian to his military advisors.

On the screen, several soldiers get out the jeeps and off the ground and walk, only to fall backwards midstride.

A general hangs up the phone and looks to Neverian, takes a breath to collect himself, like he knows he's about to deliver deeply unsatisfactory news.

"Well, uh, Mister President, you see…"

"Get on with it, General," the President interjects.

"The men on the ground are saying there is an, um…an invisible wall."

"Jesus Christ."

Neverian drops his head onto the table.

Suddenly there is the sound of a loud explosion coming from the screen. Neverian looks up and winces—a military helicopter is falling, engulfed in flames.

"Did someone shoot at our bird?" the President asks.

Relaying what he's hearing on the phone from the troops on the ground, the general responds, "No, the helicopter was flying towards the tower before it too hit an invisible wall."

"I don't believe. I just don't believe it."

A few seconds later, a younger aide, looking as pale as a ghost, walks in and drops a note in front of Neverian, before scurrying out as quickly as possible.

"Oh no. Turn on the news! Any channel!" the President pleads.

Just as the note suggests, the networks are carrying video of the helicopter crashing as well as of troops, standing befuddled, in their crashed jeeps a block from their destination.

"Well done, everyone," Neverian says, "you've made me look like a moron in front of the whole world."

"To be honest, Mister President, you did that all yourself the second you let a random citizen be a stronger force for freedom than you were willing to be," Vice President Larom says before getting out of her seat and walking out of the room. She heads into her office, a small room in the complex, to start calling friends on Capitol Hill.

Meanwhile, about 40,000 miles above Earth, Admiral Tiberius is sitting in his office, a windowless room, ten feet by twelve feet. On the wall behind his desk, he has photos from throughout his career, many with Frozos himself, as well as metals and awards, recognizing the valor of a successful career. He keeps replaying what happened in his attack on the moon, but he never had seen anything like it. At the same time, he has been briefed on the happenings on Earth and lights coming out of towers. The ship's systems are registering some sort of interference about 1,000 miles away, and he had sent out a drone to investigate, only for the drone to crash like that helicopter had.

More than anything, Tiberius feels disgusted. He has had an incredibly successful career and is a leading member of the League of Planets's military. He has overseen the successful invasion of twenty-seven planets and been at Frozos's right hand for three decades. He's due for retirement, and this was to be his last mission. This mission was supposed to be a simple task; instead it is turning into a problem of his own making. Frozos had been priming Earth for a peaceful takeover for more than ten years.

All Tiberius was supposed to do was arrive, perhaps show off his ship, and accept the terms of surrender. He didn't even bring other ships necessary to take the planet by force, because that was conceived as being out of the realm of possibility. After accepting the surrender, Frozos had agreed Tiberius would retire from active duty and he was to remain on Earth as its Governor. Now he had to explain to Frozos that he needed more troops. Tiberius was dreading this conversation; Frozos never took news of failure particularly well.

Tiberius taps a button on his desk to establish a video connection with Frozos. Thanks to hologram technology, Frozos appears standing in front of Tiberius's desk. Tiberius jumps to alert from his seat.

"Sit down, Admiral. I've been informed you don't have good news to share."

"No, sir. There appears to be a force field of some kind; we've seen nothing like it before. It protected the moon from our laser cannons, and now we are blocked outside the planet's atmosphere."

"How could this happen?"

"I think we've been betrayed by an advance scout. It's the only plausible explanation. I am deeply sorry, sir."

Frozos paces angrily across the room. The infiltration program had been his brainchild, and it had worked very successfully in recent years, speeding up the capture of planets. But those advance missions had been shorter—only one to three years on average. On Earth, and on planets central to the next phase of his expansion dreams, scouts had been sent over a decade in advance. He worries that what's occurring today on Earth could signal trouble elsewhere, and Frozos could not afford failures that would give his enemies fodder that it was time for a change atop the League Council.

"Okay, Tiberius, hold firm. My armada should be there in days."

It's now nearly 5:00 PM in Jersey City. Robert stands in his office, shirt collar popped up, putting on a red tie, fielding last minute advice from Mark and Chris, who are back in their standard suit/no-tie combo. Both men are glad that they keep spare clothes in the office, though they really hadn't quite envisioned this scenario. Robert has asked every network for several minutes of airtime to discuss what exactly is shooting out of Arbor Ridge towers. Originally, there was reluctance from some network executives to give him airtime, but then Mark threatened they would air it exclusively on *Headlines Now*, the news channel Robert had bought last year. The fear of losing all their viewers—after all, the entire world wondered what was going on—caused them to capitulate.

Robert's office is rearranged into a makeshift television studio, with cameras set up in front of his desk. A teleprompter has also been set up with the outline of Robert's prepared remarks. He will give this address sitting down.

"Here, let me help you with that." Chris leans in to help Robert get his tie perfectly straight. "Don't worry, you'll do great," he says.

"What do you think of the speech, Mark?" Robert asks as he puts his suit jacket on, straightening his American flag lapel pin.

"It's good. But trust me, be honest. The public can sniff out deceptiveness; just tell the truth. Trust them with the truth; give them, hmm, give them the chance to be brave," Mark responds.

Robert gives him a knowing nod and takes his seat. His two friends walk out of the office to watch from the adjoining room. It's now just Robert and a few cameramen in the room. The camera flips red, signaling he is now live.

"Good evening. My name is Robert Wilson; you probably know me as the CEO of Arbor Ridge. It's now been over two days since the alien ship first arrived; I know that can feel like an entire lifetime ago. In some ways, it is. You're likely wondering why there is a light shooting out of my towers. Or why I felt so confident the moon wouldn't be blown up. Well, tonight I asked for a few minutes to tell you. And I want to thank every network that is giving me the opportunity to do so.

"My goal to this point has not been to a choose a side in terms of whether we accept Anton Frozos's terms by his deadline or decline them. I have an opinion, which I will share later. But my actions have entirely been focused on ensuring that you the people of this wonderful planet we all call home get to make the choice.

"Yesterday, I sought assurances at the White House that all national borders would be respected so that each nation and each person feels safe to offer their opinion, and I was glad when President Neverian made that assurance.

"Then, Admiral Tiberius attempted to coerce a decision out of us by threatening to destroy our moon. I am proud to say that it was Arbor Ridge who stopped that from happening. My company has developed a new technology, advancing well beyond our defense shield technology into force fields. In effect, we can put an impenetrable bubble around a planet. As you may or may not know, we have a research base on the moon that has nominally been used for space mining. In reality, it existed solely to house a force field projector. This morning, for the first time, I turned it on, and we saw it worked.

"After that, with the alien ship well outside our atmosphere, I decided to turn on Earth's force field to keep the ship out. As you may know, my company for the last few years has been building twelve towers across the world, each with an identical purple spire. I had explained away this spire as a marketing symbol; in reality, these spires house the force field technology.

"Each of these towers is pumping magnetic energy nearly forty thousand miles above Earth's surface, spreading out a net around the Earth. In addition to the twelve towers, Arbor Ridge's marine research facilities in the middle of South Atlantic, Indian, and Arctic Oceans house spires of their own. These fifteen installations can keep us safe from foreign invaders for decades, potentially forever."

Robert pauses for a moment to let news of this technological breakthrough sink in to his global audience. Of all his work on Earth and on Project Ridley, the force field gives

Robert the greatest satisfaction and he had enjoyed showcasing it in such dramatic fashion today. He is confident Frozos's military has no comparable weapon. The force field is his signature accomplishment, or so he believes.

Robert continues, "Of course, if these buildings were to be destroyed, the shield would cease to exist, which is why a force field similarly extends down from the spires, around the buildings. Unfortunately, the U.S. military attempted a raid on our Jersey City tower today, resulting in a heartbreaking loss of life. I wish more than anything that this had not happened, but I hope you understand why I placed a shield around my buildings.

"My purpose in turning on the force field is to ensure the public has adequate time to determine the next course of action. Turning them on is merely a defensive action that ensures continuation of the status quo. Frozos gave us three days to decide, but now, we may have longer because we are safe from invasion. Additionally, I have attempted to unilaterally take no provocative action as I do not aim to start a conflict; I do not have a right to do that.

"Let me also be clear. No government has any knowledge of this force field technology. I've shared it with no one, and sold it to no one. I generate no revenue from turning it on. Most employees at my company had no idea it existed; this was among my most closely guarded secrets. Let me also add that if any nation invades another, as has been a constant threat of the Chinese government, I will turn off the force field over your nation and you will fend for yourself."

In reality, Robert could not do this—he could turn off a single spire to create a small hole in the shield, but he could not isolate a nation and keep everyone else protected. But he felt this bluff would be sufficient to avoid armed conflict between nations.

"You may ask how I was able to invent this technology. That requires a bit of explanation.

"For the past five years, I have been preparing for an alien invasion. Why? Because I am an alien. I was born to a family of mining slaves on a planet called Nayan. Due to high test results, I was put into a special program, a brainchild of Anton Frozos. After several years of training, we would be sent to a planet not yet under his control. Our job was to gain intelligence or influence to make it easier for him to take the planet over.

"I arrived on Earth in 2015 where I attended Yale—my background of being homeschooled in Wyoming a well laid-out fiction. I came to love this planet, particularly my new home of America. I was determined to never let happen to it what had happened to my home of Nayan. Much of my initial success came from replicating products that sold well in the League of Planets. That is why I was able to so quickly make technological innovation after innovation. The force field though is a genuine invention, I promise you.

"Earth is my adopted home, but I am not a human. That is why I've tried to avoid politics my whole life here, and why thus far, my efforts in this current crisis have been aimed solely at giving you the ability to decide for yourself. I hope you understand that."

For a moment, Robert pauses, bringing the teleprompter to a halt. He decides he needs to speak more definitively.

"Personally, I believe accepting Frozos's terms would be a terrible mistake. I've seen what he has done to other planets he has conquered. There is no such thing as peaceful coexistence. I will tell you that the force field is not the only new technology we have, and that our ability to win a fight is greater than many of our leaders have suggested. Finally, let me say this, there is never just one spy. I have strong evidence to suggest that other individuals of influence are either not human or are humans who have communicated with Frozos already."

Having made this point more clearly, Robert returns to his prepared text.

"For now, what I promise you is simple: I will keep the force field on, and I will take no provocative actions against any alien ships or any human government. If you decide that you want to take Frozos's offer, I will turn off that force field and that will be that. If, however, you decide to fight, that freedom is worth fighting for, and that one cannot be human without being free, know that I offer myself entirely and without reservation to your cause. In my life, I've encountered dozens of species of intelligent life. Mankind has its flaws, I assure you, but no species is as great as this one. Humans will fight over the pettiest of things when times are good, but when times are bad, your ability to rise to the occasion and will yourself to victory is unlike anything I've seen or studied.

"That is why Frozos has tried to quickly intimidate you into defeat. He doesn't want to give you the chance to rise to the fight because he's afraid you'll win. You know from your own history you can never appease your way to peace and security. We aren't doomed to a fate determined by some foreign species; we can write our own destiny, so long as we have the courage to pick up the pen and start writing. Thank you for your time."

The camera light switches off. He's off the air. Robert feels deeply unsatisfied. He wants to be much more explicit in naming names and urging a course of action. He finds sticking to a script to be stifling—he generally prefers to be more extemporaneous, but Chris had prevailed upon him the importance of using very precise language in these remarks. He'd love nothing more than to blow up Tiberius's ship—he is certain he could. But he had taken a vow. This was not his planet, and he would not determine the fate of seven billion people by himself. Even if his intentions were noble, that would be an indefensible course of action. He had come to believe stridently in the merit of self-government. On days like today, he did find it burdensome, but he isn't prepared to sacrifice that principle. One can't destroy freedom to preserve freedom, he had told himself. And so he worries that he had muddied his message, trying to have it both ways.

Mark and Chris, who walked back into his office, can sense he is displeased, and try to cheer him up. They heap him with praise, assuring him his message will be well received. Mark pulls out his phone and shows Robert an internal chat group for Arbor Ridge employees, which is filled with messages like "I trust Robert" and "So proud to be an Arbor Ridge employee." Robert appreciates his friends' steadfast support and loyalty, though he is anxious to see the response from the public at large.

Robert's speech sends shockwaves across the world. Governments and citizens alike are left to wonder how many other aliens are on the planet. Can Robert be trusted to keep the force field up, or would he hold them hostage? Will the planet be like this forever? Fortunately, Robert has developed a reservoir of goodwill, in part aided by Neverian's investigations, which had turned up no wrongdoing. Moreover, one in seven American households are directly or indirectly reliant on Arbor Ridge for their income. He had never done lay-offs and steadily raised pay. Within the United States at least, this provided him with tremendous credibility.

Across global capitals, people are filling up the streets, marching in solidarity with Robert's message, chanting the great cries of freedom like, "Live free or die," "We shall never surrender," "Liberty, Equality, Fraternity."

President Neverian sees one such demonstration as he looks down at the National Mall from the window of Marine One. With the threat of tsunamis having dissipated, he is able to return to the White House, leaving the Vice President in West Virginia. The Secret Service recommended they remain apart, and frankly, he was looking for an excuse to leave her behind.

Following Robert's speech, there was near unanimity among world leaders that they should not accept Frozos's terms by 6:00 PM tomorrow. Still, there was unease over the situation, as none of them knew how powerful the force field was or whether Robert would turn it off. Looking down at the crowd, a perfect idea hits Neverian; it's so obvious, he thinks to himself.

As Marine One lands on the South Lawn, it is nearly 8:00 PM. Above the noise of the helicopter's engine, the faint din of the marchers can be heard. He walks toward the West Wing as the typical throng of reporters await him. He is with his family, and urges them to walk ahead of him as he will be making brief remarks. He is glad that he freshened up on the plane ride from West Virginia—his hair, perfectly parted on the side, a clean white shirt, and a purple tie—it seemed to be the color of the hour after all (he didn't own a purple tie and had taken it from an aide).

"Mister President, Mister President, what is your response to Robert Wilson's speech?" the crowd of reporters shout.

"Good evening, I'll make brief remarks. On behalf of a grateful nation, I wish to thank Mister Wilson for unleashing a force field both around the moon and our planet. I was as shocked as you all to see this technology in use. Normally, we bleed red, white, and blue, but right now, the color of the hour is purple." Neverian smiles and points with both hands to his tie.

He continues, "Secured by his force field, the consensus of the international community at this time is that we will not accept Frozos's demands by 6:00 PM tomorrow. How we proceed beyond that is still very much being debated. To that point, let me say that I was particularly moved by how strongly Mister Wilson spoke of the need for we the people to determine our own fate. While he is not an American, it's clear that our ideals have influenced him greatly.

"To ensure that is the case, the people, not a singular man, should have control over the force field, for any one person, no matter how noble his intentions, can grow corrupt. We, of course, will rely on Robert's technological know-how for some time, but my government, the government democratically elected by the American people, formally requests that Robert Wilson and Arbor Ridge turn over operational control of the Arbor Ridge force field, namely by granting access to the Los Angeles and Jersey City towers, by 9:00 AM Eastern time tomorrow morning. By doing this, Robert Wilson will provide a powerful example to the world of how important self-government and self-determination are. Thank you and God bless you."

Robert clicks off the television. Seated behind his desk in his seventieth floor office, his shirt-sleeves are rolled up, his tie is off, and a half-eaten sandwich is off to the side of his desk.

Mark and Chris are with him as usual.

"That's one smooth operator," Mark gushes.

"I'll be honest, I thought he'd have been more rattled. I didn't see this one coming," Robert concedes.

"So are we going to let them in tomorrow? If we do, the government of every country we have a tower in will want the same treatment," Chris says.

"No, I can't. Like you said, we can't pick and choose which governments we give access, and if just one of these is turned off, there will be a hole in the shield, making us vulnerable to attack."

"Well then, we keep them out. Maybe you disenchant the public as a hypocrite rather than an idealist, but as long as the force field stays up, that's not a high price. Indeed, it is sometimes the noble thing to let oneself become the villain to protect the greater good," Mark counsels.

Robert knows Mark can sense how deeply troubled he is and is desperately trying to find advice that can comfort him to make an unpalatable choice. "You're right, Mark, if this status quo could last forever. But I fear there will come a time we need to fight Frozos head on, and if that day comes soon, I need lots of credibility."

"Is the force field not impenetrable?" Chris asks, suddenly sounding scared.

"No, I believe it is. But we could be a planet under siege shortly. And I assure you, the largest military in the galaxy, perhaps the universe, is trying to find some way to force me to turn off that force field. We need to think about that eventuality. Why else do you think I've been building a space armada?" Robert runs his right hand through his hair, and scratches the back of his head. "There's another option, but it's just, it's…"

"It's what, Robert?" Mark pushes as Robert tails off.

"Let me ask you something. If you knew a truth that would solve this problem, but it's so destructive it would cause greater problems, would you tell it?"

"Well, Robert, ask yourself, will you have to tell it at some point? If yes, then you may as well do it now," Mark offers.

Robert turns to face Chris.

"Yes," Chris says directly and emphatically to Robert.

"Why so sure?" Robert asks.

"Simple. I've known you, what, fifteen years? I know what the secret is. Tell it, and like Mark has said before, trust the public. I trust you, and they will too."

"Thank you both. I'm not going to decide anything just yet. I don't say this nearly enough, but I am so lucky to have you both as friends."

With that, the friends say goodnight, and Robert heads into his elevator to prepare for tomorrow.

CHAPTER 9

Planet Nayan
Earth Year 2004

The planet Nayan is a small planet, only about half of Earth's size. Life is relatively simple with a rural agrarian lifestyle. In addition, the planet is home to valuable mineral deposits that are critical for interplanetary space travel. These mines have helped turn Nayan into a relatively wealthy planet. The planet stays largely out of interplanetary politics, with inhabitants focused on their tribal lives. Every few months, great tankers come to purchase and ship out these minerals, in exchange trading new foods, technologies, and water.

Nayan is naturally a very dry planet, mostly consisting of an orange-colored clay, but the importation of vast water supplies has allowed life to move miles away from the few original major bodies of water. Nayans are hearty people and explorers, and a young Robert Wilson, whose native name is

Marcus Natent, is a boy in a small rural community of about four hundred, about fifty miles from the nearest mine.

To an outside observer, communities like this might seem very simple. Homes are generally just four or five rooms and one floor, often with thatched roofs. Everyone seems to know each other by name. The schoolhouse is a small building up a dirt road. Marcus and his friends are in fact bicycling back from school for the day.

At about seven years old, Marcus attends the second grade, his schooling heavy in mathematics and less focused on reading or writing. His family lives in a small, thatched roof house towards the outskirts of town, about two miles down the main road from the school. The only child of two loving parents, his father had been a college professor who married his high school sweetheart. After giving birth to Marcus, they decided they wanted a slower paced life, moving to this farming village where his father taught high school mathematics and science classes. Normally, Marcus would ride home with his father, but his father is staying after school late to help a struggling student with quantum physics, and so Marcus is riding back home with classmates.

A closer observer would note that while life in this town may seem simple, the advancements of an interplanetary existence are apparent. The vast farming fields Marcus bikes past, that stretch until the horizon, are manned entirely by robots, for instance. The cash crop being farmed is a hearty, vitamin-rich vegetable, resembling in its composition an eggplant. Flying above the village are dozens of drones: delivering packages, being used for surveillance, and so forth.

Anton Frozos had taken control of the League of Planets nearly five years ago, after a brutal and bloody civil war. The League now controls over 140 planets, up from ninety when Frozos had taken power. To this point, Nayan has avoided involvement in the League. Intergalactic wars and politics are not a priority for the Nayan people. Originally, they traded minerals with any other planet, but as more and more planets had fallen to Frozos, their trade was increasingly being done with members of the League.

There was increasing chatter throughout villages like this that the League would take over Nayan. Alongside this chatter, there were rumors of the brutality of Frozos's rule in mineral-rich planets, with the populace turned into slaves to boost production as much as possible. Frozos's vastly growing imperial ambitions required a constant supply of raw materials to enhance his military power and feed the ever-growing citizenry. Frozos had dubbed his planetary growth project the "Invest to Trade Initiative." New entrants to the League would benefit from promised substantial investment from the League to enhance their technologies, which would enable them to trade more and boost the living standards of their citizens.

In reality, there would be substantial investment, but this investment came with strings, often a League military presence. Frozos was essentially working to secure supply lines throughout the galaxy in key products and the promised "investment" was really just a purchase of influence and natural resources. With his influence, by paying off the right leaders, and on-the-ground military presence, political freedoms were quickly and easily tramped and forced labor became the norm.

While Frozos had been in power for five years, there are still rumors of a resistance. These rebel forces had been nearly snuffed out, but are said to survive on the piracy of League resources. Their reported leader comes from the water planet, Aquine, which had been the last holdout in the League Civil War, before falling and being completely destroyed by Frozos. Little does young Robert know that through this village they were smuggling minerals and supplies to resistance fighters from the mine fifty miles away. Indeed, his parents are among the leaders of the effort.

Driving past the downtown center of their village—which is really little more than a coffee shop, diner, and general store—Marcus's friends turn off the main road to head to their homes. He continues, having about a half mile to go. As he bikes along, it suddenly goes dark. Marcus looks up, confused. There hadn't been any clouds in the sky all day after all. Above him, there are no clouds but three massive spaceships, similar to the tankers Marcus had seen, which were used to ship minerals and other goods, but it was unusual for them to visit his town. Coming out of these tankers are a few dozen smaller planes, maybe twenty or thirty feet long.

Suddenly, there is a loud explosion behind him, and he's thrown from his bike.

He gets up, covered in dirt, his elbows and knees scratched up and bleeding. Fortunately for him, he is wearing a helmet, but his ears are ringing from the shock of the explosion. He turns around and sees the downtown on fire, while planes are circling and firing on the buildings. Another one lands, its back door drops down and a dozen troops of species he doesn't recognize walk out, firing upon the crowd. Screaming and crying, he runs towards his house, less than a quarter of a mile away.

As he nears his house, he sees his mother running towards him. Her usually warm, welcoming face is pinched with worry. As they meet, Robert asks, "Mommy, what's happening? I'm scared!"

"Shh, don't worry, Marcus, you'll be safe," she reassures her son as she picks him up into her arms and sprints towards the house.

Next to their home is a storm cellar—they hurry down the stairs. Marcus's mom places him on the floor and tells him, "Shh, stay absolutely silent. Not one sound. Remember that your father and I love you deeply."

Aware he may never speak to her again, Marcus takes in her long brown hair, tied back from her face; her black tunic and apron. He whispers, "I love you," nods, and she closes the door to the cellar and locks it.

Through a crack in the wooden door, Marcus can see her, walking away, then standing by the mailbox at the end of the property next to the main road, maybe fifty feet away. A voice booms, "The planet of Nayan is now part of the League of Planets. Come peacefully, and you will be treated justly. Resistance is futile. The planet of Nayan is now part of the League of Planets." The recording plays over and over again.

Marcus's mother is waiting anxiously; he can see her shifting from foot to foot as a column of troops marches down the street toward the house. Only later does Marcus realize that his mother knows if she stays it is a death sentence, but if she runs into the house, she worries that they will search throughout and find her son. She'd rather die than lose him. And so, she stands her ground, hoping beyond hope to see her husband, coming silently to terms with the inevitable.

There are a dozen troops, in orange camouflage with the blue League of Planets insignia on their right soldier.

"Nayan is now part of the League of Planets. We know this village was smuggling goods to the rebels. Tell us what you know," a soldier demands. As he asks, behind the column, another small craft lands.

"I know nothing," Marcus's mother responds, defiantly.

"Come with us then." As the soldier attempts to grab her, she pulls a small laser gun from her apron pocket, and fires at the soldier. She shoots again at another as she runs away from the house, continuing to fire. They fire back, and she is hit in the left thigh and right shoulder, falling to the ground, bleeding.

Marcus is terrified. He clamps his jaw shut, his hands over his mouth to keep it closed. Tears stream down his face as he sees his mother crawl on the ground, but he is determined to make her proud and stay absolutely silent. He sees a massive pale-blue figure walk out of the nearby spacecraft.

The blue man grabs his mother by her wounded shoulder and pulls her up as she shrieks in pain.

"Your wounds don't have to be fatal. Tell me, are some strangers who are doomed to defeat really worth dying over."

Marcus can barely hear her, as she has lost most of her strength, but staring into his evil red eyes, she is undeterred and responds clearly, "Yes, Frozos."

"So be it." He throws her to the ground and fires two shots.

Robert jumps awake. He is in his underground office, sitting back in his chair in front of the large monitors and next to the black sphere. It's nearly 5:00 AM. He must have fallen asleep down here for a few hours, awakened only by that nightmare of the past. For nearly thirty years, he had been haunted by the memory of his mother's death at Anton Frozos's hand. More than anything else, he wants to avenge her and kill Frozos. As he matured, he has realized that to truly avenge his mother's death, he needs to destroy Frozos's ideology, which distilled to its simplest form is that "might is right." Regardless, he still thirsts for Frozos's blood.

On his monitor, he notices an unread message. He clicks into it and reads:

"Message received. Understood.
Act as necessary.

—VL"

Robert is comforted by that note, exits, and looks to his live space camera feed. There is still just the one transport destroyer; he wonders how long until Frozos's other ships arrive. There is an untidy mess of papers on the desk, notes he was collating and adjusting ahead of the 9:00 AM deadline to turn over the towers. He pushes all the papers into a neat stack and opens the top left drawer. As he is about to put the papers in, he is notices a browned envelope, a bit worse for wear—after all, it is fifteen years old. He pulls out paper from inside the envelope. Typed on the page was the new name he was given, "Robert Wilson," and in red ink lies the message he had written himself, "REMEMBER THE MINE."

Taking a moment to reflect, he then puts the paper back in the envelope and back into the desk drawer. He is certain what he must do next.

CHAPTER 10

Jersey City
April 5, 2029

Robert Wilson stands in his underground office, his back to his powered-down computer monitors. It's 8:45 AM, and he's neatly dressed in a navy-blue suit and red tie with an American flag lapel pin. The black sphere is just to his right, but it is outside the view of the camera several feet in front of him. Given the security needs of the underground facility, Robert would not permit a live camera crew into his bunker. Instead, one cameraman—a balding, heavy-set man in his forties—was escorted into the room blindfolded. Robert is prerecording his remarks ahead of President Neverian's 9:00 AM deadline. When he finishes his remarks, the cameraman with the recording will be rushed back upstairs, once again blindfolded. Unlike his last remarks, there is no teleprompter to provide notes for him to refer to. On his desk behind him, Robert has etched out a rough outline of what he was going to say. It's just Robert and a lone cameraman on behalf of global media networks. After the two men nod to signal their readiness, the camera light flashes red, signaling the recording has commenced.

"Good morning. I won't bury the lede. I will not be turning over control of the force field or any critical Arbor Ridge property to the United States Government or to any other government. This technology was created by Arbor Ridge employees, paid for by Arbor Ridge shareholders, and it is the private property of this company. We do not seek to profit from it any more than we seek to profit from our annual charitable giving. That does not make it any less ours. I've consulted with our attorneys, and we see no legal authority under which the government could take it.

"Now, I will not pretend that my stand is purely a principled one on property rights grounds; I make this point to furnish this company's legal opinion should it prove necessary to fight for it in a court of law, not the court of public opinion. We cannot permit a crisis to lead us to ignore the rules and framework that have built a society that is worth saving.

"The primary reason I choose to exercise my legal right not to comply is that I do not trust the intentions of our government. As I said to you yesterday, there is never just one spy. I was trained in an elite military school on an isolated planet in Frozos's empire. We were never told how many schools on the planet there were, but there were several. I always assumed there was an obsession not to cross-pollinate because multiple people were being sent to each planet, perhaps with different missions, and Frozos wanted to avoid a cross-mingling that could lead us to conspire with each other against him.

"I was valedictorian of my training camp, and my greatest proficiency was in technology. I believe the force field above our heads is a testament to this fact. It was my assumption that Frozos would send spies with different skills to fully invade a planet from within, going after its education institutions, governments, private sector, and technological networks. I had always sworn to myself I would fight Frozos at any cost. Once here, I realized the best way to do this would be to follow the plan, use my technological knowledge to gain wealth and influence, hence my focus on defense contracting. I provided Frozos updates on my progress as scheduled right from here."

Robert points to his right, and the cameraman turns to focus on a black metallic sphere. Robert punches a few keys, a hole opens and a ramp extends to the floor. Robert walks over.

"I leveraged my spaceship's communications network to offer updates to Frozos or his advisors. However, like I said, technology, is my strong suit, so after about five years or sometime in 2020, I wired a system to track the frequency of the pulse of our messages and used that data to find other spies."

Robert now walks back to the computer monitors, punches a key and a monitor flashes on with a world map and bulging red circles emanating across the United States, Western Europe, and East Asia.

"This is every pulse I successfully tracked as a Frozos communication. Now, some emanate from the same spy who travelled. I have found at least twenty spies, myself included.

Several amounted to nothing, two have died, but several achieved successes in various industries.

"As CEO of Arbor Ridge, I was criticized for seemingly random acquisitions beginning in 2022. In actuality, the pattern was simple. I bought companies run by a Frozos spy; yes I bought a few others as well, just to cover my tracks to Frozos. That's why I kicked out every CEO; I wanted to purge individuals potentially loyal to Frozos. I did not even make my co-founders, Mark Morrison and Chris Bailey, aware of any of these facts until last November.

"The spy CEOs were people who rebounded to occupy seats of power today: Attorney General Braddock, World Bank President Johnson, Commerce Secretary Clemons, UN Ambassador Sayers, America's Council of CEOs Chairman Stewartson, the Affiliated Workers Union President Paulson. There was another who went on to enjoy life in retirement, Bill Williamson.

"I stopped all contact with Frozos in 2026, having developed enough data to track outgoing communications. There was one spy I never could identify and that one was from Washington D.C. This individual only sent written reports, most of which I was able to intercept, including one last July, saying the invasion target date was early spring 2029. By January, the date was narrowed to between March twentieth and April tenth.

"It concerned me that President Neverian appointed so many officials to his government who were Frozos spies. My concern grew on April second and April third when he proposed such a cowardly policy and yet was so confident. He did not seem like a man in a state of panic. It seemed so inconsistent. Then on his meeting with leaders April third, the retired Bill Williamson, a former Frozos spy, was in attendance—a completely forgettable man. Why would he be there?

"Last night, I looked through every communication with Frozos and noticed two that came from Beijing—there had never been a communication with China before. Unlike those in Washington, these were two-way video calls, not text reports. President Neverian was meeting Chinese President Li in Beijing when both these pings were sent. Of course, China has been actively supporting Neverian's surrender strategy while amassing its military at its border with Russia.

"In summary, I believe Frozos has compromised our government to its very top. I believe President Neverian is a spy, and that he wants our force field so he can turn it off. And I believe they have bribed the Chinese government with a promise they could rule over much of Asia. Put clearly, President Li had negotiated to be slave driver on behalf of Frozos over much of the world.

"There is only one person in government I trust—Vice President Victoria Larom, because she was outside of Washington when messages were sent, and because President Neverian has kept her at such a distance. At 2:00 this morning, I transmitted every piece of data I have to her. For transparency, I have posted at 9:00 AM on Arbor Ridge's website every interaction I have had with Frozos while on Earth.

I will never hand over control over the force field to an entity I fear is corrupted by Frozos. If that makes me a hypocrite, so be it. I have also developed a plan I am prepared to present in an open forum at the appropriate time, that I believe can defeat Frozos and secure our planet. Thank you and God bless you."

The red light turns off. Robert walks over to the door to let in Mark and Chris as well as two security officials. As the security guard walks over to the cameraman to put on his blindfold, he turns to Robert, "Well, sir, if it matters, you convinced me. And I voted for the guy!"

Robert pats the man on the shoulder and thanks him. He, Mark, and Chris follow the security guards who are guiding the cameraman to the elevator. Once back in Robert's seventieth floor office, the cameraman's blindfold is taken off, and he rushes off to get his recording ready for live television.

"Take a seat, guys," Robert gestures to his two friends. "It's not often you get to watch a speech with the guy who gave it. Plus, it will be fun to watch your facial reactions in real-time."

Right at 9:00 AM, the television cuts to Robert's speech. In households across America and the world, everyone is watching the speech, except in China, which has opted to air the speech on a fifteen-minute delay so that the government could monitor the content before determining whether to permit Chinese state media to broadcast the remarks. Robert closely watches Mark and Chris's every reaction, the slight nod or frown, to gauge their true feeling of the remarks. He can sense their rapt attention and feels more confident that the speech did in fact rise to the occasion. As his remarks conclude, his two friends turn to him and say together, "Well done!"

The sentiment on air is one of disbelief as pundits ponder the implications of the allegations against President Neverian, phrases like "Manchurian Candidate," "Constitutional Crisis," and "treason" are being thrown around. There seems to be unanimity, at least among these talking heads, that the force field is best kept in Arbor Ridge's control. As this banter goes on, Robert's phone rings; someone from the Arbor Ridge control room is calling him.

"Hello…I see," Robert nods along. "No surprise," and then pausing a moment, he says, "Well, I just bragged to the world about our technological genius. I'd like to think we could hack into their networks and force it into their broadcasts." Robert hangs up the phone, annoyed, as Mark and Chris turn to him.

"The Chinese aren't airing the remarks; just showing a snippet of me on the force field and talking about Neverian." He bounces up out of his chair with nervous energy. "They're complicit in the whole damn affair and trying to sweep it under the rug. But the dirty secrets always find their way into the light."

Mark looks up at Robert from his seat, "But is it our place to shine the light? You basically ordered a cyberattack on one of the world's most powerful nations."

"If not us, who? Our government is in chaos; who will hold them accountable? The people have a right to know what their government does."

"Maybe, but remember the greatest forest fires can start from the smallest of sparks. Don't start something you can't contain," Mark counsels.

"Listen," Chris jumps in, "I'll back you up entirely, Robert. But like it or not, you've just made yourself the most powerful person on the planet. Not only with the shield around us. You said it on global television. Every industry an alien empire sought to infiltrate to cripple us you've brought under one roof and entirely control. Arbor Ridge isn't a company, it's a nation state, and you're its ruler. There's no one, I, or Mark," Chris gestures to his friend who nods along approvingly, "or anyone else for that matter, would want in your seat. But don't lose sight of why you assembled these pieces in the first place. That's all we are saying."

Robert sits back down in his chair, absorbing their advice. "No, that's a helpful reminder. Maybe..."

Just then a bulletin flashes across the television in Robert's office as headlines appear across the screen: "WHITE HOUSE UNDER ATTACK?"

There is great commotion in Washington, D.C. Sirens are blaring. Phones are buzzing with alerts ordering all citizens to shelter in place. Fighter jets have been scrambled and can be heard making sweeps across the city, flying low in the sky. At least a half a dozen Apache and Black Hawk helicopters are circling low above the White House. Staffers from the Eisenhower Executive Office Building (EEOB), where much of a President's Administration actually works, are staring out their office windows over towards the White House, watching the circling helicopters.

Each time that a helicopter gets near the White House to land, there are some scattered shots fired from snipers on the White House rooftop. There is no return fire from the helicopter, instead it flies back up in the sky. Onlookers from the EEOB are puzzled, asking among themselves why the anti-aircraft missiles that are deployed underneath the White House lawns aren't being used. And why aren't the helicopters firing back?

Suddenly, the snipers can be seen vacating the roof of the White House. Helicopters again attempt a landing. Two Black Hawks land on the South Lawn while another lands on the White House roof. Heavily armed soldiers hop out of the helicopters, dressed head to toe in black body armor, wearing oxygen masks, and carrying rifles. Each helicopter must house ten soldiers.

A sight few Americans could have ever dreamt is being played out on national television: The White House is being overrun by armed soldiers. And they are not even meeting much apparent resistance with no sounds of gunfire evident to those near the executive mansion.

The thirty men tasked with this assignment are members of an elite regiment of the Marine Corps Special Operations Command, led by Master Sergeant Jim Kelley, a twenty-four-year veteran of the Marines. His regiment was stationed on assignment in Northern Africa but had been brought back stateside to Texas early in the week after the alien spaceship appeared. He never thought he'd be asked to do this, but here he is, in one of the helicopters to land on the South Lawn. As is his custom, he's first off the chopper and leads his men.

Kelley's men make their way towards the back doors of the Oval Office. Typically, these doors are guarded by Marines, ceremonially, when the President is at work, but this brisk

April morning, they are unattended. Kelley leads a group of ten men towards the most famous office on the planet. The group of ten from the helicopter fifteen yards east of Kelley will be swinging around the White House and proceed to the East Wing where they are to safely secure Neverian's family, believed to be in the White House Residence. Another ten Marines will be making their way down from the roof level to provide support as needed.

This task should prove straightforward if proper communications have occurred, but every solider is tense as they venture across the lawn. Kelley leads his men to the Oval Office where the curtains have been closed to block any view. They kick the door open. There is no reaction from inside the room. Kelley leads his men in.

They are greeted by the sight of President Nick Neverian seated behind his desk. Members of his Secret Service Detail are guarding the doors, guns pointed at him. A junior military officer is seated at the far end of the room with a black suitcase between his legs under his chair. Kelley signals to two of his men who cross the room toward the nuclear football. Kelley says to the lead Secret Service agent, "Athena."

The agent responds, "Catherine."

The code being answered appropriately, Kelley orders his men at ease, and they remove their oxygen masks. Kelley walks in front of Neverian's desk and says, "I have been ordered to tell you, Mister President, that the Vice President and a majority of the Cabinet have invoked the 25th Amendment that you are unable to discharge the duties of the office. You have been temporarily removed from office with Vice President Larom assuming the powers."

"Thank you, Officer," Neverian blankly responds, staring off in the distance, emotionless. "Is my family safe?"

After a brief pause as Kelley radios the East Wing unit, he turns to Neverian and says, "Yes, sir. They are safe and being held in the East Wing."

"Thank you." Neverian flatly replies.

"I've been asked to keep you here for now."

Half a world away in China, Arbor Ridge has successfully hacked into China's state media, and Robert's speech, including his allegations of complicity with Frozos by their government, has been airing while global media is focusing on developments at the White House. With an increasingly perilous situation domestically, President Li is fortunate to have completely consolidated power, politically. Seeing the situation in Washington D.C., Li senses an opening on the international stage. While Russian President Malvodov had pulled most of his troops back from the Russia-China border, China maintained its significant buildup within fifty miles of the border. Now, Li orders them to move across. He also orders troops to begin taking Mongolia. China will be moving westward.

Robert's bluff to open the force field above a nation does not intimidate Li, for he has struck a deal with Frozos. Now, his only viable political future is one in which Earth joins the League of Planets. Bringing the planet to the brink of global war is the only viable path he sees, callous to the fact it puts hundreds of millions of lives in jeopardy.

Five hundred thousand Chinese soldiers are amassed on China's western front, replete with heavy artillery, batteries of tanks, and a fleet of several hundred aircrafts. Li has transmitted orders that the attack is to commence in thirty minutes. Stage one will be aerial strikes on the Russian troops and their supply lines. Once weakened, the land assault will commence in stage two. As troops begin the race across Eastern Russia, stage three, the race across Mongolia will commence, in an effort to trap a large portion of Russia's military between two Chinese armies.

Concurrently, China has moved its air defense to the highest possible level of alert and preparedness in the event Russian President Mikhail Malvodov does the unthinkable and launches a nuclear strike on China's homeland. Russia has over 4,000 nuclear warheads, making it the second most potent nuclear power on the planet behind the United States. While Li is confident in his military's ability to shoot down a handful of missiles at any one time, a mass launching from Russia would overwhelm its system. Li accordingly has decided to only use non-nuclear weapons in his attack in the hope Russia will respond in kind.

In his office, still with Mark and Chris, Robert picks up his ringing phone, his facial expression quickly turning to one of grave concern. "Okay, I'll be right down," he says before hanging up. He stands up, gesturing to his colleagues. "Come, let's get downstairs. Something's going on with China."

After taking the secret elevator to Project Ridley, they enter a room next to Robert's underground office, a room Mark and Chris haven't been in yet. The room must be thirty-five feet deep and sixty feet wide with auditorium style seating and is filled with several dozen workers in purple jumpsuits. The outfits look to be of the same material with the same Arbor Ridge insignia as the workers Mark and Chris had seen making the jets on these basement floors over the past few months, but those workers wore navy blue, not purple.

Robert leads them down the steps at the side of the room to the bottom. On the twenty-five-foot-high wall are a dozen television screens, monitoring news stations, the twelve towers and deep-water force field spires, as well as footage from the moon, and satellites in outer space.

"Hi, Jake Thornhill, this is Mark Morrison and Chris Bailey." Robert introduces his co-founders to a man standing behind a desk who carries an aura of being in charge. He looks to be about sixty, but is as tough as nails and still cuts a lean military figure. His weathered face and tight grey hair reveal him as a man who has lived a fulsome and tiresome life in the arena. The three men exchange pleasantries. Robert sees the puzzled look on his friends' faces and realizes he hasn't explained what this room is.

"I'm sorry guys. You're probably wondering what this all is. This is our command center. They helped to build and now monitor the force field on a minute by minute basis to ensure everything is secure. Jake spent over thirty years at the DIA and has been providing his intelligence expertise for us these past few years. We also will be running our communications efforts through here. So, Jake, what is it?"

Jake hands Robert a manila folder. "Well, sir, we've intercepted Chinese orders to begin invading Russia, it's all in there. By air first, and then a ground invasion."

"Wait, we're spying on governments now?" an absolutely bewildered Chris asks.

"No more than they are trying to spy on us," Robert calmly answers while thumbing through the documents—mostly photos of troop movements, and copies of orders.

"I warned you this would happen," Mark says. "A cornered tiger is bound to bite, and you put Li in the corner."

"He put himself there, Mark, the day he sold out his home to a foreign invader. I would normally do nothing, but we're crippled," Robert responds, pointing to the images of the White House, seemingly overrun by soldiers and helicopters. "I've been clear national borders are to be respected, and we're going to ensure they are."

"So you'll turn off the force field above China?" Chris asks.

"Actually, we lack that capability," Thornhill interjects.

"Yes, Chris, that was a bluff. Besides, Li doesn't care because he's thrown his fate in with Frozos. The fool doesn't realize Frozos would blow them up anyway just to scare the rest of us. Okay, I think it's time we show off Project Ridley a bit."

"I know we've been building planes everywhere, but don't we need pilots?" Chris asks.

"Chris, all these years of focusing on the numbers have robbed you of your imagination," Mark responds, finding Chris's obliviousness nearly as frustrating as Robert's apparent cavalier attitude. "I'm sure we'll find dozens of pilots in orange jumpsuits around here somewhere."

"Red, actually," Robert deadpans. "But we're too far away, and we need to go undetected by everyone in the world except by the one person who we need to act like nothing is happening. Let's send 250 planes out of the Moscow tower."

As Thornhill is transmitting the order, another helicopter is landing at the White House.

Neverian has been sitting in the Oval Office for about twenty minutes since Jim Kelley and his Marines had informed him his Presidential powers had been temporarily turned over to Vice President Larom. During that time, not a word has been spoken, and everyone is finding the silence unbearably awkward. Minutes feel like hours. Finally, the rumbling of an engine can be heard in the background. Neverian knows that sound. He is about to look behind him when he remembers that the curtains had been drawn.

Another minute or so of silence passes, and then, led by her own Secret Service Detail, Acting President Larom walks into her new office. Neverian remains at his seat, but everyone in the room stands at attention. She is wearing a red dress and dark-blue blazer. She walks in front of Neverian's desk and does not extend her hand to shake. Nor does he.

"Mister President," she says, speaking clearly and deliberately, having precisely prepared her remarks, "Master Sergeant Kelly should have informed you that the Cabinet has invoked the 25th Amendment, which transferred the Presidential powers to me. An emergency Cabinet meeting was convened at 3:30 this morning. All members of the Presidential line of succession but Attorney General Braddock were in attendance. We reviewed materials provided by Robert Wilson and deemed you unfit to be President on a—"

"On what grounds am I unfit?" Neverian asks.

"You are not a natural born citizen, and we view you as disqualified from being President. The constitution does afford you an ability to contest this decision. However, the House and Senate are prepared to impeach and remove you from office this afternoon. You've lost. The choice you face is whether to do so with dignity."

"I haven't lost; the fight has barely begun. He is coming here and with him comes a reckoning. That said, I recognize the reality of the situation. And so I have resigned, effective immediately."

He takes a paper out of a desk drawer, temporarily putting the Secret Service and Marines on edge. As he passes it to Larom, he asks, "Tell me. How does it feel to have hitched your coattails to an invader and cheated your way to the top?"

Larom ignores the question as Neverian is escorted out of the Oval Office. He is being taken, with his family, to a top secret military prison installation in Virginia.

As Neverian walks out, a contingent of senior military personnel walk in. One steps forward, "Madam President. There is a pressing situation in China."

"Well, we have a pressing situation in the United States, too."

"Yes, but we appear to be minutes from China invading Russia."

Larom seems to age six months in six seconds as the gravity of the crisis she inherited fully sinks in. "What has Malvodov done in response?" she asks.

"Our intelligence hasn't gathered anything yet, but he has been clear only Russians will rule Russians. We can't rule anything out. We need to take decisive action," the General replies.

At this point, a young aide, a woman of about thirty in the back of the room decides to step in, fearing a catastrophic mistake. "He won't do anything!" she shouts.

The senior brass turn and give her cold icy stares. President Larom looks to her and asks, "Why are you so sure?"

The aide walks forward and hands her some satellite images of the Moscow Arbor Ridge tower. "At least a hundred planes have left the Arbor Ridge tower in Moscow. We can't identify the models. They stayed on radar just long enough to be sure the Russian military saw them and disappeared."

"Madam President," the General interjects, "this country didn't go through the pain of taking orders from an elected alien to following the lead of an unelected one."

"I agree, General, but Mister Wilson did send us his evidence against Neverian eight hours before he told the public, which is why we are standing here. We will give him fifteen minutes to clean up his mess. He put Li in a box, foolishly. During that time, I will brief the American people on what the hell has happened to their government and you will draw up options for me."

"Yes, ma'am." With that, the military officials proceed out and down to the Situation Room to prepare a response. As they leave, a press aide pops his head in the door.

"Madam President, the Chief Justice is here, and we've assembled the press in the briefing room."

"Give me a moment, Mike," the President replies.

"Take your time, Madam President," the aide replies as he shuts the door. Larom stands alone in the Oval Office, a room filled with historical moments. She kneels to the ground and says a brief prayer. Getting up, she heads out to meet the press and address the nation.

The press briefing room is filled to the brim with rows of reporters and cameras in the back. At the front, there is a blue lectern with the emblem of the White House behind it. Larom walks in alongside the Chief Justice of the Supreme Court in his court robes, an elderly man of nearly eighty years who is about to swear in a President for the seventh time.

Standing behind the Lectern with the Chief Justice to her right, Larom begins, speaking confidently from prepared remarks that she barely has to reference. "At 3:37 this morning, I chaired a Cabinet meeting to determine if President Nick Neverian should be temporarily removed as President under the 25th Amendment of the constitution. Mister Robert Wilson had shared files that he discussed this morning with us at around 1:00 AM. Attorney General Brian Braddock was not invited over concerns he would inform the President of the meeting. As nonvoting participants, we included congressional leadership of both parties: the Senate Majority and Minority Leaders, the Speaker of the House, and the House

Minority Leader. At 4:44 AM, we voted unanimously to remove the President temporarily, due to the fact we believed he was not a natural born citizen. This action enjoyed the support of the members of Congress in attendance.

"I ordered the military and Secret Service to detain Neverian in the White House, and I am pleased to say that operation was conducted without any casualties. I arrived several minutes ago; when informed of these decisions, President Neverian voluntarily resigned the Presidency, and he and his family have been taken unharmed to a military facility. For the avoidance of any doubt, the live feed from a camera on our Marines who entered the Oval Office is being shared with the media as I speak. With that, I ask the Chief Justice to step forward, and I will take the oath of office."

The Chief Justice steps forward. Larom's husband and young daughter walk over from the side of the stage to hold the Bible upon which she recites the Presidential oath of office:

> "I, Victoria Mary Larom, do solemnly swear that I will faithfully execute the Office of President of the United States, and will to the best of my ability, preserve, protect, and defend the Constitution of the United States."

With that, Larom is officially the President of the United States, no longer the acting President. She gives her husband and daughter a kiss, and then they walk off with the Chief Justice. Larom will now be giving her first official remarks as President, aware that China and Russia could be colliding in a nuclear war at any moment. Pausing for a moment, she steps back up to the lectern.

"It is my profound honor and privilege to serve you the American people as President of these United States. Let me make clear to you that my Administration has but one agenda: to ensure that I am not the last President of the United States. To the rest of the world and to our alien adversaries, let me also be clear, and say what should have been said long ago already: the United States seeks peace and friendship with all, but as a cost of this peace, we will never sacrifice our founding principles. We will never surrender our constitution nor relinquish our self-government to someone else. I hope the entire world, including the people of China, will join us in this effort.

"Those are the guiding principles of my Administration. To ensure the successful achievement of this agenda, we have begun to take action. I have removed from office Attorney General Braddock and all other individuals named by Mister Wilson, as we were able to independently corroborate his conclusions. This action will ensure that every member of this Administration is on the same team: your team. Now is not a time for partisanship, so to fill the Vice President vacancy, I have asked the leaders of the other party, the Senate and House Minority Leaders, to give me four candidates from their party, and I will choose one to join this Administration as VP.

"Additionally, we must determine the next course of action. Given the deception that has plagued our government and key institutions, I will be brutally honest with you today and in the future. I do not know if this force field is a permanent solution or if there will be war. I know nothing more about this technology or Anton Frozos than you do. Robert Wilson is the only individual who can speak to his technology. I have invited him to the White House tomorrow to discuss it and what his proposals are. Congress will be back in session tomorrow, and if appropriate, we can address these questions then.

"Our answer will have to be more than a whole of government approach. Yes, we need every branch of our federal government working together, but we need a whole-of-America approach that capitalizes upon the capabilities of our government, our entire private sector, our armed services, and our strongest asset: you, the citizenry. We will deliver this and lead this nation and world to a brighter future. Of that, I am certain. God bless you, your families, and God bless the United States of America."

Contrary to tradition, the media in the room give President Larom a standing ovation as she exits the briefing room and heads to the Situation Room to confer with her military advisors as to the goings on in China and Russia.

While Larom is speaking to the American people, Air Force base taxiways in Western China are filling up with its fighter jets prepared to take off. They are just minutes from launching phase one of the incursion into Russian territory when a sonic boom is heard. Suddenly, about 1,000 feet high in the air, dozens of planes appear just west of the base between the runway and the Russian border. They are hovering in midair, unlike any fighter jet known to man. The planes appear to have a thirty-five to forty-foot wingspan and are entirely black apart from a gold stripe down across the end of each wing. In their control tower, there is panic as planes appear on the radar screen. Officials are scrambling to understand how these planes entered Chinese airspace undetected and how anti-aircraft missiles were not tripped.

On the runway, panic ensues as mechanics and support staff run for cover. Pilots are paralyzed, sitting on the tarmac like sitting ducks but afraid to takeoff directly at the rows of planes where they would be equally easy targets. On their radios, they ask why air traffic control didn't warn them of incoming planes so they could get up in the air more quickly.

Then, they hear a booming voice, apparently coming from speakers on the planes, that in Chinese says, "Our advanced engine and cloaking technology enabled us to pass through your airspace undetected. Our weaponry is equally advanced. Evacuate these fields and withdraw all troops to one hundred miles away from the border, and we will not attack. Attempt to attack, and we will respond."

This statement is repeated again and again. After being repeated five times, it pauses for thirty seconds before restarting the pattern. The entire time, the planes just hover in mid-air. By now, radar has counted two hundred—twenty rows, ten deep—covering half a mile by a quarter mile. The base commander gets off the phone.

"Beijing says the strike is to start; there are to be no more delays. They are sitting motionless in the sky—fire the anti-aircraft placed across the front at them!"

There is hectic activity across the base as soldiers assume their battle stations, and begin the assault. Missiles from over twenty-five sites fly to the heavens to shoot down the unknown Air Force in the sky. Long guns are mounted to shoot at targets. There are booms of explosions as the shelling commences. The sky lights up in fire and the sunlight is soon overwhelmed in smoke.

The command center cheers as the radar shows no planes in the air, with fist bumps, high-fives and thumbs-ups all around. Then, after about twenty seconds with the smoke still clearing, bogeys appear again on the radar. Descending from the south down to an altitude of no more than 200 feet, a contingent of seven planes flying in a V-formation zoom across at a deafening speed with the radar trackers unable to keep pace. Their mounted cannons methodically destroy the anti-aircraft artillery. Soldiers attempt to fire from the ground but to no avail with the wind the planes leave in their wake throwing the men to the ground. Then another contingent of seven planes descends from the north, repeating the maneuver.

The Chinese frontline is now engulfed in smoke. Reports from the ground to the command center point to a near annihilation of their anti-aircraft capabilities in a strike that barely lasted two minutes. Fortunately, initial casualties appear minimal. Sirens echo across the base as fire crews attempt to put out the flames. China's armada of fighter jets remains untouched on the tarmacs with crew growing increasingly restless. With their counter-offensive completed, the sky again fills up with the same 200 planes. The Chinese military was unable to claim a single jet. The base is again subjected to a booming voice saying on repeat, "Evacuate these fields and withdraw all troops to one hundred miles away from the border, and we will not attack. Attempt to attack again, and we will respond with harsher force."

"Call Beijing again," the commander orders.

At the central headquarters of China's Government, President Li is irate. Reports from the field confound him, and his military advance is stymied before it has even begun. His mood is about to get worse. Two security aides rush in, and one says, "We need to go underground, sir."

"Why?" a frustrated Li asks.

The aide points out the window. Li walks over to see several dozen planes hovering over the city. He is grabbed back from the window, and they rush downstairs to an underground bunker. Li walks into a plain room, with a long table that he sits at the head of. On the far end, there are screens showing the Beijing skyline as well as pictures from the besieged base on China's western front. The table is filled with aides and military officials, frantically making calls trying to understand how fifty jets had entered Beijing's airspace without triggering any early-warning alarms. Their systems cannot decipher what types of planes they are or where they had come from. It is obvious that the fleet in Beijing and the front are in the same force given identical designs and hovering patterns.

Back in Washington D.C., President Larom is in the Situation Room with her top officials from the Pentagon, offering strategies as to how to best proceed. Satellites in the Far East have picked up unusual readings, but it's unclear what those readings suggest. Chinese forces near the Russian border remain at a standstill, despite expectations that a strike would be underway by now. There is also no evidence that the Russian military is preparing any aggressive actions. As a consequence, she continues to resist suggestions from the Pentagon to enhance America's military alertness.

The status quo is actually tolerable. No borders have been crossed, after all. But this equilibrium appears extremely fragile. Larom thinks to herself that she must balance two competing interests; first, ensuring America can defend herself if things go haywire, but second, not taking any action that could be viewed by the Chinese as a provocation.

In an effort to find this balance, she orders, "General, we will not be mobilizing or increasing the level of alert for any of our nuclear capabilities. However, you can mobilize all of our defense shield mechanisms and escalate the readiness of conventional forces in the Middle East and Asia Pacific."

"Yes, Madam President," the general replies.

No one in the room seems particularly pleased nor distressed by this course of action, encouraging Larom that she has found a steady course. No sooner has she ordered this than a security advisor alerts her that Russian President Mikhail Malvodov is seeking a video call. She signals to put him on the screen. He is speaking from his office in Moscow, and the camera in the Situation Room is positioned so that he can only see her, not her array of advisors. Undoubtedly, there was also an unseen group of advisors with Malvodov.

"President Larom, congratulations on taking office. You are facing a trial by fire, no doubt?" Malvodov begins. He looks unwaveringly calm, particularly considering his nation is on the edge of war. Years of service during the Cold War have numbed him to the threat of nuclear annihilation, or perhaps he just has a very adept poker face.

"Thank you, President Malvodov. Indeed, I have, though we don't seek these jobs because we like to make small decisions, now do we?" she coolly replies.

"No we do not. This is why I must ask whether your Mister Wilson is working at your behest. Or have you outsourced decisions to him?" Malvodov likely already knows the answer to this question, making it all the more cutting.

"Well, I suppose I could ask whether you have outsourced your war fighting to him?" Larom sharply responds. The hawks surrounding Larom in the Situation Room who questioned whether she was strong enough to lead at this moment show a clear appreciation for this answer. In her first minutes on the job, and she is holding serve against a seasoned foreign policy operator.

"Point taken, Miss Larom. It seems we should take for granted that our interests are aligned with Mister Wilson, but that he is a wild card."

"I think that's fair."

"You no doubt have images as do I of his jets leaving his Moscow tower. What my intelligence agencies are sharing with yours now are photos from our border with China that show these jets pinning China's Air Force to the ground. Despite the unease of some advisors, I've decided that so long as those jets are there in the sky, we will not take a solitary military action. If they do move or get destroyed, that commitment may not stand. Do I make myself understood?"

"Understood. I believe that you are taking a wise approach," President Larom replies. As she says this, an aide passes her a paper. The same occurs to Malvodov. Her paper reads in handwritten capital letters "MORE PLANES OVER BEIJING." She pauses, thinks to herself not to show any emotion. Looking back up, she can see on the TV to the left of the one showing Malvodov a live feed of Beijing with several dozen planes just hovering over the Central Headquarters.

"Well, Mister President, I suspect your aide handed you a similar paper as mine, about Beijing."

"Indeed. Your Mister Wilson is a bold man. He may be from outer space, but he's very American. I trust you to handle him. In the meantime, you understand my position, yes?"

"I do. Godspeed."

With that, they disconnect. There is now frantic energy in the room as they try to figure out what is going on in Beijing.

Larom turns to an aide. "Get me Wilson on the phone."

CHAPTER 11

Jersey City
April 5, 2029

R obert Wilson is in the command center in the basement of his Jersey City headquarters. Jake Thornhill who runs the center is calmly managing the operations, ensuring a steady flow of communication between the Jersey City Center, the Moscow Center, the aerial contingent in West China, and the one over Beijing. His years of experience have left him well prepared to keep everyone calm and following procedure. They've been training in simulations and war games to build processes and muscle memories for scenarios like this, but no drill can mimic the adrenaline rush, the high stakes, and uncertainty of an actual crisis.

Mark Morrison and Chris Bailey, neither of whom engaged in such training, are sitting off to the side in varying states of shock. Robert is trying to remain calm for their sakes, and he knows both men admire the professionalism Thornhill displays. He knows Mark is worried about the nature of high-powered politics they are entering, but he's easily able to mask his concerns, especially around strangers. Chris, on the other hand, is sweating profusely, pacing back and forth with nervous energy, and more than a few times Mark has whispered to him that he needs to sit down and get his act together.

Robert stands at the floor of the auditorium, gazing up and across the screens with his hands on his hips. Images on the main screen are from West China and Beijing. He portrays calm because he feels calm. The day is far from over, but thus far, he feels his confidence in Project Ridley is being validated. They have barely scratched the surface of the capabilities these fighter jets possess, and yet they have easily laid waste to global radar tracking and the Chinese military's capabilities. Despite some internal skepticism, his young pilot crew is performing quite well under pressure.

The goal of the West China mission has been completely accomplished thus far. Robert is proving out these weapons, and they can keep the military pinned down indefinitely. This is where the Beijing contingent must step up and push the government to de-escalate—a far trickier task. Robert is keen to not be the provocateur; his focus is on ensuring the integrity of international borders and preparing for the fight against Frozos, not internal politics. He is thinking to himself what should be broadcast from the speakers of the Beijing planes.

At that moment his cell phone rings, and he pulls it out of his right pocket, annoyed. Who could be calling now? It's an unlisted number. He knows that could only be one person.

"Hello."

"Please hold for the President of the United States."

Robert walks out the side door into his office, alone. This is not a conversation that he should be having in front of the rank and file who are implementing his strategy.

"Hello, Robert, it's Victoria. How are you?"

"Madam President. I'm glad you're the one I'm speaking to in this situation."

"Thank you, but flattery will only get you so far. And we've gotten to that point. Both President Malvodov and myself are genuinely appreciative of your actions to keep escalations from rising on the border."

"Glad to do it." Robert leans back in his chair in front of his monitors to keep an eye on his jets. The cables that had connected his spaceship to his monitors now lie on the ground, disconnected.

Meanwhile Larom is using the speaker phone of the Situation Room, while also monitoring the skies above Beijing. The room remains filled with her advisors as well as voice specialists and CIA psychologists to analyze what Robert says and how he says it. Of course, whether voice inflections from an alien mean the same as from a human is a scientific unknown.

"The point I'm getting at, Robert, is that we've given you a lot of flexibility, but we need to know why there are fifty planes in Beijing."

"Madam President, do you have an idea of how to get Li to move his troops away from Russia's border? I have no plan on waging war on China, so I am blocking his troops from advancing. But I don't want to keep my boys there forever—"

"Your boys?" the President interjects.

"Well, someone needs to fly the plane. Don't worry—when I visit the White House to discuss my plan to take on Frozos as you suggested this morning, I'll give you all the details. So where was I? Li, yes, that's right. So you tell me how to get Li to draw his troops back. I'm trying to scare him, and more importantly the rest of his government. And maybe embolden his public that his government isn't all powerful after all."

"Okay. We will try to mediate a solution with Li. But to be clear, I don't want those planes firing on Beijing. The United States Government will not condone that, and we will disavow you and everything else you want to do, force field or not. Do I make myself understood?"

"Completely. It's nice talking to someone with a backbone for a change. I will speak to you soon, Madam President."

"Thank you, Mister Wilson." President Larom hangs up the phone, and she looks across the table at her advisors. "You know, that man may be a genius but boy does he scare me. And he ought to scare you too, because he has the power to do most anything, and he's willing to use it. But you know what, I bet he's scaring all the right people too. And right now, maybe that's what we need."

Back at Arbor Ridge headquarters, Robert, feels satisfied with the call and is hopeful that Larom will prove to be a worthy

President in such trying times. He springs out of his chair and walks back into the command center.

"Who was that?" Chris asks, bewildered by the fact Robert took a call during such a crisis.

"It was the President, Chris. We aren't the only ones with satellite cameras."

He turns away from Chris and Mark to talk to Thornhill who appears unfazed by the news of a discussion with President Larom. Robert speaks in a hushed tone to ensure the analysts in the auditorium cannot hear him, "Okay, I think I know what we need to say in Beijing."

In Beijing, President Li Macous is in his underground bunker, surrounded by military officials and top political and security advisors. He feels trapped. Aligning with Anton Frozos and his pawn, Nick Neverian, seemed like a surefire bet. The odds were stacked overwhelmingly in his favor. Just four days ago, he was imagining himself as the President of the Planet; now he is wondering if he would survive the day as President of China.

Through years of political purges, Li had eliminated most potential political rivals, both in government and the military, and he had stocked the upper echelons of government structures with loyalists. These actions provided him with security against a coup, but perhaps by quelling any dissenting opinion, his government had descended into groupthink without anyone to provide reasoned challenge to Li's decisions, putting him into this predicament. While top officials are loyal to him, Li can sense resentment from the mid-level staffers in the room; the individuals who were not aware of his negotiations with Frozos and are now left trying to clean up the mess.

Flummoxed, Li implores his staff, "Does anyone have ideas for how to get these planes above us out of the sky?"

"Without withdrawing our troops away from Russia?" a younger staffer asks.

"Yes, we are all aware of that option."

The room is filled with silence, a heavy silence, and a prevailing sense of gloom when an aide whispers to Li.

"Yes, put her on the screen," Li replies.

President Larom, calling from the Situation Room, appears on a television across from Li.

"Good evening, Mister President, I'm glad we were able to connect," President Larom calmly says.

"Yes, congratulations on taking the Presidency," replies Li with a slight dig.

"I am speaking to you to try to mediate a solution to get those jets out of your sky."

"What makes you say mediate?" a genuinely curious Li asks.

"The planes in Beijing and over your troops in the west are owned and operated by Arbor Ridge. Robert Wilson is doing this unilaterally. He has assured me he will not strike preemptively and just wants your troops away from borders. Let's find a solution together."

"That's very useful to know…" Li pauses, contemplating a new idea. He continues, "We need to discuss it further. I take you at your word that he will not strike. And we will speak again shortly."

"Thank you, Mister President. This is an open line; call me as often or as quickly as need be."

Hanging up, Li looks to his advisors, a wild look in his eyes, the look of a man who sees the end growing inevitably near and seeking to do anything to stop it.

"Gentlemen, we may have our opening. Larom says Wilson is acting on his own. If we can create a wedge between Wilson and Larom, we can create pressure that forces him to recede."

"But how do we do that?" a senior advisor asks.

"Well, these planes being in our airspace is a provocative act, no matter what he says. I will announce on state television that we will launch a military airstrike in one hour on the mainland United States unless Wilson withdraws all of his planes. We'll see if the U.S. really wants to fight a war over the Russian border. The pressure on Wilson to back down will be unprecedented."

The plan is received with complete silence and uncomfortable glances among advisors who see this crazed gamble for what it is: the last-ditch effort of a power-hungry man to win a game that has already been lost. After nearly a minute, Li looks to a press aide. "Tell the media I will be making an announcement in ten minutes."

"No!" a general of about sixty years declares, rising to his feet. General Zhou Wei is a military man whose career seemed to have hit a dead-end managing sites in rural Western China until he met up with Li who helped to advance him to one of the top positions in the army. "I will not carry out these orders. Are we trying to protect China or are we trying to protect you?"

"I am China!" Li rages as he jumps to his feet and pounds his fist to the table. In that moment, Li says what has been the case for some time, but a truth that everyone at the table had tried to ignore, bringing the country to the edge of ruin. Having said it out loud, there's no going back, and so Li slumps back down into his chair, realizing defeat. At this moment, a faint rumbling can be heard, but the underground bunker keeps most sound out. An aide turns up the television volume as the state media has been broadcasting live from Beijing, where it is about 10:30 PM.

From the extraordinarily loud speakers of the jets, a voice in Chinese says, "This is Robert Wilson. We will take no provocative action and seek no external change in your government. United, we can beat Frozos. If you wish for China to join the fight, please walk outside of your homes so that your government sees you and acts accordingly." The statement is repeated again and again.

"Should we have the media take the Beijing feed down?" the young aide asks.

"No, it's too late. Once is enough to start a wildfire," Li replies. Indeed, streets of major cities across China are immediately beginning to fill up with people. In the underground bunker, the Chinese President and his leadership are confronted with videos from across the nation showing tens of millions of their citizens outside, silently protesting his leadership, an unprecedented show of defiance by a long-oppressed people.

Within ten minutes, President Li is addressing his nation. He is sitting at a long wooden desk alongside General Zhou, with flags draping the background.

"I have always had the best interest of China first and foremost in my mind. It has become clear that along the way, my decisions have strayed from the proper path. And so, I have voluntarily resigned as General Secretary of the Communist Party and as President of China. The politburo has chosen General Zhou Wei, a valued friend of mine, as interim General Secretary and President for six months to safeguard our nation."

President Zhou then continues, "I thank President Li for this selfless deed. As my first action, we are withdrawing all troops from our border with Russia, and we will play a critical role in the global response to Frozos. Thank you."

In the Jersey City command center, there is jubilation as this mission proved to be a complete success. Chris is perhaps most ecstatic, as his fear of failure proved unfounded whereas Mark is more subdued, fearing that graver risks lie ahead. Thornhill signals to all involved his pride in them for a job well done but is as even-keeled in triumph as during the depths of the crisis.

Robert feels confident that ultimate victory will be achieved. Whether his victories thus far are due to genius or rather a continued streak of good fortune is unclear. What is clear is that he is willing to take bold actions and massive wagers to achieve his aims. April fifth, 2029, he thinks to himself, is a day history will never forget, for the world's two most powerful nations lost their leaders within hours, representing unprecedented turnover on the global stage. He wonders if this will make it easier to get done what needs to be done to defeat Frozos and preserve this planet he has come to love.

CHAPTER 12

Jersey City
April 5, 2029

I t is 5:59 PM on America's East Coast, and Robert Wilson is sitting in his formal office at the top of Arbor Ridge's Global Headquarters. He is writing away at his desk, finishing plans, which he will be presenting to President Larom. When facing such high stakes, he always trusted the written word over typed out plans, perhaps as a result of a childhood where he had done so much work by hand. He thinks of his parents and hopes that they would be proud of the actions he is taking—he thinks they would be. It has been a remarkable day. There had been a peaceful transfer of power in the United States and China with leaders who had allegiance to Anton Frozos removed. His team—from the command center 1,000 feet below him to pilots in the Moscow tower—had performed admirably, and the jets themselves proved to be able in combat, although he admits to himself they had not faced the stiffest test. At least not compared to what they could be facing in the near future.

As the clock ticks towards 6:00 PM, the deadline that Frozos has set for the planet, Robert puts his pen down, pushes his chair back from his desk, and looks up to his television to see what might happen next. Undoubtedly, billions around the world are doing the same. Sure enough, as the deadline passes, the news channel cuts out in a flash of white, and there stands Anton Frozos. His red eyes burn more intensely than ever, and his face wears a frown of disgust. He appears to be standing at the conn of a spacecraft, and behind him lies a great window from which viewers can see countless stars and what appears to be the planet of Jupiter.

He begins speaking with the booming voice of a displeased but still-in-command tyrant. "People of Earth. I had given you seventy-two hours to make a decision that should not have taken a logical species a single hour to decide. And still, that was not enough. Reports from my soldiers in the field like the individual you know as Robert Wilson over the years informed me that your species is riddled with factionalism and petty squabbles, but I never realized just how foolish you were. Your society is more backwards than I thought, but I will teach you better ways.

"It seems like you have been impressed by some parlor tricks that have kept one of our ships—primarily a transport ship, mind you—from successfully attacking the moon, and yes Mister Wilson is a bright, if misguided, man. However, the League of Planets has a military that can overpower any single planet, and my personal armada will be arriving to join

Admiral Tiberius by April seventh. We will be making landfall on New York City, shortly thereafter. It's up to you how much suffering there is between now and then.

"I'm told that there is opposition to being ruled over by another species, preferring to govern over yourselves. Are you sure you believe that or is that a nice-sounding talking point coming from people who do wish to rule over you? Your history is one of war, famine, and conflict. The last five years you've enjoyed peace and unprecedented prosperity. During those years, your leading nation elected someone from the League, and your economy has been guided by another League citizen, Robert Wilson. You inherently and subconsciously seek to be ruled over by your betters.

"By joining us, we can move your standard of living forward decades, and the interspecies fights that dominated your history will be relegated to the past. Indeed, are you free now when one man maintains control over a so-called 'force-field' and sends military jets over capital cities? Maybe you should spend less time questioning my motives and more time questioning Robert Wilson's. We have been researching his records more intensely this past week and discovered his parents were anti-government zealots with illusions of grandeur who hoped to destroy their world order for their own benefit. I fear he is doing the same to yours.

"No matter the promises of back alley magicians, I assure you that resistance will be futile."

Frozos's strategy is clear: to sow doubt about Robert's own motives and capabilities, to get the public to question the honesty and sincerity of the governing class, and to intimidate the planet into submission. Whether he really can break through Robert's force field is unknowable. But will the public be willing to take that risk?

Robert gets up from the chair in his office, thinking to himself that Frozos's remarks were well crafted, as much as he hated to admit it. Rather than ponder over them alone to guess their impact, he walks out of his office, to the main elevator bank, and descends to the cafeteria floor. Thousands of employees and their families who sheltered in this building yesterday still remain here, in no rush to leave the protections these towers offer. Robert walks out of the elevator bay and into the cafeteria to meet with ordinary employees and get their opinions. Even if they are bound to have some bias in his favor, any perspective would be enlightening for him.

As he walks in to the room, the people nearest him begin to applaud, then others in the room turn to see what's causing the commotion, and begin to join in. There is a thunderous ovation, and it feels more like a political rally than an office cafeteria. Children rush up to him asking for autographs and selfies, which he happily obliges. People chant, "We're with Robert," "Keep fighting," "Don't give up," among other things. As Robert works the room, his arm is grabbed from behind. He turns around, and he sees a man in his mid-fifties with a badge signaling he is an employee.

"What's your name?" Robert asks.

"I'm John Cleveland, I work as a janitor here, Mister Wilson," he responds, voice trembling.

"Well, I'm glad to meet you. What can I do for you?"

"I was hoping I could introduce you to my father. He's sitting over there." Cleveland points towards the end of the room. "He'd very much like to make your acquaintance."

"Then I'd like to make his."

Together, they slowly make their way through the crowd and across the room. They finally arrive at Cleveland's table. Sitting there is a woman about Cleveland's age, two sons who look to be teenagers, and an older man in a wheelchair.

"Mister Wilson, this is Anna, my wife, my sons, John Jr and Michael, and this is my father, Joseph."

"Please, call me Robert," he says while shaking each of their hands. As he shakes with John's elderly father, he says, "I'm glad you're here with us."

"Please take a seat," Joseph Cleveland says, and Robert obliges him.

"I wanted to speak to you because I've lived a long life. I was born in 1942, after my father had been sent off to fight a war he'd never return from. I'm eighty-seven years old and have seen good times and bad. But I've known many Frozos's."

"What do you mean?" Robert asks, a little confused.

"Sure, this alien looks a bit different, but he's no different than Hitler, or Stalin, or Mao, whose evils I saw. But to many in this room and the world, those evils are forgotten to the past. It is easy to forget how valuable freedom is when you haven't had to fight for it. Frozos, like these other men, is a snake oil salesman, promising a better life if you just hand over those pesky freedoms. You need to reveal him for what he is. Let me ask you, why do you choose to fight him?"

Robert pauses to think, and everyone in the Cleveland family leans in, waiting intensely for his answer. "Because I've seen firsthand what the loss of freedom does to a man's soul. The bone-crushing despair when hope is snuffed out."

The elder Cleveland nods his head approvingly. "That is what I've seen. Your job, like the great leaders of my lifetime, is to make the American people understand that. If they understand why you fight, and it's for a noble cause, they will follow you, and the world will follow them."

Robert gets up from his seat, puts his hand on the elder Cleveland, and says, "Thank you, very much." He thanks everyone at the table, slowly makes his way back to the elevator, and heads back to the office to put the finishing touches on his plans. He will be off to Washington D.C. first thing in the morning to meet with the President and potentially Congress as well.

While working on his plan, Joseph Cleveland's question keeps popping up in his head as does a line from Frozos's speech, that Frozos "discovered his parents were anti-government zealots with illusions of grandeur who hoped to destroy their world order for their own benefit." That line is infuriating to Robert, and he keeps thinking of his father and the values he believed in and taught to his only son.

CHAPTER 13

Planet Nayan
Earth Year 2004

t's nightfall, and young Robert, or as he is known on Nayan, Marcus Natent, has fallen asleep in the storm cellar. It's been about eight hours since his mother was murdered, and during that time he has stayed silently in the cellar, afraid that the soldiers may investigate the house. He's hopeful that his father or a friend of his parents will return to get him. After several hours of waiting, exhausted and traumatized, Marcus falls asleep. He is lying in the back corner of the cramped, damp space when there is suddenly an abrupt noise, a rattling, outside the cellar, which startles Marcus awake. Scared, he hides in the corner of the storm cellar hoping that whoever opens the door is a friend. The door opens, and there is a man, it is too dark to see who, holding a flashlight, scanning desperately across the room. When the light shines on Marcus, the man rushes down the cellar, crouches down, and gives him a giant bear hug. It is his father after all!

Marcus's father, Jesse, is a man who looks to be about forty with a slight build and the same short black hair his son will later have. While now a local school teacher, he normally carries the appearance of a professor, usually preferring a bowtie and sweater alongside his horn-rimmed glasses. But tonight, he is wearing hiking boots, cargo pants, and a fleece jacket. After holding his son tight for at least thirty seconds, he gets down on a knee, looks at Marcus, and wipes away tears from his dust-covered face.

"Don't worry son, you're safe now. The soldiers have moved out of town towards the mine," he says in the most reassuring way possible to hide his own fear and uncertainty.

"But Dad, what are we going to do? They, they…" Marcus's voice quivers as his lips tremble.

"I know. But Marcus, I hope you realize just how much your mother loved you, and how much I love you. Those men don't understood love, but you will never forget it, right?"

"Right, Dad! But I'm scared."

"I know, and I understand. But you know what your mom would want you to be right now? Brave, like she was. Can you be brave? For her?" Jesse asks his son.

"I will," Marcus says with a smile.

"Okay, then let's go, it's a little dingy in here, don't you think?" and his father gets off his knee, holds his hand, and they quietly venture out of the storm cellar. The night is dark and completely silent. In the distance towards town, smoke is still billowing from the embers of Frozos's destruction. Nayan has no moon, so while the night sky is filled with a voluminous number of stars and constellations, this night is exceptionally dark. They walk behind the house, where Jesse has brought his and Marcus's bicycles. He's filled up the baskets of each bike with water and other essential supplies and fixed a flashlight on top of the handle bars. There are also two backpacks, a large hiking pack that Jesse puts on, and a smaller one that Marcus can wear while biking.

As they mount their bikes, Jesse turns on each of the flashlights, and looks to his son. "Just stay right behind me. We'll take it nice and slowly."

Marcus nods in agreement, and they begin biking across the backyard and towards the large agricultural fields. They bike for several hours as the agricultural fields stretch for hundreds of acres. Rather than riding on the clearly cut paths, they ride between rows of plants just in case soldiers have been left behind to monitor activity. Every forty-five minutes or so, Jesse stops to give Marcus a few minutes break—a chance to drink water and catch his breath. Occasionally, a siren or the thud of a distant blast is heard emanating from the faraway mine that Frozos is securing.

After about an hour and a half of riding, they come to the end of the fields. As they break for water, Marcus is desperate to stop but even more desperate to hide that fact from his father. But Jesse can see his exhaustion. Putting his hand on Marcus's shoulder, he encourages him, "Don't worry. We're almost there."

Marcus's young face quickly turns to one of relief, but he defiantly insists, "I can ride like this for a lot longer, Dad."

Smiling, his father tells him it is time to go, and they venture onward. They pass through stretches of desolation before coming to a wildlife preserve that extends for over fifty miles deep and seven miles wide. Biking into the wood, the terrain gets increasingly rugged and rocky. It is incredibly dark. The woods are filled with an uncountable number of Nayan Pines, similar to pine trees on Earth, but often passing a hundred feet in height. The tree coverings block out what little light there is in the night sky, leaving Jesse and Marcus to be guided just by their flashlights. It is nearly impossible to avoid the stray rock on the paths, and Marcus occasionally tumbles off his bike, scraping his elbows and knees. He refuses to show his pain, and he hopes his father can't hear him sniffling.

Finally, after about an hour of biking through the forest, they stop. They've long left the official hiking paths, heading onto a trail that would barely be visible in the full light of day. Jesse is only able to lead from knowledge and the few esoteric markings that he and his wife had left. On foot, they walk their bikes carefully down the side of a steep embankment. At the base of the slope, they walk down to the right behind some trees. Jesse pulls aside some brush to reveal about a three-foot-high opening to a cave and pushes through the bikes on their side. Then, Marcus crawls through the hole followed by his father, revealing a cave that must be underneath the slope they had just climbed down.

Once Jesse crawls through the opening, he pushes a button, turning on lights hung against the cavern walls. Marcus is surprised at the size of the cave, about twenty feet wide and thirty-five feet deep. The ceiling is generally seven to eleven feet high; it's actually a comfortable space. Most importantly, Jesse tells Marcus, it's a space one is highly unlikely to find without already knowing where it is. As far as Jesse knows, there are only two people alive who know its location. Marcus is shocked to see two cots, a reserve of canned foods and water, some playing cards and board games, and what appears to be a two-way radio that he had seen in old textbooks but never in person. In addition to these goods, under the cots, there are dozens of textbooks which Marcus will be acquainting himself with in coming years.

But for now, after a frightening day and exhausting night of riding, it is time for some well-deserved sleep, so Jesse tucks Marcus into bed and kisses him goodnight. His father would stay awake watching over his son for several hours, periodically peering out the covered entrances of the cave to ensure they weren't followed. He had deliberately taken a roundabout way in case they were being tracked, but it appears they had not been followed.

The next day, Marcus eventually awakens—it is past noon, but his father let him sleep in, given the rigors of the night. During the morning, he quietly takes to assembling some odds and ends in the cave, unpacking bags, essentially trying to make it a bit more of a home for the two of them, not that they were ever likely to return to normal or anything like it. As Marcus gets out of bed, his father makes him a breakfast of an oatmeal-like substance. There is a small wooden table in the back corner of the cave next to a simple kitchen with hot plates and a fire pit, though they couldn't cook large meals without causing smoke to fill the cave. They'd be living on simple dishes and off the land, which was fine as Jesse was never much of a cook anyway. Sitting down, Marcus stares longingly at the empty third chair where his mother is supposed to be sitting. Having let his son eat and regain some strength, Jesse decides it is time to explain circumstances to his son.

"Marcus, I need to explain to why your mother was killed and why we are here."

"Okay, Dad."

And so, Jesse begins telling snippets of a story he would repeat often and expound upon in coming years.

Marcus's parents worked for years as members of Nayan's resistance. The resistance was a multi-planetary group of freedom fighters, loosely connected. For several years, Marcus's parents helped to house members from other planets. Prior to his birth, they had lived in the mining city where the university was located. Resistance fighters needed minerals from Nayan's mines to power their ships and would arrive discreetly to secure supplies. After Marcus was born, his mother felt this was too dangerous.

So they moved to a rural town and had left the resistance, though they were always loyal to its cause. After about two years out of the fight, word was coming that Frozos's rule was becoming ever more brutal. There were food shortages throughout the League, and so he was aggressively expanding his empire and utilizing more and more slave labor to produce the necessary supplies to keep the populace happy and fed. Fearing that Nayan with its resource-rich nature would become a target, both in terms of minerals and agriculture,

Marcus's parents felt that they had to get back into the fight. Their rural town became a resistance outpost with raw materials smuggled from the mine into the village, and then picked up by supply ships friendly to the resistance.

Indeed, much of the town was involved, but it was never spoken of, particularly in front of the children, to avoid loose remarks in front of the occasional visitor that could sink the effort. Over the past five years, there would go periods of months when no contact with members of the resistance had been heard, causing fear that the effort had totally collapsed against the weight of Frozos's unmatched military power, which grew by the day. Fortunately, contact would eventually resume.

In the past two years, hope had been building that anti-Frozos forces were getting more organized. One planet, an aquatic world, had mounted an unmatched fight against the invading forces. They had destroyed seven transport destroyers, countless supply ships, and withstood an over seven month siege. By tying up so much of the League's resources, resistance activity had been flourishing with the volumes of shipments out of Nayan surging. More material was being taken than could be used, so it appeared the resistance was stockpiling resources to prepare for a prolonged effort, or so was Jesse's theory.

About three months ago, word came that the aquatic planet, entirely covered in oceans, had fallen, giving Frozos a critical reserve of water. However, rumors had been flying that the planet's ruler, known as King Hammerhead, always regarded as among the galaxy's wisest and most just had escaped prior to the fall of the planet, along with several dozen ships. The valiant effort of his military had bought resistance efforts elsewhere invaluable time, and if he had escaped, perhaps he could unify anti-Frozos forces and help bring peace and freedom back to this enslaved portion of the galaxy.

Jesse speculated that with Frozos having secured a supply of water, his focus shifted to cracking down on the resistance and securing other supplies. Increased smuggling out of this village and elsewhere was also likely not to go unnoticed, so Frozos conquered Nayan to snuff out rebel towns and secure the resources necessary to sustain his fleet. Knowing this day was bound to come, Marcus's parents had been scouting out a refuge for them to hide during and after the invasion, which is why they had filled this cave with supplies. Unfortunately, Marcus's mother was not here to be with them.

For the next four years, Marcus and his father would live together in these woods. As a mathematics professor, Jesse was well equipped to teach Marcus advanced math and science, and these lessons dominated much of their days while they lived in the woods. Jesse believed that somehow, some way, education would provide Marcus with a path to a better life. Aside from math, there was a healthy dose of stories of his mother, the resistance, and training for how to sustain himself in the outdoors.

Not a week would go by these four years without Jesse reminding his son that the greatest weapon against Frozos is love. It is for love that people, like his mother, make true sacrifice and accomplish the impossible. Love can drive people to do the impossible, creating boundless opportunity to do good. Indeed, Jesse's last words to Marcus were, "Don't let them embitter you or drive you to hate. Let them hate. Act out of love, and they can never beat you."

CHAPTER 14

Washington D.C.
April 6, 2029

R obert Wilson and Chris Bailey are sitting in a waiting room next to the Oval Office in the White House. Both men are in black suits, Robert in a red tie with thin black stripes, and Chris in a green tie. The two men flew down this morning on an Arbor Ridge owned plane while Mark Morrison remained in the Jersey City office tower. Despite the precautions he had taken, Robert is not comfortable with all three co-founders out of the office at any one time. Robert has a thick manila folder on his lap, with the proposal he has drafted. They are sitting silently, aware that the room is undoubtedly bugged and not wanting any of their thinking known. It is nearly 10:15 AM, and they've been waiting a while. Finally, the secretary signals they can go in.

They walk in, Robert first, Chris second. President Victoria Larom, wearing a navy-blue skirt suit, gets up from behind her desk to greet them. Across from her large, wooden desk are two empty chairs, and behind them are two couches where several aides and military officials are sitting.

"Welcome, Mister Wilson. I didn't realize Mister Bailey was coming as well." Larom walks over to greet them and shake hands.

"Madam President. Yes, it's important for Chris to be here. I don't decide much without Chris or Mark Morrison, who couldn't be here today, being involved."

"It's a pleasure, Madam President," Chris says.

"Please sit down," she gestures. Once everyone is seated, Larom jokes, "You know some in the Pentagon felt I should just hold you hostage until you give us the force field."

Turning around to address the officials behind him, Robert says, "I figured as much, which is why the force field automatically powers off if I am not back by midnight." He says it in just such a way that it seems like a joke but no one can be completely sure.

Chris lets out an awkward laugh.

"Well, let's get back to the issues at hand. Tell me, Mister Wilson, why do we need to do anything beyond just getting used to life with a force field around us?"

"If you're asking me what will break the force field, I don't know. But that's how the French felt in the 1930s after they built the Maginot Line. Problem was, once the Germans got past it, there was nothing that stopped them from reaching Paris. I want to be sure that New York isn't lost the day we discover the force field may not be impenetrable."

"Well, from a risk management perspective, that seems sound. What do you recommend?"

Robert pulls the plan out of his manila folder. There's one copy for Larom, one for her aides to review, one for Chris, and one for himself. He passes them around. "This is my proposal. You said your Administration's priority is ensuring you aren't the last President. This will achieve that I think. Shall we walk through it?" Robert sits silently as Larom and her aides thumb through the four-page document.

Putting the document down, President Larom says, "Let me ask you a question, Mister Wilson. It seems to me you want to wage war on Frozos. Am I wrong?"

"War with him is inevitable, and I want to be sure we win it," Robert responds after a brief pause.

"Yes, but is it a good or a bad inevitability? We, or at least I, need to understand your motivations."

"Frozos murdered my mother and enslaved my birth planet. I won't pretend to hold him in anything but contempt. But I don't relish the idea of others dying on behalf of a personal vendetta. I seek justice, not revenge. I do know that if we beat him here; it can be a rallying cry across the galaxy. That's why he will need to expend every resource to take over Earth. If he lets us go on with our lives, we will be a symbol to the resistance. To him, me putting a force field around this planet was a provocative—not a defensive—act."

"How do we know you won't take further provocative action?"

"You have to trust me. And the fact is, I could blow Tiberius up right now, but we haven't. You don't have to accept my terms. I can walk out of here and go on with my life. But if you want me involved, those are my terms."

"And why aren't we using Air Force pilots?" asks a military advisor on the couch.

"For the mission at hand, I believe my pilots are the best trained. We can't have people in the planes who've never seen them before."

"I'll need to get Congress; they'll have questions, and then there's the rest of the world," Larom says.

"If you back this agreement, let me address Congress, and I'll let you sign up the world. I'd think Malvodov will join given we've already saved his country once," Robert says.

The negotiations continue for two hours before Robert, Chris, and Larom sign a memorandum of understanding to be ratified by the U.S. Congress and immediately joinable by any other foreign nation. Project Ridley, which houses Robert's top secret jet program, moon base, and force field—essentially the weapons of war—would be separated from the rest of Arbor Ridge. The U.S. government would pay $150 billion, a quarter of their cost, for a 50 percent stake in a new legal entity that would own all of these assets. Arbor Ridge would own the other 50 percent. The U.S. government was essentially buying in at a half-off discount. With Robert having control over Arbor Ridge, this amounted to a personal stake in the endeavor. The U.S. government could sell half of its own stake to other nations who wished to participate to ensure it truly is a global security cooperative.

All of the employees of Arbor Ridge who worked on Project Ridley would be moved into this new entity. As a fee for the force field, participating nations would contribute enough funds to grow the jet count from 10,000 to at least 50,000 and sustain at that level. Project Ridley forces would only be allowed to fire weapons outside of the force field (nearly 40,000 miles above the Earth's surface) unless alien ships were inside the force field. It is only authorized to act if the force field or the planet face imminent danger. If three months pass with no alien contact and no presence of alien ships within 2.5 million miles of Earth (for perspective the moon is about 240,000 miles away), a 75 percent vote among the government ownership of the entity would trigger its dissolution with the jets distributed on a pro rata basis to participating governments and ownership of the force field returned to Arbor Ridge.

Robert Wilson will be the Commander of Project Ridley, which is being renamed PEACE (Protecting Earth against Alien Conquest and Exploitation). While serving as Commander of PEACE, he would resign as Chairman and CEO of Arbor Ridge, hand over day-to-day operational decisions to Chris and Mark, and would not exercise any control over its business, excepting its stake in PEACE. He is guaranteed to remain Commander for a term of six months effective immediately. After six months, a 75 percent vote among the government ownership can trigger a leadership change, at which point Robert would have the right to dissolve the partnership under the same terms as a government dissolution. A representative of each government's military would be able to participate in military strategy and operations meetings but would not have the ability to overrule Robert's, or a future commander's, decisions.

These terms leave no one thrilled, but everyone comfortable. Members of the military are not comfortable with the creation of a new military organization out of their control, though the restrictions on its ability to operate within Earth's atmosphere help to placate them. President Larom is not pleased about the cash contributions, but Chris Bailey is insistent that legally Arbor Ridge needs to ensure it acts in the interests in shareholders, even if Robert is uninterested in the financials. Robert is saddened to be taking a leave of absence from the company he had built, but he recognizes that there is no other way to proceed. Besides, he trusts the company will be in good hands with Mark and Chris as co-CEOs.

Each party signs the agreement, but Congress will need to approve the spending to make it official. Larom is also eager to bring other nations on board to share in the cost of the program. Financially, there would be a strong incentive to free-ride, but she is hopeful that leaders will want to be involved in the program as a point of national pride.

It is now 7:00 PM in Washington D.C. Robert is sitting in an office in the U.S. Capitol building; an ornate room with portraits of esteemed congressional leaders of the past adorning its walls. Robert is wearing the same red tie with thin black stripes, and his suit jacket with an American flag lapel pin is hanging on the back of his chair. He is reviewing a final draft of an address to Congress and the nation he will be making shortly. The last seven hours since signing the initial memorandum of understanding have been very productive. President Larom gave brief remarks of the agreement from the White House Briefing Room where she enthusiastically endorsed the deal. The text of the agreement has been made available; Congress has seemed warm to it, though he will need to close the deal tonight.

Internationally, there has been a rush to join the pact. Within thirty minutes of Larom's announcement, Russian President Mikhail Malvodov announced he would sign on, likely seeing this an opportunity to further burnish Russia's standing on the world stage. China and much of Europe followed suit. As of now, it appears that PEACE will be owned 50 percent by Arbor Ridge, 25 percent by the United States, 2 percent by Russia, and 1 percent each by China, Japan, Canada, France, Germany, Italy, the United Kingdom, Australia, Brazil, Taiwan, Indonesia, Vietnam, Chile, South Africa, Israel, Saudi Arabia, India, and Mexico. The remaining 5 percent would be owned by a consortium of other nations with smaller individual stakes.

Chris sits next to Robert, eating a sandwich. He has been an invaluable asset today, hammering out the agreement and taking the necessary legal steps. Procedure is where he shines, and he's also an effective "bad cop" on financial matters in these negotiations. As someone not versed in military matters, he has also offered useful feedback on an earlier draft of Robert's speech to ensure it will hit the right notes with viewers across the social spectrum.

Robert puts the speech down and turns to him. "Chris, I hope you know how appreciative I am to have you as a friend. I know with you running operations at Arbor Ridge, things will be smooth. And that matters just as much as what I'm doing at PEACE. We need the power to run, phones to work, goods to be delivered, for civil society to function. I rest easy, knowing our company and the world is in good hands."

Chris smiles. "Thank you, Robert. I know but I appreciate you saying it. Just win this thing quickly, so that you'll be back in your corner office before cobwebs start growing."

A man walks in to tell Robert that it is time. Chris and Robert walk out of the office. Chris is led by another gentleman to the balcony from which he can watch the speech. Robert, meanwhile, is accompanied down a marble hallway to the Hall of the House of Representatives where a joint session of Congress has been called. These gatherings only occur for the annual State of the Union address by the President and occasional remarks by foreign dignitaries.

The room is cavernous with seating emanating in a semi-circular pattern, and seats are filled to the brim with 435 members of the House and one hundred members of the Senate. At the front of the room, there is a brown lectern from which Robert will speak, with a background of a hanging American flag adorning a white marble façade. Behind him sit the Speaker of the House and the President Pro Tempore of the Senate. Above the chamber, there is a balcony where invited guests, like Chris Bailey, are seated.

At 7:02, the House sergeant at arms loudly declares "the honorable Robert Wilson." There is a polite standing ovation from Congress. Normally, there is a raucous cheer, but the mood tonight is more subdued, given both the nature of the moment and some unease about Robert Wilson's plans. During the day, President Larom's telephone diplomacy with other heads of state has been a resounding success, signing on most of the world. Now Robert needs to replicate that success for a domestic audience as Congress will need to authorize the first $75 billion to launch PEACE. He calmly walks down the aisle, nodding his head and smiling at lawmakers, many of whom he's met over the years, given Arbor Ridge's work as a defense contractor.

Upon reaching the lectern, Robert hands two copies of the speech, which have been sitting atop it, to the Speaker and President Pro Tempore, as is the custom. After a few moments, the applause dies down, the audience takes its seat, and Robert is set to begin a speech that is likely being watched by over ninety million Americans and over 1.5 billion worldwide.

"Mister Speaker, Mister President, and esteemed members of Congress, thank you for inviting me to address you and the American people tonight. It is genuinely a profound honor. I am here to offer my thoughts on Protecting Earth against Alien Conquest and Exploitation, or as I prefer to call it, PEACE.

"I have worked throughout the day with President Victoria Larom on this government and private sector partnership. I am grateful for her trust and her work to win the support of nations big and small across the world for this endeavor. The text of the agreement has been available for hours, and she has eloquently explained its terms. PEACE will be co-owned by world governments with the United States controlling twenty-five percent and Arbor Ridge owning half. I will serve as its Commander for an initial term of six months, and our focus will be solely on protecting this planet from the threat posed by Anton Frozos and the military of the League of Planets.

"I feel that there are three questions I need to answer tonight to earn your support: why should you trust me, why should we fight, and what is my plan for victory. I plan on answering these questions tonight, and I hope these answers will in fact win your support.

"First, why should you trust me to lead this effort? Well, every action I have taken has made it harder for Frozos to conquer this planet. I think it's safe to say I am not a double agent. I will also be blunt: I can offer technology and military readiness that no one else can. If you believe we will need to fight, there is no other person or entity that can provide the resources I can. This may not be an inspiring answer, but it is the truth. I hate Frozos with every fiber of my being because I've seen the evil of his oppressive rule firsthand and the false promise of progress and prosperity that he is now offering this planet.

"My home planet of Nayan was conquered by Frozos. He murdered my mother in cold blood when I was seven years old. Eventually, my father and I were enslaved in a mine, which provided critical minerals for his space fleet. There, I witnessed firsthand what enslavement does to a free man's soul, the destructiveness of tyranny. It would be in this mine where my father died after years of backbreaking work. I entered

Frozos's spy program with the sole purpose of coming to a free planet and doing everything I could to ready and protect it.

"You have every right to know the motives of whom you are partnering with, and these are mine. I want to protect this planet and will dedicate myself entirely to this effort. I want to defeat Frozos and his cowardly ilk. I have a personal vendetta, yes, but it is not my right to spill another's blood to settle the score. But because this is personal, know that I offer myself in a way no one else will. I swear to you an undying loyalty to our mission, and will spend every last ounce of energy and courage I have to deliver victory.

"We speak often of 'dictators,' but where does the term dictator come from? Well, dictators originated in Ancient Rome, which was a republic. When under threat, the Republic gave broad powers to one man to eradicate the threat and then hand back power to the people. This worked until one man, Julius Caesar, decided he wouldn't hand back the power. As in Ancient Rome, the barbarians are at the gates. What we have crafted is a plan that gives me the power to police those gates effectively while curtailing that power so that you can rest assured I will be no Caesar."

Robert pauses. A real hush had fallen over the room when he disclosed that Frozos had murdered his mother. As he takes a sip of water, there is scattered applause that builds into a fulsome ovation. He looks up to the balcony to find Chris who gives him a subtle thumbs-up.

"Thank you," Robert continues, settling the audience down. "If you'll oblige me. I am next going to answer my third question. What is my plan for victory? Well, the first tenet is the force field. I believe this will shield us from an invasion, perhaps forever. However, I think it unwise for us to bet the entire planet on that fact. Just because a city builds strong walls does not mean it can forgo a military. At the least, I believe the force field will buy us time to develop the capabilities necessary to win a war against Frozos's forces in space. Given our mandate, PEACE will not have nor train ground forces, merely an aerial assault team.

"I have built a fleet of ten thousand space fighter jets: we call them the SF-01 as they are our first model of space fighters. Video of these jets floating over Beijing and easily dismantling the military defense of China on their western border have gone viral, but the SF-01 can do much more. Namely, they can reach and operate in space, armed with laser cannons, and an assortment of other artillery, and go twice as fast as a space shuttle when exiting the atmosphere.

"I have a fully trained labor force that will begin expanding this fleet tomorrow. We will be training more workers and fully leveraging the supply chain of the entire global defense industry with the aim of reaching fifty thousand within three months. Now you may be wondering who will be flying these planes. How can we train pilots to operate in space? The answer is that we already have.

"As you know, Arbor Ridge is a leading manufacturer of video games. Our most popular game is *Galactic Flyer: Invasion* with over 250 million active users. This game has been our training ground, which is why we always made it so lifelike. The SF-01 is the *Galactic Flyer* fighter jet. As we made and designed the SF-01, we analyzed all the data from this game. Maneuvers that worked and those that didn't were used to develop this, Earth's most powerful jet, and ensured it would incorporate all the benefits of the human element—the pilot. You have been training for this very moment for years; you just never realized it.

"Indeed, you will meet our squadron commanders who are walking out into the balcony now." Robert motions to the balcony, and everyone in the room turns around. Chris is standing up in the balcony, and opens the door. Ten young men and women walk in, wearing red jumpsuits.

Robert continues, "If you remember, last year, we ran a contest where those who led the best squadrons in *Invasion* would win an internship at Arbor Ridge. The 'internship' was really entrance into Project Ridley as squadron commanders. I am proud to introduce you to Mike Murphy, Anna Small, Jerome Smith, and Angela Perez of the United States, Adrian Murray of England, Dmitry Ivanov of Russia, Paulo Cruz of Brazil, Samantha Sharp of Australia, Kim Ji-Yoo of South Korea, and Karl Muller of Germany."

The room takes to its feet with a sustained and hearty standing ovation for these young men and women of about twenty years of age. They are all smiles as they stand in the balcony before walking down several steps to take seats next to Chris.

"I told them," Robert continues, "that while tonight's ovation was going to be memorable, just wait for the reception they receive once they kick Frozos out of our solar system." This line causes another mass ovation. Robert's confidence is growing as he realizes that he isn't so much winning the audience over. Rather, this is an audience looking for a reason to hope and to believe, and they are finding it in his message. He takes a sip of water while the cameras are on the ten commanders and then continues.

"In particular, I wish to commend Karl Muller and Dmitry Ivanov, who oversaw yesterday's mission in China. We have just over twelve hundred pilots currently, mainly game developers, these ten commanders, and other high scorers whom they had flown missions with. Over the next forty-eight hours, we will be reaching out to our most promising players, prioritizing those with military experience, and those under forty, to sign up for PEACE. We expect having no problem putting a qualified pilot in every one of the fifty thousand SF-01s we will be building.

"That is how we will win, utilizing human pilots, an unmatched fleet of planes, and the force field to protect the planet.

"I hope I have explained why I am worthy partner and why I believe we can win. Last, I must answer the most important of all questions. 'Why should we fight?' I have tried to answer this in past remarks, and hopefully I can put aside any doubt that this is a noble effort.

"Last night, Frozos tried to shake your doubt in the virtue of self-government. He is correct that Earth's history features much war and conflict. I assure you that is no different than the history of any other planet or than his League of Planets, itself. Indeed, the instigator of these conflicts has generally been a person or nation that seeks to rule over another. In studying Earth's history, I have read of men risking their own lives to free another people. This nation has sent its army abroad as liberators not as conquerors. That is the act of a bold and noble species, and is a sentiment that Frozos cannot grasp.

"People like him view that decision—to sacrifice oneself to help another—as weak; in reality, it is strong.

"Why do we do it? I saw it firsthand when my mother took the time to lock me in a cellar as a seven-year-old boy as Frozos was invading, giving her life to save mine. She did it out of love. Love is our secret weapon; the true arsenal of a democracy. The love for your fellow man that is implicit in the belief that they should have the ability to rule over themselves is what makes us strong; it is what makes us dig a bit deeper when our back is against the wall, to chart our own destiny when fate seems tilted again us.

"The history of self-government may not always be pretty, and progress does not move in a straight line. There are fits and starts, no doubt. But, at least we get to chart our own course rather than have it decided by someone else. There is a reason why no matter how strong the oppressor, there is always a resistance effort to regain liberty. The thirst for freedom is unquenchable and universal because the human soul is starved when it is enslaved.

"So, I ask that you look to your children and your children's children. Do you want to let them rule their own lives or serve a foreign master? I hope you choose to join with me because the preservation of freedom is a fight worth having whatever the odds. That is why I am prepared to fight this battle no matter the cost to preserve Earth as a free planet and hopefully earn the most flattering of all titles, one which

I have pretended to hold these past few years: citizen of these United States of America."

The polite but tepid applause that Robert received when he walked onto the House floor is replaced with a resounding, emphatic roar as he prepares to walk out. He turns around to shake hands with the Speaker and President Pro Tempore of the Senate who congratulate him on a job well done.

The walk down to the exit is slow, as members of Congress crowd the aisle to shake his hands and get his autograph as they often do after the President delivers a State of the Union. It takes nearly five minutes to get out of the House Chamber. He is led back through the marble hallway and into the office where Chris and the ten squadron commanders are waiting for him. Chris gives him a big hug, and the former "interns" offer a nice round of applause. After a few minutes of chitchat, it is time to get going.

It is now nearly midnight, and Robert is in his office at the top of Arbor Ridge's Jersey City headquarters. In the background, the television shows that Congress has passed a bill by a vote of 411–24 in the House of Representatives and 97–3 in the Senate that makes PEACE official under the terms agreed to by President Larom and himself. It should be a happy moment, all things considered, but right now Robert looks somber as he stares at old photos of himself, Chris, and Mark during key moments in the company's history, from its first product launch to its initial public offering.

There is a knock at his office door. Robert turns around to find Mark and Chris standing there with a pizza and some soda in hand.

"We wanted to check in," Mark says.

Robert is thankful—his friends know that having to officially step aside at Arbor Ridge was a bitter pill for Robert to swallow, even if functionally he had been focusing 80 percent of his time on Project Ridley anyway for the past few months.

"I was just thinking," Robert says, "I hope you guys don't run this company too well while I'm gone."

"Why's that?" Mark asks.

"Well, if you do, maybe they won't have me back," Robert responds with a smile.

"The nice thing about owning most of the company is you get to do whatever you want anyway," Chris retorts with a smile.

"Do you remember what you asked us back at Yale when you asked us to cofound a company with you?" Mark asks.

"I do," Chris chimes in.

"Not exactly," Robert says. This is a bit of a fib as Robert has a good idea what the answer is, but he knows Mark will relish saying it, and besides, it would do him some good to hear it.

"You didn't tell us we'd become some of the world's richest people, though that's admittedly been a nice side effect, or promise power. You asked, and I quote, 'Would you like to join me in building the most important company on the planet?' You certainly didn't oversell it!" Mark adds with smile.

Knowing it could be some months before Robert will be sitting in this office again depending on how Frozos responds to the formation of PEACE, the three co-founders sit down, and reminisce about some of the highlights of the past decade over some pizza.

CHAPTER 15

Jersey City
April 7, 2029

R obert Wilson stands in the basement of the Jersey City Arbor Ridge Headquarters, which is now the headquarters for PEACE. He's wearing a navy-blue suit with an American flag lapel pin, blue button-down shirt, and no tie. Now that it is time to actually get things done and not simply give speeches, Robert is glad to leave neckties in his closet.

It's nearly noon; less than twelve hours since this new initiative was created. Robert has barely slept a minute. After reminiscing into the early hours of the night with Mark Morrison and Chris Bailey, the real work began. The tent city that had been occupying much of the factory floor this week has been taken down, and the railway tunnels have been reopened. There is a din of activity on the floor as production resumes, with workers in their blue jumpsuits returning to the positions they've occupied for much of the past year building the first fleet of SF-01s. A similar scene is being played out across the other eleven manufacturing facilities under Arbor Ridge towers.

Together, they should be able to produce 500 SF-01s a week, perhaps with supply chain prioritizations and more shifts, it could be pushed to 750. Robert though is seeking 40,000 new jets over the next three months. That's 13,333 a month, or over 3,000 per week. To get that type of run rate going, the manufacturing of these planes would need to become the global manufacturing priority. To that point, President Victoria Larom had said two days ago that we needed a "whole of America" approach to win this war, leveraging not merely the resources of government but also of the vast private sector.

Consequently, Robert has spent the past few hours talking with executives of large companies to lock-in supply chains. He and the President are taking a carrot and a stick approach to these negotiations. Robert is appealing to their patriotism and the promise of public recognition for their assistance, knowing that if they deny him help, Larom can legally force them to begin production under her national emergency powers. Other world leaders have offered similar assistance. Thus far, the carrot approach has been working. Competing defense contractors have offered their facilities as assembly lines for the SF-01, so Robert is sending senior supervisors from the existing production sites to oversee the ramp-up of activity at these ten new locations. Steel mills from North Carolina to India and China have offered the expedited delivery of fabricated metal to these sites. Chemical producers on the

Arabian Sea will begin exporting the necessary product next week as they adjust refinery runs. Auto plants in Germany and Michigan are building the landing gear while Arbor Ridge has set aside video game console manufacturing to exclusively build the communications equipment needed to operate the SF-01 fleet.

Even more quickly than global governments, the world's private sector is unifying behind a singular mission: to build these planes. By April 14, the first SF-01 off this enhanced production platform will be completed. Over the first four weeks of the program, Robert hoped to get to a 4,000 plane per week production rate on top of 750 from existing basement sites and hold there to get to the 50,000 in less than three months. It's an ambitious plan, but with the manufacturing industry mobilized in a way not seen since World War II, Robert is feeling optimistic.

On top of this, the 756 planes stored under each of Arbor Ridge's towers are beginning to be moved to training facilities across the globe, generally leveraging the existing infrastructure of nations' military. While about one hundred planes would be operated from each tower, the remainder and those made at new locations will be taken to military bases in South Carolina, New Mexico, Southern France, Qatar, Guam, Chile, Norway, Australia, and Japan, among others.

Recruitment emails have already been sent out to over 15,000 qualified players who have performed exceptionally well on *Galactic Flyer: Invasion*. Of the 15,000, 4,750 are currently serving in a branch of a participating nation's military. When Robert had last checked about thirty minutes ago, there were 12,873 replies, 11,411 had accepted the invite, including 4,687 of those actively serving in the military. The response rate was extremely gratifying—he was pleased to see mankind excited to join this effort, for he felt only a willing army would be a winning army. These new pilots would be sent to the facilities that PEACE was establishing on military bases to undergo the necessary training and be assigned a squadron. Ultimately, Robert felt he had a pool of 240,000 qualified potential-pilots in his desired age group of eighteen to forty, which at the current response rate meant there was a more than adequate supply of talent, given estimated needs for 75,000 pilots. Not to mention, millions more began playing the game just today, suggesting that more talent could unveil itself in coming months should the battle prove to be long-lived.

There had been some hiccups along the way, and Robert had faced some close calls, whether it be calling out the President on live television, telling the world he is actually an alien, or attacking a Chinese military base, but thus far, all of his gambles had been paying off. Whether this had been a stroke of good fortune or a sign of his talent, it is still too early to tell, but Robert is about to be reminded that he can't afford for his streak to turn south anytime soon.

"Commander Wilson," a youngish aide in a purple jumpsuit (though the insignia on the sleeve has been changed from Arbor Ridge's logo to PEACE's), says as he taps Robert from behind. Robert turns around, startled—he hasn't quite gotten used to his title as Commander of PEACE, having always thought of himself as a Mr. Wilson or preferably, Robert.

ROBERT WILSON AND THE INVASION FROM WITHIN

"Does Thornhill need me?" Robert responds, knowing that the purple meant this aide worked in the command center.

"Yes—he said it is very urgent."

"Okay, let's head over." Robert walks with the aide toward the elevator to head down a floor to the command center. As they walk, Robert asks him, "How have you liked your time here?"

"Very much, sir. Major General Thornhill is a fair man, and I've learned a lot from him."

"Good, I'm glad to hear it. He isn't working you too hard, is he? We need to be prepared for a marathon, not a sprint," Robert replies as they get into the elevator.

"No, sir. He works us hard, but we can take it," the aide confidently replies, knowing it is both the truth and what he has to say as he shouldn't criticize his senior officer to his boss.

"Good. So, tell me, do you think we'll win?" This is the first time Robert asks this question of a PEACE employee, though he will continue to ask it of line workers, pilots, leaders, and communications specialists many times in the days and weeks ahead to gauge sentiment.

"Absolutely sir," the aide confidently replies as they get off the elevator and walk towards the command center.

"Why are you so confident?" Robert asks.

"Because we have to win. Frozos doesn't. We're fighting for our lives; he's fighting for some dirt. Who'd you pick in that fight, Commander?"

Robert pats the aide on his shoulder and says, "I like our odds too." Together, they walk into the command center; the aide slips over to his seat while Robert walks down the steps to the stage where Thornhill is poring over some charts.

"Morning, Jake. Or is it the afternoon already? What bad news do you bring me today?" Robert asks with a smile.

Thornhill pulls his weathered face up from his papers, hands pushing down on his desk. He may look weathered and weary but he can outwork just about any man half his age and Robert knows it—that's why he picked him. "Well, I only have the news; you tell me how bad it is." Turning to the row of workers behind him, he says, "Pull up sector 1401."

On the main screen on the wall, a satellite feed from the edge of the force field is projected.

"Why that's Tiberius's ship." Robert says, unimpressed but knowing there's more.

"Pan out," Thornhill orders. There are two more transport destroyers—white oblong tanks mounted upon red semi-spheres. Surrounding them, there were at least one hundred small ships. Likely between fifty and two hundred feet based on their relative size, they are in all shapes and sizes: black spheres like the one in Robert's office, only larger, thin white disks, orange fighter jet ships. A varied armada of small vessels, likely perfected to offer a variety of tactical capabilities and bolster the defenses of the transport destroyers that carried planet-busting artillery and potentially even tens of thousands of ground soldiers.

Hovering behind the transport destroyers, there is a hulking presence—a ship nearly twice as long and equally as wide as the destroyers. At its front, there's a long red nose, sloping down to a narrow point, behind that a bulking black body, armed underneath with four long, blaster cannons, perhaps seventy-five feet long each, and at the rear of the ship, a wing extends, from which four giant turbo blasters sit. This space-ship is an engineering marvel that few on Earth could have even imagined, let alone built. Surrounding this ship, there are at least another one hundred small crafts to safely escort it across the galaxy.

"That's Frozos's ship," Robert says coolly and confidently. It looked to be updated and expanded from the one that had struck terror across the League of Planets when he was a student on Killjorn some fifteen years ago, but it had all his markings.

A hole opens from the red semi-spheres in the front of each of the destroyers with fifty-foot-long cannons extending, just as the day Tiberius struck at the moon. One fires at Earth. The force field holds. The second fires; the shield holds. The third fires; it holds again. On the screen, the computer is able to show the trajectory of the laser beam, which, had it broken through the force field, would still have just missed the planet.

"Interesting," Thornhill ponders, "they are firing glancing blows at the force field."

"Yes," Robert says, "they want to be sure they don't blow up the planet if the beam succeeds in penetrating the shield. They need the planet intact as a base to operate from next to their speedway entrance."

Now, all three destroyers fire at the same time, hitting first the same exact spot on the force field, apparently testing if they can overpower it. Once again, the force field holds. There is a bifurcated feeling in the command center. Robert and Thornhill are relaxed, Robert trusting his technology and Thornhill long experienced in high stakes moments. Behind them though, there is palpable anxiety among the rank-and-file, less sure of the force field's durability.

After a few minutes pause, the three ships fire on different locations, perhaps testing if the force field weakens in other areas when facing an attack elsewhere. Yet again, the shield absorbs the attacks. While the command center is getting a close-up view of the attempted attack, on the streets of Earth from London to Singapore, slight rumbles can be heard and flashes of light seen as the attacks ricochet around the force field and dissipate out into space. People, far and wide, stop and look to the sky to see if alien forces are about to pour down. As none arrive, they hesitantly try to resume what they were doing, from grocery shopping to golfing or working, wondering if this would be a new normal they would have to grow used to.

At the top of Arbor Ridge's Jersey City headquarters, Mark and Chris call everyone back to their seats in the large boardroom. Robert is grateful for their faith in what he is doing; if anyone should feel such faith, it is they, for who else knows him better? They want to get operations back to normal, and that starts with not sidetracking every meeting every moment there may or may not be a military development, large or small.

About 1,000 feet below them back in the command center, they see that the cannons are being pulled back into the red spheres. "Okay folks, show's over," Robert says, clapping his hands together. "Back to our regularly scheduled programming, please."

"But don't you think Frozos's ship will try to pierce the force field?" a mid-level strategist in the front row asks.

"No. That ship is meant to intimidate. It's part military weapon, part propaganda tool. If they try to fire and fail, as Frozos now is assuredly worried it would, the symbolic impact of his impotence would carry far and wide. That's why he uses his own ship's weaponry very sparingly. No one knows for sure what it can actually do, and the rumors are more powerful than any actual display of force."

"I'm reminded of a program from the 1980s I worked on that most of you likely read about in history books," Thornhill says as he turns to his team. "It was President Reagan's Strategic Defense Initiative, using lasers to strike down nuclear weapons, an idea we actually are implementing now. It didn't matter that it didn't actually work great then. What mattered was the Soviets feared it might, and that changed the calculus of the entire Cold War. The appearance of strength can be just as important as actual strength."

"Yes, that's a good analogy," Robert concurs.

"But won't people see Frozos not firing as a sign of weakness?" the aide asks.

"No, I'm sure they'll spin it as 'the weapons are so powerful they are worried that a strike would also blow up the planet.' That's another reason the initial strikes were specifically aimed to avoid Earth."

Robert heads out up the stairs to walk out of the command center, but at the top, he turns and says, "We should release all this footage to the press. Let's accompany the full video with a simple three sentences. Quote 'Additional League of Planets invasionary forces, including what we believe to be Frozos's own ship with him presumably commanding it, have arrived. Multiple strikes were attempted on the force field, which easily withstood the attacks. Recognizing the futility of the effort, Frozos avoided the embarrassment of a failed strike from his own ship.' End quote. We may as well try to counteract the narrative he'll make up. I want that sent out on our longest wave frequencies too. Thanks, everyone, for a job well done."

In the sky, high above Earth, Supreme General Frozos is standing in the conn of his great warship, named *Magnus*, looking down in disgust at a planet that is proving to be a stubborn thorn in his side.

"Petulant, insignificant children," he mutters to himself.

This was not how today was supposed to go. Admiral Tyrone Tiberius was to have signed the surrender terms yesterday, and Frozos was to make a grand entrance today, welcoming the planet into the League of Nations with Presidents Neverian and Li at his side. Construction on the speedway portal just beyond Earth's outer atmosphere would have begun imminently.

Instead, here he stands, locked out of a planet that is technologically centuries behind the League and diminutive in size. He walks away from the giant window where he was gazing down upon North America and towards the captain's chair. The conn is a great buzzing room. From floor to ceiling, it stands forty feet tall. The floor is shiny, black stone—an elegance reserved alone for his ship. There are two rows of curved desks emanating out from his chair—to his right sits the team who steer and operate *Magnus*, while to his left are the radar and communications team. The walls on each side of the room are mounted with two floors of monitors, manned by several dozen crew. These crew manage the weapons. Serving on *Magnus* is the highest of honors in Frozos's space fleet, and these crew are the most highly trained and skilled fighters the League has. Frozos tolerates nothing less than excellence.

Given his exacting standards, he is in an exceptionally foul mood today, after the embarrassing display of impotence he has been subjected to the past forty-five minutes. He clicks a button on the side of glossy white chair, and within ten seconds, a hologram of Tiberius is standing in front him, looking ill at ease, his reptilian eyes darting all across the room, avoiding eye contact with Frozos, his head bowed ever so slightly, and hands fidgeting with each other at his waist.

"Well, Admiral, how much did we fire at the so-called force field?" a beleaguered Frozos asks.

"Umm, Supreme General, we fired a total of seventeen shots, the last ten at full power. We tried firing in quick succession, with a longer delay, at different spots at the same time, at the same spot. Our attacks had no measurable impact."

"Well, clearly we aren't trying hard enough."

"But sir, we have fired the most powerful weapons the transport destroyers possess." Tiberius emphasizes "transport destroyers," holding out hope that *Magnus* may have more powerful, advanced weaponry that could take down the shield.

"No, but there is no such thing as an impenetrable force field. We are just firing the wrong thing at it. What have we learned about its make-up? You've been here several days with nothing to do but stare at it. You must have run tests?"

"Why yes, of course, sir. Our scientists continue to work through it. It seems to be a type of magnetized light, repelling forces like a magnet while moving through the air and space like light. No one has come across anything quite like it."

While Tiberius and Frozos are talking, there has been chatter over at the communications desk among five or six crew members. A young sailor, the most junior rank of the team, walks up to Frozos. She can't be more than twenty-three and looks absolutely petrified. He turns to her, annoyed at being disturbed, and grabs a paper from her hand. It's the statement that Robert dictated, which is being projected as far out into space as PEACE's satellites can reach. Frozos crumples the paper into his massive palm.

Continuing to look at Tiberius, rather than make eye contact with the sailor, Frozos tells her, "Tell your cowardly senior officer, that obviously, he is to block the message of this propagandist. Once you convey that message, you may take leave for the remainder of your shift. You've done your officer's job; he can do yours."

She immediately scurries back to her desk to repeat his message, though he spoke loudly enough for the entire room to hear him. Returning to his conversation with Tiberius, he continues, "We need to begin construction in the next week as scheduled. I'll have no more delays. You are continuing to lead the military effort. I expect better answers on how you're going to get through that shield by then. This planet must not be allowed to resist."

"Yes, Supreme General." And with that, Tiberius signs off.

It's quite clear to everyone in all of these ships as well as to members of the League Council on the Capital Planet of Centurem that Frozos cannot afford to let Earth hold out, as word would spread like wildfire throughout the federation and could inspire mass resistance. At 478 planets, the military is stretched extremely thin. Having added fifty-four planets in just the past year, Frozos's breakneck pace of expansion has pushed the military to the edge of its policing capacity. Rebellions and food disruptions could quickly snowball into an uncontrollable disaster.

Beyond the symbolism, Frozos has explained the importance of a friendly ground presence on Earth to patrol the speedway gates and ensure safe loading and passages for transport ships. This is true, but not quite as important as he made it out to be. In reality, Frozos is here to confirm reports and data received from Nick Neverian several years ago that deep beneath Earth's crust lies an element that mankind has yet to discover.

The matter is so sensitive that Frozos banned Neverian from speaking of it any further three years ago and has kept the information even from Tiberius, his most trusted advisor. Due to these precautions, Frozos is confident that neither his own political rivals nor Robert Wilson are aware of it. His ship has been conducting deep planetary scans the past two hours, and they confirmed Neverian's suspicion: Earth is home to a motherlode of the most precious metal in the known universe: raptium. If this is discovered and coordinated with the resistance, Frozos's very rule could be threatened. But if Earth can be subdued, Frozos can rest, secure in his throne, consolidate power across his expanded League, boost military capacity, and cease his expedition across the vast expanses of the galaxy.

Earth must fall.

CHAPTER 16

New Mexico
April 17, 2029

It has been over two weeks since Planet Earth first learned of the existence of intelligent life when a ship from the League of Planets appeared over the skies of Manhattan. The first five days in the wake of this revelation were defined by the chaos of ever-changing developments. The President of the United States, Nick Neverian, proposed a peace plan, which was blocked in the UN. There were rumors of China invading Russia, only for those to dissipate, and within days, the nations were back at the brink of war. The moon was to be destroyed, but it survived. A force field surrounded the Earth, revealing that the leader of the planet's greatest company, Robert Wilson, is actually an alien. The leaders of the two most powerful nations, the United States and China, were deposed in a matter of hours. A new pan-global military super force, PEACE, rose like a phoenix from the ashes of fallen governments. And now, a burgeoning space armada is orbiting Earth like a pack of sharks circling an ailing boat, awaiting its capsizing.

It has been said that history does not move steadily through time; there are certain years where it stops and unfurls a multitude of dramatic events: 33, 1066, 1492, 1776, 1945, to name a few. 2029 is likely to go down as one such year, if there is a history to write. Events that together might amount to one of the most consequential years in human history occurred in rapid succession in the same week; it could be forgiven if most inhabitants would struggle to name every event that they had just experienced. However, everyone on the planet knows that life will never be the same, and that is sufficient enough.

If the first five days were defined by chaotic birth of a new era, the next ten days have been defined by the gradual return to normalcy, or at least what can be considered normal in this new world. On Sunday April 8, President Victoria Larom, in conjunction with leaders of the Group of 20 (or G-20, the nineteen leading nations and European Union) that it would be the leading priority of global governments to return civil society and the economy to a normal footing. To that end, domestic travel restrictions and curfews were gradually lifted over the course of the next week, though international restrictions were largely kept in place. Alongside this, most regular economic activity was ordered to resume as normal, and key symbolic cultural institutions from professional sporting leagues like Major League Baseball and Premier League Football to concerts and Broadway theatrical performances returned to normal schedules.

On Tuesday, April 10, world financial markets and banks reopened after a one week holiday. There was grave concern that the events of the past week could cause mass panic and a death spiral in financial markets that could shatter fragile nerves and confidence. Needless to say, in the financial halls of power from Shanghai to London, Frankfurt, and New York, there was quite significant pressure from governmental and regulatory bodies on major banks, insurance companies, sovereign wealth funds, and asset managers to limit selling and do their patriotic duty. Of course, on Monday, the world's major central banks, led by the Federal Reserve announced coordinated policy actions to support the global economy, including lowering interest rates and promising to inject a combined $16 trillion in liquidity, which buoyed investor sentiment heading into Tuesday's market open. In an emergency press conference on Monday, the Chairman of the Federal Reserve put it thusly: "Our government has gone on a wartime footing against an alien enemy to protect life, liberty, and the pursuit of happiness. Today, I can assure the American people and the people of all nations that the world's central banks are similarly assuming a war footing, using all of our tools to insulate this economy from attack."

Perhaps, no one is more nervous on that Tuesday morning ahead of the 9:30 AM stock market open than Chris Bailey, now co-CEO of Arbor Ridge. On Monday, the company's entire workforce showed up for work, a fact that he and co-CEO Mark Morrison are rather proud of. Alongside PEACE, government policy, and central banks, Chris and Mark had been putting Arbor Ridge on a wartime footing as well over the weekend, increasing shifts at its food and beverage plants, expecting a run on goods at grocery stores, prepping increased investment plans in the utility and communications division to harden the grid, and of course, ramping up activity at its manufacturing facilities that would be supplying PEACE with products. By getting this company operating at full capacity, they knew that would facilitate a return to normalcy throughout the global economy—the company is just that big. By announcing they would not lay off any employees, they put pressure on other companies to follow suit, and dozens have.

Coming into Tuesday, Arbor Ridge is worth about $12 trillion, meaning its shares account for about 17 percent of the value of the U.S. stock market. How would its shares respond to news that its leading founder is an alien? Not only that, but he had to leave the company to run PEACE. On top of all that, the Project Ridley assets had been valued at $600 billion, but a 50 percent stake in them had been sold for $150 billion, meaning the company would be writing down the value of its assets by $300 billion. Chris is prepared to see the stock plunge. Indeed at the open, shares were down 9.7 percent (or nearly $1.2 trillion), but they began to bounce mid-morning on news that ordinary investors are buying stocks. There are reports that dinner reservation activities, hotel bookings, and online shopping are running at or above the normal pace.

By the day's close, Arbor Ridge shares are down less than 2 percent, and the stock market less than 1 percent, which is hailed as a tremendous victory. The much-feared chaos did not materialize. Instead, in their own small way, billions of people showed they would not be cowed into submission by Frozos's bullying, instead choosing to try to continue with ordinary life, attempting to "keep calm and carry on" as they had during past conflicts.

From that day forward, the fears of social unrest, economic collapse, or rolling government lockdown policies faded away. Commuter trains filled up; offices went back to work. There were, of course, some signs of underlying stress, from elevated toilet paper sales to increased attendance of church services, but the contingency plans that governments across the globe had formed have proved unnecessary for now. Would this last or would a breach of the force field shatter this calm? No one quite knew. But for the time being, the steely calmness of ordinary men and women everywhere flew upwards to their elected and unelected leaders who realized they had underestimated the guts and grit of the people they lead.

The relative normality of civil society is of great relief to Robert Wilson, though he had hoped for as much, allowing him to spend his days focused entirely on PEACE's mission: ramping up production of the SF-01, rounding out recruitment of pilots, and introducing himself via a series of video conferences with the assigned nonvoting military representative of each participating nation. He doesn't need their support to do anything during these six months, but it would make his life easier and bolster the legitimacy of his actions, or so he feels, if his major decisions are backed by the majority of the participants.

Ten days have passed now since PEACE was officially formed, and new plants are progressing as expected. They should be producing the hoped-for 4,750 planes per week in three weeks' time. Hitting the target of 50,000 planes will still be ambitious, but things are going successfully enough that this "reach" goal does continue to seem attainable.

On this Tuesday morning, Robert is walking off a plane at a joint Air Force-PEACE base and training facility in the New Mexico desert. It is 10:00 AM local time and an unusually warm eighty-two degrees, though temperatures are set to drop below fifty degrees tonight. Robert is wearing a green button-down shirt and khaki pants, a business casual look that has become his go-to as the Commander of PEACE, as he walks across the tarmac. He's introduced to Major Alan Thompson of the Air Force on the way to the main building, the highest ranking official on the base and its official liaison to PEACE. Thompson is a stern man in his mid-fifties, proud that his base will be home to such a critical war effort but also wary of having non-Air Force personnel roaming its grounds.

Major Thompson leads Robert into the main facility, and off in the distance, Robert sees the sun reflecting off over 200 SF-01s, made in the Los Angeles Project Ridley basement. This giant hanger has been converted from housing planes to dozens of simulators. Here, over 700 recruits are training in their assigned squadrons.

The simulators are essentially enhanced versions of the *Galactic Flyer: Invasion* virtual reality video game. The SF-01 control panel is already identical to that of the flyer in the game. In these simulations however, all of the individual simulators are linked into one game, so that each member of a squadron is working alongside fellow members of a squadron. Additionally, the game's developers have been intensely updating levels and war games based on incoming data from the ships above Earth, as well as the likeliest battles, either attempting to exit the Earth's atmosphere to fight out in space or a simulation where the force field has fallen and they are defending Earth's major cities in low-altitude skirmishes.

A key element that PEACE recruiters screened on in gameplay data was a player's willingness when fighting within a squadron to sacrifice one's plane and life if that would enable other flyers to advance. It is a harsh reality of war that not everyone will come home. However, it's one thing to make a calculated sacrifice in a video game and another in real life. The most pressing question of this entire endeavor is whether pilots could put aside the natural instinct of self-preservation and sacrifice themselves or go for the riskier route that offers an attractive risk/reward.

These simulations are intended to hash that out and weed out those pilots who play the game well but can't translate that into real-life success. Indeed, a key aspect of these hours of games is for each pilot to "die" at least once, and then to measure whether their strategy changes in future rounds as the realization they may not come home sinks in. Several dozen recruits across the program just in the past twenty-four hours have been removed from the talent pool because they become overly conservative, to the detriment of the mission's success, after suffering a fatal attack in previous simulations.

Robert is convinced to his core that civilians can be just as heroic as those in the military—after all, members of the military are all former civilians. It is due to this belief that he has largely raised a civilian army. However, he appreciates that those in the military have—prior to the offer from PEACE—already signaled a willingness to die for a cause and been trained to act rationally and for the good of the mission when under duress. Therefore, in every squadron of twenty-four planes, they have attempted to have at least three members of the military in a hope that their training could prove contagious to the broader group.

Additionally, as experienced by China, Robert has already developed a talent pool of 1,200 pilots. To help train and motivate these new recruits, Robert has sprinkled around many of these pilots to the new PEACE bases to lead in simulations and offer advice about taking the game play to the battlefield.

At this base, Anna Small, one of the Arbor Ridge "interns" along with the squadron she directly leads in her role as a group commander, is here to speed up the recruits' training. The recruits at this base who pass through the training will fold into Anna Small's group. It is accordingly valuable for her to have some face-to-face interaction and develop a sense of trust and comradery with them.

Anna is a red-blooded Midwestern American. She was born and raised in Missouri with a father who was a shift supervisor at the nearby auto plant and a mother who was the school nurse at her town's middle school. At twenty-two, she is the second-oldest of four children and the only girl, and she took a gap year from her senior year at Washington University in St. Louis to accept the Arbor Ridge internship, which admittedly has not been what she expected.

She led the third highest scoring squadron in the *Galactic Flyer* competition, and her training results over the past six months have been extremely strong. She has a bold flying style, preferring to take riskier routes and press the advantage in battle to capitalize on momentum and distress in the opponents. The recruits at this base have exhibited a similar style, which should allow for a cohesive group formation.

She is standing in the front of the hanger, watching on the screen the battle simulation play out. In this game, the fighters are trying to protect the West Coast of the United States from an invasion of one transport destroyer and the dozens of small crafts whom escort it. She has been alternating between participating in simulations and observing to see how the recruits fly and what common mistakes are made. This is the second time they are running this simulation. The first was a disaster with pilots acting as individuals rather than as a group, and the coastal cities were destroyed inside forty-five minutes. This round has been a more even fight, though Anna is keenly aware that even is not good enough when the future of humanity is on the line.

Major Thompson leads Robert to her. She, like all the PEACE soldiers, is wearing the red jumpsuit to differentiate them from Air Force personnel. Recruits wear a bright yellow band on their left sleeve to signal they have not yet passed training and are effectively on a trial period.

"Group Commander Small, I believe you've met Commander Wilson," Major Thompson says.

"Yes, I have, though not as Commander," Anna responds as she shakes his hand.

"Well, I'm the same guy. Tell me, how are the recruits doing?" Robert asks.

"They are working hard. It's a steep learning curve, but most are showing progress."

"That's good. Now be honest, do you think many are scared?"

"Everyone is. But most are as scared of failure as of dying."

"Well, I guess that's good?" Robert asks.

"That depends," Thompson interjects. He's not a member of PEACE, but as this is his base and he has been training pilots for over two decades, he's entitled to speak. "Fear of dying can cause excess conservatism. But fear of failure can cause a pilot to tense up and miss his shot, similar to a hitter choking in the bottom of the ninth."

"Thanks for your perspective, Major. Which of the two fears do you prefer in a new recruit?" Robert asks, sincerely curious to hear his response.

"Fear of failure, no doubt, because that's easier to train away. Success will breed success."

"I know, and that's the challenge of this entire operation. There won't be many battles, and losing the first one could be the end. It's hard to have early success that breeds other ones."

The three ponder over that while watching the battle simulation play out on the screen. There is no simple answer apparent to any of them about how to address that concern. One or two minutes later, an aide in a purple jumpsuit signaling a role in communications, rushes over to Robert.

"Thornhill needs to speak to you, sir," he says with a strong sense of urgency.

"Very well. Major Thompson, where is the secure PEACE communications facility at this base?"

"It's in the basement level underneath our main office complex. I can take you there."

"Thank you, Major. Group Commander Small, you're free to join us; I think this may be of interest to you."

"Thank you, I will."

Together, they walk out past the rows of training recruits and across the tarmac to a brick office building and into its basement. Robert can't help but think to himself how ironic it is that he is spending almost all of his time below ground when the threat is far above it. This communications room is a small, soundproof room of ten by twelve feet with a simple wooden table surrounded by folding chairs. Thompson is not permitted in the room, so just Robert, Anna, and a communications aide walk in. There are already three communications workers who are stationed here full-time, in the event there is an order from headquarters to deploy the pilots. Robert acknowledges them and sits at the center of the table across from a large, closed circuit television with a direct feed to Jake Thornhill's command center in Jersey City.

Yesterday, two more ships from the League of Planets had arrived to join Frozos's forces. These ships were ones that Robert had recognized from his days on Nayan: supertanker transporters. They are more than 50 percent larger than the hull of the transport destroyers, which Admiral Tiberius captains, and have a similar hull design and coloring, but they lack the semi-red spheres on which the destroyers sit. These ships are the backbone of the League's interplanetary supply chains, moving food and raw materials across the galaxy. Transport destroyers would often escort a handful of these ships when moving through contested zones.

"Good morning, Jake," Robert begins. "I suspect you have news for me regarding those supertankers?"

"Yes, good morning to you. About three hours ago, we began monitoring activity on these ships as the rear of the hulls opened and small crafts began taking materials out." Thornhill flips the feed to a split screen between the command center and the satellite feed of the goings-on in space. Small drone crafts are pulling metal piping from out of the transport ship and assembling it so that Frozos's fleet is between Earth and the space construction site. Very little is apparent as construction is very early stages, but it does appear to be in the shape of a curve.

"Okay, Jake. We need to begin prepping Operation Selena, obviously very discreetly. Let's also alert the military representatives of all participating nations that we will be holding a conference call in thirty minutes. Please pull together all the pictures or video images you can to buttress our case."

Robert turns to Anna. "There likely will be military action today. Your group won't be involved, so I want you here to watch it as I think that will be valuable experience. However, I don't want the military officials to know I have a pilot with me."

"I can leave and you can bring me back," she offers.

"No, I don't want to do anything that could possibly arouse suspicion. There's no margin for error in this part of the game. So, I'm sorry, but could you sit over in the corner of the room so you are out of sight of the camera?"

"Yes, no problem."

"Thanks."

CHAPTER 17

New Mexico
April 17, 2029

Robert Wilson is sitting in the makeshift communications office of the joint PEACE-Air Force Base in New Mexico. In the dingy room, it is just him, a few communications aides, and Group Commander Anna Small who is sitting out of sight of the camera; Robert is sure she thinks him overly cautious or paranoid. On the screen, there are three images, that of Jake Thornhill, images from outer space, showing the space construction, and a mosaic of faces from all the military representatives. There are 117 nations in PEACE, and ninety-eight military officials have logged in. It's possible more will join, but it is 11:17 AM, two minutes after the scheduled start time, so Robert is eager to begin.

"Thank you for all being here. I am hoping to get your input and support on a planned PEACE operation to respond to what I view an imminent threat occurring more than forty thousand miles from Earth's surface, which is our primary function. First, though, I will turn it to Jake Thornhill to provide the facts of the situation before I offer my analysis."

Thornhill goes through a ten-minute presentation, showing the arrival of the supertanker transporters, the nature of the ships—as cargo-carrying vessels rather than ships of war—and the construction developments that are now nearing their fourth hour. It is a to-the-point, just-the-facts presentation that is appreciated as credible and even-handed by all on the call. As Thornhill prepares to turn it over to Robert, the South Korean representative interrupts.

"Thank you, General Thornhill. Tell me though, how the arrival of nonmilitary spacecrafts would constitute an imminent military threat."

"I'll take that," Robert says. "We know Frozos wants to build a speedway above Earth. I do not know the technical nature of speedways or hyperdrive, but I would suggest they are beginning to build the opening of a portal they can control. Based on the extrapolated dimensions of the curve, it could fit two of those supertankers at one time. If we let them build it, they could bring in dozens of ships in a short order, which could overwhelm any military capacity we could build." The part about not knowing the technical details is a bit of a fib, but he needs to get these people on his side.

In response, the American representative enters the conversation. "I sympathize with this perspective, Commander Wilson. But it seems you are laying out a potential future military threat rather than what I think we meant for imminent to mean."

"Yes, but I'd rather strike now to impair their potential to develop not just an imminent threat but an insurmountable one, General," Robert says, bitingly.

Thornhill reinserts himself before tensions flare. "If I may add a point. The question of imminence gets to motivations. If they build a portal for commercial purposes primarily but which could be used for military purposes, that's a potential but not imminent threat. But a portal intended primarily for military purposes with other secondary uses would be imminent. We know that Frozos has said we will face repercussions, and they have already launched multiple strikes on the force field, seventeen in one day last week and in recent days several strikes, admittedly for apparent research purposes. The motive of the capacity buildout to me is clearly military."

"Tell me," the Russian Defense Minister asks, "Do you have knowledge the force field is not impenetrable? Otherwise, no threat outside it would be imminent."

"No, Madam Secretary," Robert replies. "To my knowledge and everyone who has worked on it, we do not see a way through. But I don't think the existence of bulletproof glass should make one tolerate an ever-increasing number of guns pointed in their direction."

"Yes, but I want to get to the risk versus reward of the operation. Tell me, if you wanted to fly a squadron from, let's say, your New Mexico base to blow it up, you'd have to at least temporarily turn off the force field to let them through, no?"

"That's correct."

"While the force field is off, it would be possible for their ships to enter our atmosphere, no?"

"Correct, though only briefly. Likely under two minutes," Robert responds, confidently. He had been hoping for this line of questioning.

"So, I agree a speedway portal is an imminent threat, but it may not be realizable. To combat this threat, you'd create a realizable imminent threat by turning off our best protection, temporarily. That's poor risk versus reward."

Murmurs on the call indicate broad agreement for this point.

"I can sympathize with that point, Madam Secretary. Let me ask a question back. If I could launch an attack, only on the supertanker transport ships to signal our opposition to a speedway but without engaging in provocative action against the military vessels, and without ever having to turn off Earth's force field, would that be a risk versus reward you would support?"

"Well, I suppose, yes I would, but that's not this situation."

"Actually," Thornhill chimes in, as planned, "we have a contingency plan, Selena, that I believe will meet your criteria."

Dovetailing the retired General, Robert adds, "I do not need your approval, but I very much want it. It is important that PEACE be seen as acting legitimately to ensure support on Earth and to signal to our opponents that were united as one planet. I think you will find this plan is low-risk and will take out an imminent threat to our ability to prevail in potential further military conflicts."

After a further ten minutes of discussion, there is an anonymous nonbinding vote of 84–17. It is then agreed that the participating nations would provide unanimous support for

PEACE's operation when details are disclosed subsequent to its completion.

Admiral Tyrone Tiberius is standing in the conn of his ship, staring at Earth. Every few minutes, he peppers his radar and communications teams with demands for an update. Earlier, at about 10:50 AM in New Mexico, Tiberius's satellite cameras discovered that SF-01s were being moved from storage and onto active runways. Tiberius hopes that Robert has taken the bait and will try to blow up the beginnings of the speedway gate. Tiberius has amassed all of his fleet's firepower pointed down at Earth to capitalize on what he assumed would be a brief few minutes to get as many ships as possible inside of Earth's atmosphere to reap devastation. He doubts he could get enough ships in to conquer the planet, but just enough to destroy several cities. He hopes that will be sufficient to torpedo confidence in Robert's leadership and cause the planet to capitulate. At the least, it will show much needed progress to an increasingly agitated Frozos.

It's now 11:35 AM, and there is still no sign of action from Earth's runways. Tiberius is nervously pacing back and forth across the conn, wondering what is taking so long.

"Planes are taking off, Admiral!" a radar specialist shouts.

"Are they near the edge of the atmosphere?" Tiberius asks, prepared to send his ships even closer to the edge of the force field.

"No, they appear to be circling low, waiting for more jets to take off."

"Smart," Tiberius concedes. "He wants them flying tight together to minimize the time he turns off the force field. Tell all ships to inch closer to the atmosphere's edge." The entire fleet, except for Frozos's ship, *Magnus*, are within 1,000 miles of the force field and more than 100,000 miles away from the portal. *Magnus* is about 25,000 miles behind Tiberius's destroyer. Suddenly, a massive explosion shakes the entire conn.

"What was that?!" Tiberius demands. Mayday calls are pouring in from one of the supertankers, which is on fire. 500 SF-01s are flying around the nascent construction site, making quick work of the cursory defense force of seventy-five small crafts.

"Admiral! What should we do? Supertanker 1's shields have suffered catastrophic breaches. Supertanker 2 is trying to fly toward us, but two hundred bogies are attacking it." The communications team shouts as the conn descends into near panic.

Tiberius is momentarily frozen. He doesn't understand how so many ships slipped past his radar but is afraid this is a trap to get him to turn his back on Earth and leave himself vulnerable to the building assault. "Send Destroyer C and its team of small crafts, full speed. Maximize enemy casualties. A and B hold positions to prepare for a second wave from Earth."

Meanwhile, the 500 SF-01s are zig-zagging across the construction site, shredding the metal frame. One fighter has been lost to sixty-eight League planes who were totally unprepared for an attack from their rear. Just as Destroyer C turns to head to the construction site, there is a massive explosion from the already burning, rudderless Supertanker 1. The fires apparently reached the fuel cells, causing the entire ship to explode in a blindingly bright ball of fire, that must be visible from the Asian nations the fleet is flying above.

Supertanker 2, virtually defenseless against the high-speed SF-01, is enduring waves of attacks. Nearly 200 SF-01s are flying in a series of V-formations of twenty-four planes firing down at the top of the hull, before rolling and circling back to hit its underside. The repeated sprayings of hundreds of laser bullets have pierced through the outer shields. The supertanker's engines have stopped, and the ship is now floating helplessly away from Earth with ever-intensifying fires.

With the speediest crafts from Destroyer C Group nearing the fleet of SF-01s, they are recalled to base, having achieved the mission. They turn away from the second supertanker and move full-speed to the moon. At full speed, they seem to travel at least as fast as the League's small crafts. By the time the last of the SF-01s is close enough to the moon for the force field to be turned on, the nearest League plane is still over 30,000 miles away. Just subsequent to the reemergence of the moon's force field, the second supertanker explodes, its fires having grown uncontrollable.

Utterly defeated and humiliated, Tiberius collapses into his captain's chair in the conn, head resting on his hand. "Tell me, have the planes on Earth landed yet?"

With a gulp, the radar aide says, "Yes, the jets are landing and tarmacs clearing. It was a diversion." Tiberius is beside himself; he had never contemplated the possibility of an already-existing base of SF-01s on the moon. At the same time, he is puzzled that Robert spared the entire fleet when he could have launched a devastating attack on the transport destroyers or *Magnus* even, in all likelihood. This defeat was a horrible psychological blow and would greatly slow the military ramp-up outside Earth, but it did not impair their existing capabilities.

"Sir," the communications team reads out, "We have a message from *Magnus*. Supreme General demands the fleet return to *Magnus* and for Admiral Tiberius's attendance immediately."

"Steering, bring the ship back twenty thousand miles, and prepare my personal vessel." Tiberius fears his end is near in the retirement-assignment from Hell. Still, he is holding out a little hope that his one last gamble could buy him a bit more time.

Back in New Mexico and Jersey City, the mood is ebullient. Operation Selena was a tremendous success. Tiberius fell for the earthly diversions, allowing the fleet of SF-01s from Arbor Ridge's old moon base, now a PEACE property, to launch a sneak attack. There are over 600 planes on the moon, having been secretly flown up in December before Nick Neverian took office as President. Robert had kept this close to the chest, knowing they only had one chance for a moon sneak attack. To Chris Bailey, Mark Morrison, and Jake Thornhill, he had always alluded to the presence of jets in three locations away from the twelve Arbor Ridge towers, but never informed

SCOTT RUESTERHOLZ

them of the moon's facility until two weeks ago to allow for some strategic planning.

Robert is glad to see the mission accomplished with relative ease. PEACE lost two planes and pilots; he has already requested the names of next of kin to place personal phone calls. But, the League of Planets lost two supertanker transporters, all material, and men on board, likely over 100,000 lives, seventy-five small crafts, and the first bit of construction on the speedway portal. Robert is glad to see the SF-01 perform this well in a true combat mission. The moon pilots are his most experienced, so he never doubted their ability to perform under pressure.

Robert does feel a tinge of regret that he did not go after Tiberius's ships. He could only launch a surprise attack from the moon once, and he has now played that card. But, it was critical to deliver a win to give mankind confidence, and he needed a military plan that could win the support of the nations of the world and have a very high probability of success. Going after a Destroyer group or *Magnus* didn't meet those qualifications. All in all, it was a successful day.

Robert congratulates everyone on the video conference. He asks Thornhill's team to compile video for public release and will make a press statement in roughly one hour at 2:00 PM local time.

Robert turns to Anna, "So, what did you think?"

"I think the SF-01 proved itself capable of what we thought. It's the fastest ship in the sky and packs enough punch to damage large carrier ships," she replies.

"And?" Robert asks, sensing she is holding something back.

"Well, sir, we know what we can do, but I still don't know what they can do. We destroyed unarmed, overwhelmed targets. We won't have that luxury again."

"That's an astute point. But hopefully, seeing success will give our recruits confidence that we can win and to stop fearing failure quite as much."

"I will be conveying that message for sure!" Anna says, smiling, as she gets up to leave.

"Very good. Godspeed, Group Commander Small."

At 2:00 PM, Robert is standing out on the tarmac behind a thin metal lectern with about a dozen local reporters seated in front of him. Several television cameras are feeding national news outlets. About ten minutes ago, PEACE released videos from the battle, including the explosions of each of the supertankers, along with a brief statement, that he is about to expound upon.

"Good afternoon, everyone. Thank you for making it here on such short notice. I am speaking to you from Holloman Air Force Base, which is now a joint PEACE facility. I am glad to tell you our recruiting and training programs have progressed nicely this past week, and I thank the U.S. Air Force and all our military partners globally for their help and cooperation.

"Today, in my judgment, the world faced an imminent military threat in space. I conferred with the military representatives as a courtesy before taking action, and there was unanimous support for today's operation. Yesterday, two supertanker transport ships arrived to join Frozos's military fleet.

Today, they began construction on a speedway portal, which could lead to the arrival of significantly more military ships.

"We will not tolerate an ever-increasing number of guns pointed at our gates. To drive this point home, we took action against the construction site and the two supertankers while not engaging the existing military spacecraft. We launched a strike of 500 SF-01s from PEACE's moon base, which is part of Arbor Ridge's longstanding lunar facilities.

"At no time did we lower Earth's force field, nor did we use any ships from Earth. I am pleased to report that this mission was a tremendous success, destroying the two tankers and all construction, as well as at least seventy enemy aircrafts. We suffered two casualties, a brave American and Austrian citizen, who gave their lives heroically to protect ours. We will be releasing their names shortly.

"I have believed from the outset that we possessed the skill and determination to prevail in conflict with any enemy; my conviction in this only grows stronger by the day. I urge Supreme General Frozos to end his acts of aggression and leave our planet alone. PEACE stands ready to protect this planet, and our readiness is only strengthening. Our resolve will not be broken. Thank you and God bless."

While Robert was speaking to the press, Admiral Tiberius had boarded his personal ship, a black sphere similar to that in Robert's underground office, and gone aboard *Magnus*. He is standing in front of Frozos who is seated behind a desk, on top of which plans are strewn everywhere.

"I believe this strategy is our best way to end the nuisance of this force field." Tiberius concludes.

"Interesting, Admiral. I commend the out of the box thinking. And you say two weeks?" Frozos inquires.

"Yes, sir. Two weeks for the first phase of the operation."

"This reminds me of my childhood on the family farm. Have I told you about that farm, Tiberius?"

"No, sir." A half-truth from the Admiral, who has learnt that when Frozos has a story he wishes to tell it is best to let him tell it.

"We had a family of foxes who, despite my father's best efforts, kept getting into the hen house, killing our chickens. So, one day, we dropped a smoke bomb down into their den, and I shot each one as they ran out, panicked. We never had a fox problem again. We'll give your plan a chance. Make the necessary arrangements back at headquarters."

"Thank you, Supreme General."

Tiberius bows and walks to the door of the office. As he is about to open the door, Frozos says, "Tiberius. You've had a long and faithful career, for which I am grateful. It is for that reason alone I am giving you a final chance to take this meddlesome planet and undo your wrong. Your next failure will be your last."

Tiberius nods in understanding and leaves.

CHAPTER 18

Jersey City
April 29, 2029

Twelve days have passed since PEACE's first military engagement. The success in space has, as Robert Wilson hoped, greatly boosted morale both among his recruits and the broader population. Public polling showed that over 80 percent had confidence in his leadership and over 70 percent "feel safe from alien attack." More important than any opinion survey, daily life is seeming increasingly normal—the strongest sign yet that people do indeed feel safe.

After an initial rush to hoard goods, grocery store sales are entirely average, restaurants are filled. Financial market volatility has largely subsided. Topics of conversation at the office water cooler, local bar, and family dinner table have mostly reverted back to the daily dramas of life, the latest episodes of popular television shows, and how the local sports team is faring. From an outsider's perspective, life would seem totally normal. Still untested, of course, is how durable this calm is or whether a military snafu could bring with it mass panic.

Life, of course, is not normal for those working at PEACE, but operations are progressing smoothly. Weekly plane production between new facilities and existing ones is set to pass 3,800 this week, leaving PEACE on pace to hit peak production of 4,750 within two weeks. Private sector partners have stepped up to the occasion mightily, integrating complex supply chains in days, sharing information and employees, to get product out the door and shipped as quickly as possible. Critically, diagnostic and flight tests show no deviation in quality from legacy Arbor Ridge sites and new facilities. There are now over 17,000 planes in PEACE's fleet. This sum exceeds the combined Air Forces of the United States, Russia, and China. The fleet is nearing critical capacity to be able to defend the majority of the planet from attack should the force field fail, but there still are not enough planes to successfully wage a battle in space.

Pilot recruiting has been another source of optimism. There have been over 40,000 recruits thus far, out of 45,725 offers. Of these 40,000, 7,191 have passed through training, generally a two-week process, been enlisted, and assigned to a squadron and group command. That gives PEACE nearly 9,000 active pilots, including 1,200 legacy pilots on Earth and 550 on the moon. Of the 9,000, about 2,700 are either active or retired members of their nation's military. Just over 3,300 recruits have failed out, primarily because the fear of death altered and impaired the way they flew from how they had performed in the virtual reality game. That leaves over

29,000 recruits who are progressing through training at various stages. Based on pass rates thus far, Robert expects about 110,000 recruits will be needed to achieve a fighting force of 75,000 pilots, well within the tolerance bands given 240,000 qualified game players, and he expects, should current trends hold, about 20 to 23 percent of recruits to be active or retired military officers, with a heavy skew towards the active force. At that penetration rate, there should be at least two or three military members in each squadron, a presence which he hopes will make it easier for trained civilians to cope with enlisted life.

Today, Robert is sitting in his office in the Jersey City headquarters of PEACE. It has been a whirlwind ten days for him. After the success of the first strike, he toured around PEACE bases across several nations to energize recruits and poll group commanders about how training was progressing. Equally important, he was meeting with the heads of state or defense minister in each country he visited: Canada, Japan, China, Vietnam, Russia, Austria, France, Nigeria, and Brazil.

The debate prior to the last military battle had opened Robert's eyes to the reticence with which the national delegates viewed opening Earth's force field. Of course, that was never the plan for the speedway portal operation, but the national representatives didn't originally know that. There could be a time where PEACE needed to launch a strike from Earth that could briefly open the force field, and Robert worried he would lack the necessary national government support. While he technically had unilateral authority, he did recognize that acting contrary to the overwhelming view of the world's governments would undermine his credibility, particularly if the operation was anything other than a clear success.

Robert has been meeting with world leaders to encourage them to deploy aircraft carrier groups, fighter jets, and anti-craft missiles to major cities. During these briefings, he always emphasized that the force field would be opened for mere minutes, so there would be very few enemy ships that would get through before the shield would be closed again, particularly given the rush of PEACE jets flying out into space. PEACE jets would continue to be the primary line of defense, but by deploying conventional militaries to major cities, there would be a secondary line of defense, which could hopefully engage a handful of ships, successfully. By adding this "insurance layer" to Earth's defenses, he hoped that there would be greater willingness to open the force field if and when it is necessary to do so.

Meeting with these leaders proved to be a frustrating experience for Robert. Most leaders were reluctant to deploy militaries in a way that civilians would notice in their everyday life, like posting a battleship a few hundred yards from shore. The degree of calm from citizens has been a pleasant surprise to world leaders who did not want to take any policy that would upset that calm. They feared deploying the military would scare the public or be seen as a sign there was doubt about the impenetrability of the force field.

While this was the primary reason given to Robert in meeting after meeting, there was an additional reason. Many, particularly within national militaries, were wary of Robert and uncomfortable outsourcing so much of the globe's defense to him. Some nations joined PEACE to monitor his actions rather than because they were supportive of the idea, not to mention fear of being left out if the initiative proved to be a popular success, as it has been thus far. To that end, they feared deploying their own militaries as supplemental defenses would make it too easy to launch an offensive against Frozos— an action for which they feared Robert was overly eager.

In these dealings, President Victoria Larom has been a helpful partner, able to supplement deft diplomacy with Robert's more blunt style. Before engaging in this global tour, Robert met President Larom at the White House where he first laid out the idea of deploying national militaries. She was sympathetic to his idea, in part because Nick Neverian had been so uncooperative under constant interrogation, much more so than the other detained spies. Neverian was insistent that Frozos would stop at nothing to take Earth and he was prepared to wait patiently in jail for that day to come, certain a life of luxury and power awaited him.

Neverian never offered details for why he felt this way, just saying that Earth would be a "crown jewel" in Frozos's empire. Larom didn't divulge this information to Robert who was already sufficiently hawkish on military affairs. However, it did underpin her view that the planet should be planning for a long haul and that it would be wise to enhance defenses. She, though, did understand concerns from other leaders that overly blatant displays of force could upset the calm among civilians.

So, after Robert's meetings with foreign leaders, where he offered his proposal and faced pushback, she would phone the relevant leaders to offer a compromise path that the U.S. was pursuing. It is highly unlikely that Robert would be opening the force field on a moment's notice. He would likely be able to give at least one day's notice before opening the force field to launch an attack. As a consequence, Larom proposed a "T+1 strategy"—essentially a plan whereby the military would be sufficiently ready to deploy to major cities within one day. This meant the U.S. was moving its aircraft carrier groups within one hundred miles of shore, close enough to protect cities within hours but sufficiently far away that they would go unnoticed by the public. Similarly, additional troops and mobile anti-aircraft systems were being sent near major cities so that they could be rapidly deployed.

The one drawback of this approach is that cities would not be immediately protected if Frozos broke through the shield. This is the risk they needed to balance against the risk of public panic. At this point, they continue to view the force field as impenetrable, so Larom viewed this risk as acceptable against the need to keep the public calm. Indeed, her middle-ground proposal has largely been met with approval from her fellow world leaders, particularly compared to Robert's more aggressive proposals. Alongside the U.S., most nations have secretly agreed to this partial deployment strategy so that their militaries could be able to supplement PEACE's defenses in one day's notice.

Robert is heartened to have a partner like President Larom in the White House to deal with other world leaders, and he feels comfortable that her proposal is both prudent and sufficient to address his concern that world leaders would be overly hesitant to support a brief opening of the force field. With that matter settled and Larom promising her help where possible, Robert is able to focus entirely on PEACE's mission.

Sitting in his office today, he is reviewing intelligence reports and photos compiled by Jake Thornhill's team. Subsequent to the battle on April 17, there has been virtually no action by Frozos's forces. That night, Tiberius deployed one of the transport destroyer groups to the moon to pin down the lunar forces, a move Robert expected. The remaining two groups and *Magnus* just sat in orbit around Earth's atmosphere. All of the ships moved just enough to avoid being an easy target in the event Earth had deep space laser capability, which it does not. Otherwise, there was no action whatsoever; Robert had been beginning to find the degree of complacency among the enemy forces unsettling.

Then, yesterday, three more supertanker transporters arrived, escorted by an additional transport destroyer group. Up through this morning, there had been no activity from the supertankers, and speculation around their purpose has been rife. Robert has been dismissive of the theory that they are here to make another attempt at building the speedway portal. He is certain that Frozos or Tiberius has something else planned. For the past three weeks, the League's top scientific minds must have been spending every waking hour trying to find a way through or around the force field, and this is likely to be their answer.

There is a knock at the door connecting Robert's office to the command center.

"Come in."

Thornhill walks in. "There's action. Come over when you have a minute. Not imminent."

"Thanks, Jake. I'll be there shortly."

After paging through the last bits of the intelligence reports, Robert gets up from behind his desk and walks into the command center. Up on the screen, the satellite feeds are being transmitted. There is finally movement. The supertankers have moved closer to Earth than in the photos from overnight that Robert had just been reviewing. From the opening in the rear of the supertankers, small crafts are pulling a dark fiber out. They appear to be welding the edges of these fiber sheets to create a larger sheet.

"Where are the ships?" Robert asks.

"About 200 miles from the edge of the force field, sir," an officer in the front row says.

"Yes, but what part of the planet are they over?" Robert asks, a bit more urgently.

"Sir, they are about 250 miles south of Tokyo."

"And what time is it, there?"

"11:43 PM"

"So no sunlight, then?" Robert asks rhetorically.

"No, it's the dead of night," the officer answers unnecessarily.

Robert looks to Jake in a state of genuine horror. "And, do we have any idea what type of material that is?"

Thornhill motions to the over-eager officer to button up, "No, it's impossible to do any real testing, but our preliminary scans show no active weaponry. The only military ships are from the escorting, single destroyer group about 2,500 miles behind the supertankers. Elsewhere, one destroyer is stationed by the moon, another over South Africa, one over New York, and Frozos's ship is over Finland."

"Well, I'm not sure what we can do other than monitor it. All of this material is coming out of just one supertanker, correct?" Robert confirms.

"Yes, that's right."

"My goodness, that sheet looks gigantic."

"Yes, they're adding tens of thousands of square yards per minute," Thornhill replies.

"Okay, keep me abreast of any developments. Otherwise, I want to know the second it is daybreak above Tokyo."

With that command, Robert walks back into his office and picks up his phone.

"Madam President, this is Robert Wilson.... I'm afraid the day we've worried about is coming. They are trying to work around the force field. I'm ashamed to admit I didn't see this one coming...."

After a few minutes of back and forth with President Larom, Robert hangs up the phone. He stares at the phone for a moment, hesitates, and then picks it up.

"Mark, it's Robert.... Yes, yes, I know I'm not supposed to. Just make sure the utilities charge the excess energy batteries to their full capacity today.... Trust me on this, and make sure other utilities do the same. Thanks."

Technically, this phone call is in breach of the agreement that Robert had signed incorporating PEACE, but now is not the time to worry about details. Robert knows that Mark would be more understanding of the occasional slipup than

Chris, who by his nature is a letter-of-the-law type of guy. He just hopes that his advice is heeded. A battle for Earth is all but inevitable now, Robert fears.

CHAPTER 19

Jersey City
April 30, 2029

It is now 4:00 AM in Jersey City, and Robert is standing in the command center. Like all the individuals in the room, from retired General Jake Thornhill to the lowliest aide, Robert hasn't slept all night, and he looks it. The group is tired, unshaven, working off adrenaline and caffeine. Indeed, Robert has a cup of coffee in hand as he stares up at the screen. He doesn't even care for coffee, but his taste buds have long gone to sleep.

Robert's hunch from yesterday morning has been confirmed: Frozos's army is deploying a shade around the planet. The nature of the material is still unknown but it appears extremely thin and light-weight—that is the only way one supertanker could carry so much of the material. From preliminary tests since sunrise, the material does an exceptional job at blocking sunlight and reflecting the heat away from the

Earth. The project has been underway for nearly twenty hours and enough space has been blocked off to block the sunlight from hitting 0.7 percent of the Earth.

Fortunately, there is significant cloud cover over most of Asia this morning, so the impact from the lost sunlight isn't being felt on the ground. When clouds dissipate, there will essentially be a black blotch on the top of the sky, and it will continue to grow. This "sunsheet," as the command center has taken to calling it, also appears to be motorized and rather than orbiting over a stationary spot on the Earth, it is moving alongside the sun so that it will be blocking its life-giving rays twenty-four hours a day. As an aide noted, this feature means that Frozos needn't build a sheet around the entire planet to block out the sun. However, such a feat wouldn't be necessary; Earth's resistance would collapse well before then.

Indeed, Frozos can have a crippling impact on daily life on Earth, endangering its habitability, with a sunsheet that is far smaller than the planet's surface area. By blocking around 10 percent of sunlight from reaching the Earth's surface, models show Robert that global temperatures could fall by more than seventeen degrees Fahrenheit on average. That would make the Earth colder than during the Ice Age, which would greatly shock the nature and quality of life across much of the planet. Parts of North America and Europe could remain snow-covered year-round with beach summer vacations a thing of the past.

While this would undoubtedly be an unpleasant change and it would likely lead to death as societies readjusted themselves, wearing a winter coat all year is the least of humanity's problems. Solar power is now a critical supply of energy for utilities. Some areas are likely to lack the generation capacity to keep the lights on without new investment. Sunlight also provides the energy for plants to grow, which provide the backbone of global nutrition and recycles CO_2 into oxygen in the atmosphere.

Keeping 10 percent of Earth shielded from sunlight is likely to cause massive crop failures and a loss of vegetation not seen since an asteroid wiped out the dinosaurs millions of years ago. Worse, if Frozos continued to expand the sun shield past 25 percent of the Earth's surface, the losses could be irreversible. Mass hunger, potential shifts in the composition of the atmosphere, and unprecedented cold risked mass unrest and global war amongst nations over the fight to secure food and other critical natural resources.

Frozos could set in motion a cataclysmic series of events where Earth falls from within. Obviously disgusted by the callous disregard for the loss of over one billion souls, Robert could nonetheless appreciate the ingeniousness and simplicity of the plan. While a strike would be preemptive, it is clear to Robert, having looked through the models and now sifting through presentation materials crafted by PEACE's scientific research wing, that Frozos's forces now pose exactly the type of imminent threat that PEACE was constructed to stop.

"You know," Thornhill says to Robert, "When we think of besieged cities that fall, we think of Troy where the enemy attackers sneak their way in behind the guarded walls. In reality, throughout history, besieged cities fall because they are gradually and methodically starved of resources from the outside."

"I've always thought of our planet as self-reliant," Robert replies, "given there is no intergalactic commerce we partake in. I never realized that we were entirely reliant on another entity the whole time—the sun. So foolish of me."

"Not just you, sir. Not one of us who worked on the force field foresaw this. Perhaps we all just lacked the imagination that there could be enough raw materials to effectively implement a solar blockade."

Taking little solace in Thornhill's attempt to comfort him, he attempts to pivot back to the plan of action. "Is May twelfth still our best guess as to when ten percent of sunlight is going to be blocked?"

"Yes," the same junior aide who just a few weeks ago told Robert he was sure Earth would be victorious replies. Robert takes heart in his vigor—at least one man hasn't lost confidence in the ultimate outcome of this effort.

"Well, Jake. You should freshen up. I'm going to take a quick shower and shave. I think we have a better chance of success if we don't look like the crazed, sleep-deprived souls that we are." Robert gives Thornhill a pat on the back and heads back into his office to freshen up before a 6:00 AM conference call.

At 6:00 AM in Jersey City, Robert is sitting behind his desk, having put on a black suit with a light blue tie. Thornhill is taking the video conference from his own office on the other side of the command center, wearing his standard purple jumpsuit with commander insignia. Given Robert sees the situation as a near military threat but not yet an imminent one, he has requested heads of state instead of the standard military representatives. In the mosaic of faces on his screen, he is relieved to see that President Victoria Larom is on the call. He needs her presence more than ever. There are 108 countries on the call with what looks to be eighty-one heads of state and twenty-seven military representatives—a strong showing, though Robert is left to wonder what those government leaders could be doing that is more important than the briefing he is about to give.

"I thank you all for being here on such short notice. I realize for many of you it isn't a convenient hour. I'm going to ask Jake Thornhill to begin to provide all the technical details for today's briefing."

In his just-the-facts style, Thornhill runs through all the developments of the past forty-eight hours, from the supertankers' arrival to the nature of the sunsheet that is now being strewn across Earth's skies. Following these details, he summarizes the scientific consensus of the impact of the lost sunlight, from colder temperatures to lost agriculture.

"Thank you, Jake, before we open it up to questions on our plan of action, I just want to highlight two numbers," Robert says. "The first is ten percent of sunlight. That is when we will start to feel the loss of sun noticeably on temperatures, solar energy production, and some crops. The journey to that first ten percent really shouldn't impact daily life. The second is twenty-five percent of sunlight. Based on the scientific consensus, that is catastrophic, if not species threatening. Essentially, we need to destroy the sunsheet somewhere between the ten and twenty-five percent thresholds, which best guess would put us in the May twelfth to May thirtieth time period."

Russian President Mikhail Malvodov is the first to speak up. "Why don't we just destroy it now? Not that we in Russia mind our winters, but what's the purpose in waiting?"

"A few reasons, Mister President," Robert replies. "Each day, we're now building 500 planes and graduating several hundred pilots. Each day enhances our military capacity, and we see little real-world impact of waiting at least ten days. Second, based on our roughest of estimates, the three supertankers may carry enough sunsheet to cover fifteen to twenty-five percent of the Earth. If we destroy it too soon, they could deploy a new one of sufficient scale. I want to waste more of their material. Third, I think it's everyone's consensus that we should only open Earth's force field when it is essential to do so. We haven't met that criteria yet."

"Why do we need to use earthbound planes?" asks Ecuador's President. "Can't we use the lunar fighters again, to mitigate the risk?"

"I wish, Mister President. With a destroyer stationed against the moon, I fear those planes are pinned down. They'd have to travel two hundred thousand miles with Frozos's military pointing at them. The probability of success is very low. There are few enemy crafts between the force field and the sun shield, which sits just a few hundred miles from the edge of force field. This has to be an earthbound mission."

A solemnity hangs over the room. Many had hoped that direct military conflict between Frozos and Earth's fighters could be avoided. It is now painfully clear that will not be the case. There will be at least one battle, and in all likelihood, more than one.

"How can we help you?" Portugal's Prime Minister asks.

"To be frank, sir, don't worry about the military aspect. We have high confidence we can win this battle, assuming the basic dynamics that Jake and I have laid out remain the same. Maintaining the element of surprise is critical. I believe our communications are secure from Frozos's interception, but we will not divulge all details as a precaution. Know that between May ninth and May twenty-fifth, we will be taking action to destroy the sunsheet. That will be the sole focus of this mission. I ask you to do what is necessary to inform the public and keep calm. There is going to be a giant black spot in the sky; the public will find out what's going on. I think you need to proactively communicate to the people you represent in a calming, reassuring way. You alone can do that; it's outside my mandate. I leave it to you whether to invoke the T+1 plan, though I prefer you don't just yet that way they don't know that our strike will come from Earth. Leave the military matters as my concern, and I will leave the public as your concern."

"That's sounds like a fair deal," President Larom concludes. She adds, "The United States will not be invoking T+1 unless you advise us otherwise." She knows that by stating this position clearly that the rest of the world will follow.

"I thank you for your time." Robert turns off the video conference. He knows his next move and is now just waiting to hear what world governments have to say.

At 7:00 AM in Washington D.C., President Larom has stepped behind the lectern of the White House Briefing Room, wearing a golden-yellow skirt suit. The room is filled to the brim with reporters and cameras. Over the past twenty minutes, leaders in Europe and Asia have been taking to the airwaves to discuss that mysterious black spot hovering above the skies in most European capitals. The world now waits to see what the American President has to say on the matter.

"Good morning. This morning, leaders of all nations in the PEACE coalition conferred with PEACE leadership over developments in space outside of our force field. I will begin with the good news. The actions being taken by General Frozos's military seem to indicate they too believe the shield is impenetrable. Rather than attempt to break through, they are attempting to place a sunsheet over our planet to block sunlight.

"They are seeking to lay siege to our planet, and by limiting the sunlight, cool global temperatures, destroy crops, underwhelm solar energy facilities, and kill oxygen-producing plant life. This strategy, if we do nothing, would take weeks to have any impact on our lives. Indeed, PEACE commander Robert Wilson told me the best thing the public can do for the war effort is to remain calm and carry on with daily life because these actions in no way are a danger to you.

"We, of course, will not stand idly by and do nothing. Rather, we have already formulated plans to ensure sunlight continues to Earth uninterrupted. To ensure the success of military operations, I cannot provide any details publicly of the nature or timing of our plans. Just rest assured they are coming.

"I encourage all Americans to begin this workweek as they would any other. Thank you and God bless the United States of America."

As President Larom walks out of the room, reporters shout questions at her with variations of, "Why isn't Commander Wilson answering questions?"

Sitting in his office in PEACE headquarters, Robert hears these questions as the cable news channel cuts out of the briefing and back to their New York City studio where pundits are asking the same question, wondering if his silence signals a disagreement between elected officials and himself, which of course couldn't be further from the truth. Robert can envision this narrative snowballing over the course of the day, so he decides he needs to nip it in the bud.

It's funny, Robert thinks to himself. Most of mankind has never travelled to space and likely never will. And yet somehow, having space closed off like it is now makes one feel so utterly claustrophobic. Robert himself has that same feeling of being trapped, even though they still have an entire planet, closed off safely and securely. He tries to ponder over what message to tell the world in this time of strife.

He thinks of his father.

CHAPTER 20

Planet Nayan
Earth Year 2008

It has been just about four years since Marcus's mother was murdered and Nayan had fallen to Frozos's forces. During that time, Marcus and his father, Jesse, have lived together in the cave in the woods. In the back corner near the makeshift kitchen, Marcus and Jesse are working through complex physics problems at the kitchen table. There are still three chairs here, one of which neither has sat in: the chair that was supposed to belong to Marcus's mother. In their first days in the cave, a young Marcus, noting there were no family photos or pictures of his mother, asked that they keep the chair to ensure they never forgot his mom. The chair has remained in its place, unoccupied, ever since; an ever-present reminder of his mother's sacrifice. Aside from that, many of their nights passed with Jesse telling and retelling stories of their past, little anecdotes that revealed the character of his mother from their first date to her efforts smuggling resistance fighters through mining towns across Nayan.

The father and son passed most nights by playing board games and telling stories. Aside from his mother, Marcus's favorite topic was of the resistance, and the heroic fighters who led it. Undoubtedly, Jesse took some literary license in these tellings to keep his son engaged, and often greater truth lies in fiction than fact. As the years passed, he at times forgot which stories were true and which had been exaggerated. Occasionally, Jesse would try to use his old radio to see if he could find resistance chatter away from the propaganda that the League of Planets pumped out. As the years went by, resistance chatter grew sparser and sparser, but there was the periodic snippet that kept hope alive. To this day, rumors that this King Hammerhead, whose planet, Aquine, was said to have held out longer than any other against Frozos, is alive and keeping rebel forces aligned, striking where possible, and patiently biding their time until there's an opportunity to capitalize on the internal strife in the League, persisted.

Jesse consistently told his son that a day would come when Frozos would be toppled, repeatedly preaching to Marcus, "Intelligent life is not meant to be oppressed. The number who want to fight against Frozos far outnumber those who will fight on his behalf. But, the people need to believe that the fight can be won before they will muster the courage to challenge him. Until someone can light that spark, Frozos's darkness will endure."

While nights were occupied with stories and games, the days were hard work. Jesse was adamant that his son be educated, and given his background as a college professor, he was well equipped to teach him the maths and sciences. And so, Marcus spent every day from early morning to midafternoon on schoolwork. There were no summer breaks, and weekends were half-days. Marcus spent two-thirds of his time on math and science and the remainder covering a smattering of English and history with a focus on the history of democracies in this part of the galaxy. Jesse's expertise was in mathematics, and he knew that passing that expertise on to Marcus would be his only ticket off this planet. But, he also wanted to ensure that Marcus knew right from wrong and would use that expertise for noble ends. Fortunately given Marcus's natural proficiencies and the intensive tutoring his father provided, he excelled in the sciences and mathematics. As an eleven-year-old, he was already solving physics problems that would elude the greatest of Earth's scientists.

After school, the father and son spend time carefully out of the cave, filling up their water reserve, picking berries and vegetables that grow naturally throughout the forest. Several times a week, they fish and trap small game to supplement their diet as the stock of food and supplies that had filled the cave to the brim have largely been consumed these past four years. Having spent his formative years in the forest, Marcus is an adept hunter and gatherer, able to move throughout the woods without making a sound. He stands at about five feet tall, which would place him just above average on Nayan. He has untidy, long hair, a natural result of living alone with one's father, who now sports a beard to go with untidy lengthy hair of his own.

In their first weeks in the cave, there was an abundance of aerial activity as Frozos consolidated his control over Nayan and rounded up those who had fled to work as slaves in the mine. There were even several ground patrols through the woods. As a consequence, during those first two months, Marcus never left the cave and Jesse did only sparingly. However after about a month, the patrols and air raids nearly came to a halt; Frozos's forces must have been confident they had rounded up or killed substantially all of the holdouts on the planet. For the following three years, there were virtually no patrols through the forest and planes could only be heard from above occasionally. Generally, these patrols occurred after an escape from the mine; Jesse and Marcus would not run across a single soul during these three-plus years. However, in recent months, activity had been ticking up with several air patrols a week and ground patrols once every eight or nine days. It is unclear to Jesse and Marcus why there was an increase; Marcus hoped it was a sign there was increasing smuggling to resistance forces. While Jesse wanted to believe this as well, the lack of communication he could come across on his radio left him more circumspect.

Today is a hot, summer day on Nayan. It is mid-afternoon, and Marcus is wearing a green tunic and cargo pants, barefoot, his feet having outgrown shoes quite some time ago. His father is wearing a badly-fraying, faded yellow button-down shirt, torn khaki pants, and hiking boots badly in need of repair. Marcus is sitting anxiously as his father grades a celestial physics test. Jesse always maintains a perfect poker face while grading, enjoying the nervous anxiety building in his son. After several agonizing minutes, he puts his red pen down.

"Not bad, but you can do better. A ninety-one. We need to review gravitational forces on multi-star solar systems, but that can wait until tomorrow."

"Okay, I guess," Marcus says with a sigh, "but it's still an A-. You know what that means!"

"I know; I'll get the water," his father replies. To incentivize his son to learn to the fullest of his potential, anytime he did better than a ninety on a test, his father would do that day's main chore, which today was going to the river and refilling the water tank. This happened to be Marcus's least favorite chore; it was a quarter-mile walk to the river. He had to carry a five-gallon tank like a backpack and a one-gallon bottle in each hand, which would give them several days' worth of water. For an eleven-year-old, it is an exhausting project. Knowing this, Jesse had taken to scheduling tests on water fill-up days, to give his son a bit of extra motivation to study and excel. He is more than happy to carry the water if it meant his son achieving his academic potential.

Throwing the empty water bag over his shoulder, and with the two empty canisters in hand, his father heads out. Marcus pulls a beaten-up deck of cards to entertain himself with a game of Nayan solitaire—not the most exciting of pastimes, but it is something to do when alone. As time passes, Marcus realizes he is on his sixth game of solitaire; normally, after three, his father is back. Worried, he decides to go look for his dad, crawling through the opening, and rushing through the trees, toward the river.

As he nears the river, he slows down, remembering his father's demand to always be cautious, particularly in daylight. Crouching down, he moves silently, but swiftly, through the tall grass and bushes, until he settles under a bush and behind a tree, about seventy-five yards from the water's edge. Looking out, he sees exactly what he feared most. His father is on his knees, hands tied behind his back. The right side of his face is swollen and some blood is coming down from the corner of his lips. His clothes are covered in dirt and dust, apparently, all from some scuffle. Surrounding him, there are eight League of Planets soldiers. Marcus had seen them from afar but never this close. They are entirely in black, from the soles of the army boots to their face shield, a black composite Kevlar-like helmet from which a black bullet-resistant glass visor descends just below a soldier's chin. This made it impossible to see the eyes or read the facial expressions of a soldier. Seven of the soldiers are carrying laser rifles across the arms, while the eighth only has a pistol holstered on his right hip. This soldier, assuredly the group leader, is standing in front of Jesse, about five feet away, while five of his troops are positioned in a circle around Jesse, and the remaining two are ripping through the water containers, trying to find contraband or communications material. Marcus feels both intense anger and deep fear.

One of the soldiers examining Jesse's bags tells his superior officer, "There is nothing here."

"I told you that fifteen minutes ago," an exasperated but defiant Jesse says.

"Shut up. I'll ask you again. Where have you been hiding?" the lead soldier asks.

"I've told you already. I am alone. I just am passing through; I didn't realize the woods are private property. I'm sorry."

"Enough lies!"

The officer looks in the direction of a soldier standing behind Jesse who bangs him in the head with the butt of his gun, knocking Jesse to the ground with a cry of pain. Marcus nearly screams out, but bites his lips to stay quiet. A solider pulls Jesse back up to his knees as he winces in pain. The superior officer pulls the pistol out of its holster and points it right between Jesse's eyes.

"Last chance. Who are you working for and where are you staying?" the soldier demands. Jesse closes his eyes and puffs up his chest, prepared to die an unbroken man.

"One...Two...Th—"

"Wait!" Marcus shouts as he tumbles out from under the bush, running towards his father.

"Run away, Marcus! Please!" his father begs before Marcus reaches the ring of soldiers, but Marcus ignores his pleas. He has seen one parent murdered and won't sit back to watch another die. He runs past the soldiers, hugs his father, and stands between him and the loaded gun.

"It's just my dad, and I. No one else. We just live a life in a cave back in the woods. We don't bother anyone, leave us alone."

The commanding officer crouches down onto one knee, flips his visor up, revealing a pale white face, disfigured from severe burn trauma that never properly healed.

"You know, something, I believe you. What's your name, boy?"

"Marcus."

"Well, Marcus I believe you. I really do. I just wish your father had been as honest with us as you are because we could have let him go on his way and return to your little cave. But we can't have people lying to the military, now can we? That would just incite chaos. So, we have to take him to the mine to work, and we can't leave you all alone in the woods. How old are you, twelve?"

"Eleven."

"Yes, that's far too young to be on your own. So because your father lied, you'll have to come with us, and work the mine alongside him. I used to work the mine; it can be a dangerous place, as you can probably guess. But work hard, like me, and you could join Supreme General Frozos's army one day."

As the soldier stands back upright, Marcus tries to push him out of the way while yelling, "Liar!"

The commanding officer throws Marcus to the ground. "Clearly, living in the woods has robbed you of good manners. No worry, you'll learn discipline. If you touch an officer of the League of Planets again, you'll find the punishment far more severe."

Marcus gets up and hugs his father. "I couldn't let them kill you, Dad; I'm sorry."

Jesse pacifies him, "You're a good son, Marcus; you'll be a great man someday. It's okay. Everything will work out."

A soldier pulls Jesse up to his feet. Escorted by the soldiers, Jesse and Marcus lead the way down the river for about three-quarters of a mile before coming to a small transport plane. Its back door opens downward to the ground, making a ramp that they walk up into the plane's fuselage. After they take seats, the plane lifts off from the ground, and Marcus looks down at his forest home of the past four years for the final time.

It is only about a ten-minute flight before the mine comes into view—a giant complex that stretches all the way through to the horizon. As Marcus will soon learn, it is broken down into three "Blocks." Block A is about 185,000 acres, Block B to the west is about 410,000 acres, and Block C, which is north of Blocks A and B before stretching out to the east, spans 715,000 acres. There is active mining and production coming from Blocks A and B. Block C is home to further exploration activity as the geology is suggestive of rich mineral deposits as well as a refinery system to process and purify some of the minerals before products are loaded on supertankers to be brought to the shipyards scattered across Frozos's empire.

As they fly in, Marcus sees a deep, giant hole, almost like the crater of a massive asteroid. This open-pit mine is the centerpiece of Block A. Here, they are mining for nayanite, the dominant metal and third most abundant element on the planet's crust. When fused with carbon, it is three times as strong as steel but only half the mass, making it the perfect outer case for spacecrafts and battleships. In the past, Jesse has explained to Marcus that this mine has been producing nayanite for over sixty years, and its reserve life is expected to last another forty years at least, not even counting the potential for further discoveries in Block C. The pit is almost one mile deep and covers nearly seventeen square miles. The walls of the mine are "stepped" with each level about thirty feet thick. Marcus is amazed at the engineering marvel, having never seen the mine in his life.

While nayanite reserves made this planet a critical player in the galactic supply chain, its true treasure lies in the underground pits deep below the planet's surface in Block B. About twenty-five years ago, the mining company discovered an extraordinarily rare and valuable element: raptium. An extremely dense metal with a dull, goldish coloring, this metal can cause extremely powerful explosions for which scientists have been able to develop a controlled apparatus. Raptium is now the primary fuel of Frozos's fleet, enabling ships to enter a series of "speedways" and enter hyperdrive, which permits ships to fold spacetime and travel faster than the speed of light. Developing these routes had become a critical element of Frozos's security strategy, allowing him to quickly move resources and manpower across the galaxy to quell the faintest of internal rebellions and continue to fold new planets into his sphere of influence.

Of the 227 planets within his realm, only five have reserves of raptium, and Nayan alone has 43 percent of the total reserves, making this planet among the most critical in the League of Planets. Officers in the League's army carefully guard and patrol the mine to ensure that raptium is not snuck out to support rebel forces and keep their planes in the sky. Increased smuggling indeed was the reason for the enhanced patrol schedule that Jesse and Marcus had observed in the forest the past few months. Raptium is extremely expensive in the black market, so it is unclear whether the element is being smuggled onto the black market for profit or funneled to the resistance. Either way, Frozos directed the security team to take whatever measures were needed to bring smuggling back down to zero.

After the plane lands, Jesse and Marcus are brought through for processing. They are handed new uniforms: ill-fitting grey button-down shirts, a white t-shirt, grey pants, and work boots. The boots are to last six months and clothing three months, so they are told to be careful. Looking around the camp, workers are seen dressed in clothes of various states of disrepair, given the grueling nature of the work. At his age, Marcus will work in the underground mine of Block B where he will mainly be doing menial tasks, like bringing around water to the crew, moving rubble off mine cart tracks, helping to load the carts with raptium ore for refinement and processing, and whatever tasks supervisory workers and military personnel need. As he grows older and more familiar with the mine, his responsibilities will grow, and by the age of sixteen could become a miner, and eventually, a supervisory worker, or if he is particularly fortunate move over into a military position.

Marcus is fortunate to be working in the raptium mine, for it is among the easiest assignments. The mine is nearly two miles below the surface, and as a consequence, it has a natural climate of fifty to sixty-five degrees, though it can get warmer from the heat thrown off by the heavy machinery. Throughout the mine are a series of deep tunnels, ranging from thirty feet tall to five feet. The complex maze has tunnels stretching for hundreds of miles. It can take years to master the routes.

Marcus learns he will be working on crew #1949. This team of twenty-five men has been working together since before Frozos took over Nayan. Originally, they were employees of the mine, and subsequent to the occupation, they were drafted into service. Marcus will be meeting the group tomorrow at the entrance of mine shaft three, and they would be working in the midsection of the mine, which has been producing raptium for thirteen years now.

His father is less lucky. He will be operating in the processing plants and refineries in Block C that meld nayanite with carbon. Jesse will discover that the working conditions in these facilities are poor, with safety standards criminally negligent. Rarely does a week go by without at least one fatality. The blast furnaces will exceed 1,600 degrees Fahrenheit, and as a consequence, temperatures throughout the facility frequently eclipse a hundred degrees. Heat exhaustion and severe dehydration are common maladies. The machinery is poorly maintained, and so accidents of hot metal falling onto workers are not infrequent either. Working in these facilities is functionally a death sentence as the average worker only lasts fifteen months in these conditions. Workers who are caught trying to escape or smuggle goods get sent to this facility. Seen as a fugitive from Frozos, Jesse is being sent to this facility and presumably to his death.

Jesse—whose hands have been uncuffed—and Marcus are standing at the processing office where they are being given their assignments.

A diminutive guard tells Jesse, "From now on, you will be identified as NJ272. Write that marking on all your clothes to identify your possessions. Report to Entrance C of Mill 4 at 7:00 AM tomorrow. Your shift is 7:00 AM to 6:30 PM with thirty minutes for lunch."

Turning to Marcus, he says, "You will be NJ273. You will report to Shaft 3 of the Block B mine. Look for crew number 1949; you will be joining them. You have the same shift as your father. You will live in Barrack 47. Follow this officer."

Jesse and Marcus follow the officer out the building and down a dirt road. The officer points them to a dilapidated brick building. It is there where meals of gruel, dried bread, and occasionally a single slice of salted meat, are served promptly at 6:00 AM and 7:30 PM. From here, there is row upon row of wooden longhouses, standing about fifteen feet high, thirty feet wide, and one hundred feet long. After about a half mile walk, they get to Barrack 47, a wooden structure that they will now call home.

Inside the building, there is a dirt floor and two rows of bunk beds, fifteen deep. In the back, there is a bathroom that doesn't look the least bit sanitary. The building is empty with everyone at work. The officer tells them they are assigned to the first bunk on the right and leaves them alone in the barrack. On each of the beds, there is a two-inch thick mattress and one single paper-thin sheet.

Jesse turns to his down-trodden son, "So top or bottom bunk, Marcus?"

"Bottom, I guess?" Marcus says as he sits on the bed.

Jesse sits next to him, "Don't worry. I know you probably feel trapped. But better days will come."

"How do you know, Dad?" Marcus asks, feeling trapped in every sense of the word.

"Because I know you aren't meant to spend all your days here, and I know Mom is looking down on us and will protect you. Remember, the character of a man is forged in the tough times, by how he perseveres and sticks to his principles, even when it seems all is lost. The strongest metals are forged in the hottest furnaces. Together, we'll get through this and be stronger than ever. I promise." Jesse puts his arm around Marcus, and hugs him. Silently, they sit there as Jesse says a prayer to his wife, hoping and believing she is with them always.

CHAPTER 21

Manhattan, New York
April 30, 2029

I t is just a few seconds before noon on the East Coast. Robert Wilson is sitting in a sleek television studio. Behind him, there is a giant window, from which the bustle of fifth avenue can be seen. Having watched the reaction to President Larom's speech, Robert feels like he may need to attempt a more public strategy as the fragile calm that has benefitted everyone appears to be teetering. Financial markets are down 7 percent, having already been halted from trading once. Chris Bailey also discreetly sent Robert a text at 10:30, saying that 13 percent of Arbor Ridge's nondefense employees hadn't shown up for work today. Robert knew that Chris must have been worried to break their no-communications rule.

Robert is about to give his first interview since assuming command of PEACE. His objective is simple: to maintain the civilian calm that has been a genuine asset in the war-building effort. He is still wearing a black suit with an American flag lapel pin but has swapped out the light blue tie for a red-and-blue striped one. Robert hates TV studios, but he felt it important symbolism to leave the safety of a PEACE facility. Sitting across from him is Jim Storks, clad in a navy-blue suit and dark blue-and-white tie. Storks was Robert's go-to interviewer when he ran Arbor Ridge, as the long-running, respected anchor of America's top morning business show. It seemed only natural to offer him the interview.

At 12:01 PM, having received the cue from the hour's typical anchor, the red light flips on, signaling they are live.

"Thank you, Mary. Sorry to cut in on your hour, but we have a special interview for you, with PEACE Commander Robert Wilson," Storks says to the camera. Turning to Robert, he continues, "This is your first interview since forming PEACE, right commander?"

"It is," Robert begins. "If you remember, Jim, back in November, when you harangued me about acquiring a news network, I promised you'd always get my exclusives. Never let it be said I'm not a man of my word."

"Well, we appreciate that. Now tell me, why have you avoided the press in the three weeks since you formed PEACE?"

"It's simple, Jim. My objective is to ensure Earth is safe and has the military resources to guarantee we win this war. It's not my job to govern over civilian life. That's for civilian authorities, your government leaders and elected officials, to do."

"So, are there restrictions on your communications as part of the PEACE formation agreement?"

"No. I can speak to whomever I want, whenever I want. I just do not wish to cause confusion in the chain of command. But I am here today solely because I want to be."

"So why now? Is there truth to reports that you are unhappy with what President Larom and other leaders said today?"

"No. First, there are no reports that say this, just the conjecture of TV pundits who do nothing but talk all day."

"That's not entirely fair to—" Storks says as Robert cuts him off.

"No, it is fair. I've talked to no one about my opinions on this matter. There were two PEACE officials on the briefing this morning. All of my suggestions were accepted, and we have complete unanimity."

"Fine. So, what do you make of the sunsheet. How worried should we be?"

"First, I agree with President Larom's conclusion that Frozos does not believe he can get in through the force field. That means we never have to let him in if we don't want, and it would take months to starve us out, if we did nothing, which we won't."

"So, what will you do?"

"PEACE has the capability to get rid of the sheet, and we will do that. We may do it today, we may do it tomorrow. We may use planes, we may use lasers, or I may have other tricks up my sleeve. I really can't tell you."

"Now, some cynics are going to say you're delaying because you actually don't have a plan. What do you say to them?"

"I would remind them that time is on our side. Each day, I am churning out hundreds of new planes, certifying hundreds of pilots, and studying their spacecrafts' every move. As long as the public will allow me to, we can fight this war on our timeline to maximize our probability of success."

"I want to explore this further," Storks prods, deviating away from his notes. "What do you mean 'as long as the public will allow me to?'"

"It's simple. I can continue to play the long game and build military strength as long as civilian society is united and calm. If there is disorder and division that threatens our alliance or could cause us to tear each other down, I will be forced to act against Frozos, perhaps before PEACE is at full strength. I know it doesn't feel like it, but every person going about their day makes it easier for our brave men and women to prepare for the day when they will protect you."

"So, it sounds like you do share President Larom's sentiment about getting to work."

"I do." Robert turns to the camera. "I know I'm not the CEO of Arbor Ridge anymore, but I hope those employees know I would not say, 'feel safe, go about your lives, we will protect you,' if I did not mean it from the bottom of my heart and in every ounce of my being. So, I ask that tomorrow you be leaders in your community. Go to work like you always do. Drop your kids off at school. Buy sufficient groceries, but not four months' worth of toilet paper."

"I think I speak for many viewers when I say I am grateful for your insights. We recognize you are very busy, but we stand united at this critical hour," Storks concludes, reaching his hand out to shake Robert's, who does in kind.

"Thank you, Jim. If I may add one more thing. I know what it is like to be trapped. Many years ago, I was sentenced with my father to work as a slave on a League of Planets mine. I understand what it is like to feel contained and controlled; it's the worst feeling in the world. I remember so clearly him telling me that character is forged in the tough times, by persevering and adhering to one's principles. Only in retrospect, do we realize how these trials made us better and stronger. Let me just end by saying, the universe is about to discover the humanity's character is unlike anything Frozos has come across before."

The following day, not one Arbor Ridge employee fails to show up for work. Vacation travel is curtailed, yes, and some financial market jitters remain, but the prevailing calm proves to be more durable than Frozos had hoped and frankly than many of the world's leaders had feared.

CHAPTER 22

Jersey City
May 12, 2029

Twelve days have passed since Admiral Tyrone Tiberius deployed his last-ditch effort to get back into Supreme General Anton Frozos's good graces: the sunsheet. Nearly 10 percent of sunlight is blocked from getting to Earth on a daily basis. Temperatures are a few degrees below the daily average for this time of year, but that's largely not noticeable to the public given normal deviations, though it could have significant long-term effects if sustained.

The concerted effort by world leaders, with an assist from Robert Wilson, has helped to keep the public calm. Indeed, remaining calm has been hailed as an act of patriotism and bravery, which for the time being has strengthened the public's resolve. Assisting this, of course, has been the fact that daily life still does continue as normal. This may not last forever; how the public will respond then is a question weighing on the political leadership.

PEACE has been using the past two weeks to continually expand its capacity. Its fleet of combat-ready SF-01s now stands at 26,000, and the pilot count has just passed 26,000, meaning that every one of these planes could be used in battle. Waiting two weeks to attack the sunsheet has been critical in delaying the apparently inevitable conflict and developing enough militarily strength to make it a fairer fight.

Since this began, Jake Thornhill and Robert had circled May 11 to 14 as the optimal window for attack. Delaying until then allowed PEACE's forces to essentially double in size while not allowing the sunsheet to grow so large that it posed a true danger to Earth. Despite hours upon hours of analysis and conjecture, no one could figure out why Tiberius built the sunsheet so near the Earth's force field and why he left it unguarded. Admittedly, his military strategy had been lacking during this entire conflict, but this move seemed particularly odd. Nonetheless, this past afternoon, Robert informed Thornhill's team that he would not suffer analysis paralysis, and that they would strike tonight.

Recognizing there could be a trap of some sort, it has been agreed that maintaining some element of surprise is critical. The best assumption is that Tiberius is monitoring the Arbor Ridge towers as well as military bases that his forces have discovered. Consequently, they have agreed to deploy forces from one of their two existing production sites outside of the Arbor Ridge towers: an Arbor Ridge research facility in the South Indian Ocean that also helps support the force field.

There are 547 SF-01s housed in this facility. To an outsider above sea level, this facility looks like an offshore oil rig, production platform and all. Underneath the ocean though, the facility expands into a large warehouse where Robert has been storing planes since December. The group commander stationed at this facility is Kim Ji-Yoo of South Korea, one of the winners of the *Galactic Flyer* internship contest. Now twenty-three, she graduated college in mechanical engineering with honors. Her flying style is calculated and methodical, conservative but not timid. She trains harder than most other commanders on simulators to play out scenarios as much as possible. She relies less on "feel" and more based on playing the odds. She should be well-suited to lead what ought to be a straight forward mission without growing overly cocky and letting her guard down.

It is nearly 11:00 PM in Jersey City, making it about 8:30 AM at the PEACE base in the Indian Ocean. Robert is standing in the command center to watch the mission, codenamed Icarus. He has already given his blessing to proceed and should be merely an observer. About one hundred planes can fit on the platform at any one time. They are being brought up in a series of elevators, pilots already in the cockpit. Rather than having to take off, they are able to lift themselves into the sky from a stationary position, thanks to a fully rotational engine.

Getting the first hundred birds in the air was simple, and things are now moving a bit slower. Once airborne, the planes fly to their designated spot over the ocean in a grid like pattern. Importantly, and one reason why today was chosen to initiate Icarus, the sky is filled with low lying clouds. It has even begun to rain over the "drilling platform." Finally, after about twenty minutes, all the SF-01s are in the air at their assigned spot. It is now 11:07 PM. On the screen in the command center, they see a live stream from satellites in space as well as from Kim's cockpit. Over the speakers, they hear Kim order her group: "Begin ascent."

The 547 SF-01s shoot upwards at a speed greater than that of a space shuttle. It will take them exactly twenty-two minutes and twelve seconds to get 38,995 miles above the Earth. That will be about five miles inside of the force field line and 205 miles away from the sunsheet. At exactly 11:30 PM Eastern time, or about twenty seconds after their arrival, the force field projectors from the South Indian Ocean, Tokyo, Hanoi, and Sydney will turn off. This will create a hole in the force field well in excess of the size of the sunshade while keeping the rest of the planet protected from an assault away from the shield. They will be given ninety seconds to fire their laser cannons repeatedly in each pilot's assigned target area to destroy most if not all of the sunsheet. In his hand, Robert is holding a black remote with a red button on it. He alone can click it and give another sixty seconds to blow up more of the sunsheet if necessary, but after that, the force field will be automatically redeployed and locked from being opened again for thirty minutes.

At 11:29:40 PM in Jersey City (8:29:40 AM local time), Kim's ship comes to a halt. It automatically locks its position to avoid an inadvertent drift across the force field line. "Be calm and methodical everyone," she says as she tightens her right hand around the firing trigger.

Above them, there is nothing but darkness with the sunsheet blocking all light. Their systems do not recognize any enemy ships, an encouraging sign. With two seconds to go, she says, "Fire."

There is an array of light as volleys of laser cannons shoot 200 miles into space before erupting the sunsheet, which disintegrates at the point of attack. With each passing shot, the view from Kim and her fellow pilots' cockpits brightens as sunlight passes through where it once was blocked. Firing once per second, over 4,500 shots are fired at the sunsheet, each strong enough to level a sixty-story building. There is no resistance from Tiberius's forces.

In the command center, excitement builds as the assembled crowd cheers the sunlight. Robert puts the remote control in his pocket. At ninety seconds, the force field is once again fired from the four PEACE ground locations, and Kim orders "Cease fire." Looking 200 miles above them, they see the remnants of the sunsheet aflame. Over 70 percent has been destroyed, and by the time they make the twenty-two-minute journey back to the base, the rest will have been burnt to ashes. Project Icarus has been a complete success, it would seem.

While much of the room is in celebration, an aide walks over to Thornhill. Together, they comb through videos on a computer. After two minutes, he shouts, "Put satellite camera twenty-three on the screen." This satellite is orbiting above Western Europe. Video from it during the attack on the sun shield shows ships from the League of Planets testing to see if they could pass through the force field.

"Look," Thornhill says to Robert, "they were testing to see if we could open the force field in one area or if there would be openings globally."

"So," Robert responds, "We thought they were laying the groundwork for a long-term siege campaign when in reality it too was a Trojan Horse, aiming to let them in. That's why they left it undefended so we would only send ships from one location."

"I'm not sure entirely of their motivation. They aren't testing with enough crafts to have been able to successfully conquer the planet if indeed the entire shield was down. It feels as though the entire thing was just a test-run."

"Tell me Jake, are you a sports fan?"

"Why yes, I love baseball."

"Well, today it feels like we won a spring training game, a contest that really didn't matter. Worse, we used our star players, giving away our game plan, while they only fielded minor leaguers."

"Yes, it is an unsatisfying victory," Thornhill says. That sentiment has been gradually building throughout the command center as realization deepens that Tiberius never intended to defend the sunsheet. This was merely an opening salvo. But to what end?

"Okay. Well, regardless, let's send a memo to the military contacts. Quote: 'Mission a success. Sunsheet destroyed. Attacks on force field failed. Further actions likely.' End quote. I don't want too many details. I'll go out to the press and spin a nice story. We should at least be able to stiffen public confidence thanks to this."

About thirty minutes later, Robert is standing about a block outside the Arbor Ridge building in Jersey City. It's lightly misting outside so he is holding an umbrella. There is a gaggle of press in front of him with nearly a dozen cameras. It was clear to the public that something was going on when the black spot over the sky in Asia disappeared, so Robert is really here to put a face behind the good news.

"Good evening. Thank you for assembling at this late hour. I am happy to report that as promised, PEACE took action against the sunsheet. Using about 550 planes from a secure facility in the Indian Ocean, we launched an attack on the sunsheet and found minimal resistance. Our fleet of SF-01s stayed within the force field for the entirety of the strike. The force field over part of the planet was lifted for between one and two minutes; for security reasons, I cannot be more specific than that.

"In this short time, thanks to the efficiency of our pilots and strength of our technology platform, we were able to lay waste to the sunsheet, restoring sunlight back to normal immediately. We promised action, and we have delivered it. There have been no disruptions to daily life, and during these two weeks, we have added thousands of pilots and fighter jets.

"I can say without a doubt our resistance has been among the most effective and least costly of any that Frozos has faced in his years of conquest. I do not expect that to deter him, and we should prepare ourselves for them to adapt the sunsheet strategy. I continue to thank the public for the calm, work-manlike attitude they have maintained frankly since the first ship arrived on April second. Let's continue to plow forward until this threat is relegated to history's trash can. Thank you and God bless."

Meanwhile in the sky above Earth, Tiberius is sitting in his office, reviewing the data from the attack. He had suspected the attack on another part of the shield would prove futile, but it was a low-cost Hail Mary. Right on time, a hologram of a General Frozos appears in front him. Frozos appears neither pleased nor displeased today.

"Tell me, Admiral, did you collect the necessary data?"

"Yes, Supreme General. As we expected, the force field only opened in certain areas, but our sensors should now be able to detect when it turns off and on."

"Good. And on their jets?"

"Yes, we have a better understanding of their laser's fire-power, average, and speed, above-average. Defense capabilities are of course not fully understood."

"And how long for the next phase of construction?"

"Given the incremental distance, it will likely not be as productive as the first sunsheet, so I would estimate fifteen days to get where we were today in terms of coverage. But may I suggest, we wait a day or two to begin, that way it seems like we are evaluating options. Their arrogance is their gravest liability. We should be certain to exploit it."

"Yes, that's fine. You still have operational control over this military operation I remind you, so I defer to your judgment."

Tiberius knows Frozos is saying this to distance himself from further failure and leave him as the fall man should there be another issue. This next move had to work, and he was confident that it would.

"Yes I understand, Supreme General."

CHAPTER 23

Jersey City
June 2, 2029

Three weeks have passed since the successful attack on the first sunsheet. In that time, there has been much activity on both sides of the force field. 42,000 miles above Earth, the League of Planets's forces have begun construction in the upper atmosphere once more. This construction began on the afternoon of May 15, New York time. The material for the original sunsheet had been carried to Earth on the first super-tanker transporters, but more of the fiber is being used from the other two ships to construct Admiral Tyrone Tiberius' second project. There are two main differences in this second sunsheet iteration.

First, rather than build one massive sunsheet that follows the sun, the League is building fifteen sunsheets. The center of each one is a force field launcher: the twelve Arbor Ridge towers and the three research facilities in the South Indian,

Arctic, and South Atlantic oceans. From each center point, drone ships have been building outwards, so that there will be fifteen sizable and ever-growing circular sunsheets above the planet. Because these sunsheets orbit over the same spot on the planet, they block less sunlight over the course of twenty-four hours, spending eight to fourteen hours in darkness in a given day.

This fact means that even though they now cover 10 percent of the Earth's surface, like the first sunsheet did when it was attacked, they have less of an impact on global temperatures, energy production, and agriculture. Tiberius has exhausted all of the material in the second supertanker, and he will soon be beginning to use the inventory aboard the final supertanker to continue to grow each of these fifteen miniature sunsheets so that they have the necessary impact on life on Earth.

Second, while the first sunsheet was built just about 200 miles above the force field line, this variation is being constructed about 3,000 miles above the force field line. At this distance, the sunsheet is outside of the range of the SF-01 weapons, which is closer to 1,200 miles, meaning that to destroy the sunsheet, the fleet would have to traverse beyond the force field line.

During this construction period, an additional transport destroyer group has arrived. That means there are now five transport destroyers, each accompanied by about one hundred smaller ships of all shapes and sizes and the several thousand unmanned attack drones they could carry. With the additional destroyer, Tiberius has shifted positioning somewhat.

One destroyer group continues to pin down the lunar base, Tiberius' own ship sits above the Eastern Seaboard of the United States, one is above Moscow, one above Rio de Janeiro, and one above Bangkok. Each of these ships is hovering about 10,000 miles beyond the edge of the force field. *Magnus* has withdrawn by about 75,000 miles, orbiting on the opposite side of the planet as the moon. Whether Frozos has done this for strategic reasons or to signify he is primarily an observer rather than the lead commander is unclear to combatants aboard the destroyers as well as fighters on Earth.

While there has been much activity high in space, the pace on the ground has been equally busy. First, PEACE Commander Robert Wilson and Jake Thornhill have spent much of their time determining the challenge posed by this new sunsheet structure. From what they've discovered, Tiberius' new construction will take longer to reach critical mass, which has bought PEACE time to continue to expand its military capacity. Indeed, they have been doing just that, building an additional 14,000 combat ready SF-01s over the last three weeks, bringing the total plane count to 40,000. This leaves them well on pace to hit the 50,000-plane target inside of the three month timeline. Pilot training has also been progressing quite nicely. There are 51,000 approved pilots, of which 13,424 are either active or retired military officers. There are another 33,000 recruits undergoing training, and 17,000 have failed out. Given the approved pilot count and likelihood that recruits will bring the number near the 75,000 target, additional recruiting has come to a halt, giving group commander and squadron commanders more time to train in simulators rather than worrying about rallying and exciting new recruits.

Robert is pleased with where PEACE is today; in all honesty, it has exceeded his expectations. They have managed to avoid direct conflict with Frozos, and delivered two confidence-inspiring victories, destroying two supertanker transporters, the speedway portal construction site, and the first sunsheet. These victories have given new recruits and pilots a tremendous confidence boost. Importantly, they have given the public confidence, with over 75 percent of people globally confident in PEACE and Robert's leadership. This mass public support has given him the ability to act largely independently of the demands of elected governments and their military representatives should he so choose—although to this point, he hasn't. While at first Robert felt he needed the nonbinding support of governments to provide legitimacy for his actions, the public's trust provides legitimacy in and of itself, or so he feels. This reality has been appreciated by governments globally, some of whom are comfortable deferring to Robert and others wary of the power he has been amassing.

Aside from PEACE's military buildup, the past few weeks have been uneventful on Earth. There was some disappointment but no surprise from the public when new sunsheets began to pop up in the sky. Indeed, there has been remarkable calm bordering upon complacency, bolstered by the belief that the force field is impenetrable and that PEACE under the great Commander Robert Wilson could blow up any sunsheet outside of the force field. Yes, there are armies at the gates, ready to storm through any opening, but the walls are high enough, trenches deep enough, so it is safe to continue to party in the city. That at least appears to be the sentiment held by most of the public—a sentiment that national governments have been happy to cement rather than deal with domestic strife. For his part, Robert is relieved to have a calmed populace even if more danger is lurking than they might appreciate.

But today, June 2, 2029, is going to be a day that interrupts the calm. With sunsheet coverage of Earth at 10 percent, it is time for another strike on the sunsheet. This mission cannot be as straightforward as the last one. To destroy all of the sunsheets would require turning off the entire force field at one time. That simply is not a plausible strategy. It would leave the planet extremely vulnerable to invasion and require nearly sending out the entire fleet of planes.

Instead, Jake Thornhill and Robert agree that the smartest approach is to launch a strike on a single sunsheet with a subset of the fleet. They can continue to launch these precision attacks and gradually chip away at the shield. Given each individual sunsheet is relatively small, one hundred SF-01s should do the job, especially as the small crafts in the destroyer groups are stretched thin trying to patrol so many areas.

The tentative plan had been to launch the first strike on the sunsheet above Moscow given it has among the longest days at this time of year. However, Robert has opted for a different strategy. Yesterday, intelligence photos revealed that one of the supertanker transporters, emptied of sunsheet materials, has begun the journey back to the League of Planets. The remaining supertanker sits above Los Angeles, well removed from the five transport destroyers. It is just now starting to be emptied of the sunsheet material it carries.

If PEACE can destroy this ship in addition to the Los Angeles sunsheet, Tiberius's ability to expand his sunsheet would be greatly diminished, buying Earth potentially weeks of time to further expand its military preparation and destroy the other sunsheets. This will be the sunsheet they target.

Given she is based in New Mexico and has a reputation for being among the most competent and aggressive pilots, Robert has selected Group Commander Anna Small to lead this mission, giving her team just twelve hours to prepare. While destroying the sunsheet should only require one hundred SF-01s, taking on the supertanker will expand the complexity of the mission and give Tiberius's military more time to rally its defenses. Consequently, Robert has decided to send up nearly 900 fighters.

It is about 3:00 PM in Jersey City, 1:00 PM in New Mexico, and noon in Los Angeles. As they were for Operation Icarus, Robert and Thornhill are standing on the base of the command center, prepared to monitor events from the live feeds of satellites and planes on the giant screens in front of them. Robert is standing calmly in a dark suit, red tie loosened from his collar, and top button open. He has just briefed the military representatives that PEACE would be launching a "targeted attack" on the sunsheet to mitigate the imminent threat it poses. This briefing was much more cursory than past ones, lasting less than thirty minutes and with scant operational details. Robert did not even have Thornhill on to discuss the technical aspects and intelligence as in past briefings, instead treating it as a formality. As no representative could dispute the threat posed by the sunsheet and recognized the strong public support Robert enjoys, he faced minimal resistance. Still, his newfound laxness did not go unnoticed.

As Robert sees it, the primary operational challenge of this mission is to try to maintain an element of surprise so that Tiberius cannot begin to move defenses during the twenty-two minutes it takes airborne fighters to reach the edge of the force field. Thornhill's team have devised a solution to this challenge. They would launch the global SF-01 fleet from bases all over the world. In total, 28,000 of the 40,000 planes in the fleet will be used. By launching globally, Tiberius will be forced to hold his defenses everywhere, thinking a global strike is coming or in hopes that he can send planes through a globally opened force field. This launch pattern offers the clearest avenue to keeping the supertanker unguarded.

Right at 3:08, the global fleet, which had launched from the various runways and bases on which they resided, began the ascent to the force field. Over the next twenty-two minutes, Robert and Jake continuously confer with the satellite specialist team in the front left of the auditorium, while also monitoring the satellite feeds up above. Exactly as hoped, there is no major movement in Tiberius's fleet, with small crafts merely tightening their patrol patterns around the nearest sunsheet—unsurprising defensive behavior.

Group Commander Small has led her squadron to the edge of the force field. Internally, she is filled with nervous energy, but she trusts her team and her training, giving her confidence in the mission's success. Externally, she projects steadiness and calm, radioing the force she is leading, "Get ready; this is the day we've trained for. Let's show them what we can do."

Exactly at 3:30 PM, the force field projector in Los Angeles turns off. Seconds later, Group Commander Small flies out of the force field zone and into the hostile territory of space, the first individual from Earth to do so during this entire conflict. As was her style, she is at the very front of her group formation. Each squadron of twenty-four planes is flying in a V-shaped formation with row upon row of squadrons pouring into space.

Anna runs through their mission as she travels further from the atmosphere. The first section of about 400 planes will head for the sunsheet and destroy attacking enemy ships. About 250 miles behind them, a group of 500 planes who, at about 1,000 miles out from the sunsheet, will veer off and make a straight-run at the supertanker. Given the lack of gravity and atmospheric resistance in space, these space jets can fly at extraordinary speeds. It should take under two minutes for the second group to reach the supertanker absent any resistance.

As they near the breakaway points, the mission is going well. The first group has only encountered a few dozen small unpiloted drones, and several squadrons have peeled off to deal with them tidily. Thornhill radios Small to alert her to the fact that Tiberius is moving the transport destroyer over the Eastern Seaboard towards the Los Angeles sunsheet, alongside supporting crafts. At this pace, they should be back inside the force field before the destroyer is upon them, but there is little time to waste.

As the first group is firing on the sunsheet, tearing it to shreds, and the second nears the supertanker, the supertanker's gigantic bay doors open. Hundreds of shots are fired upon the attacking SF-01 group. Thousands of spherical drones and midsize crafts catapult out of the behemoth of a ship!

Anna curses into her headset, which connects her to the fleet of SF-01s as well as the command center where Robert and Thornhill are carefully tracking the attack. It isn't carrying sunsheet material at all.

"We've been set up!" Anna warns.

Squadron Leader 27 shouts into her intercom, "ENEMY FIRE! ENEMY FIRE! INITIATE EVASIVE MANEVEURS."

Several dozen SF-01s are flying out of control, aflame, the laser attack frying systems and piercing their shields. The remaining 400 in Group 2 scatter, engaging in mass combat against the over 3,000 enemy ships.

Seeing this, Anna yells into her headset, "Group 1: attack the Supertanker. Assist Group 2."

The 400 planes in Group 1 turn from the destroyed sunsheet and head toward the battle around the supertanker to provide relief to their overwhelmed friends.

Anna can't believe the supertanker was a trap all along and is certain Robert is in a similar state of shock given his lack of communications. She evades another ship, taking a quick look up towards where the destroyer is approaching. They need to withdraw, before it's too late, otherwise she fears the entire force could be lost.

She hears a voice in her headset: "Commander Small," Thornhill says, "this is an order to retreat immediately. A destroyer group is fast approaching. Commander Wilson is reopening the force field."

While being tailed by two drones, she calmly orders her group to withdraw. In the process of flipping her plane 180 degrees, she fires her laser cannon to take the two drones out.

About 625 SF-01s make an all-out dash for the force field. In a straight shot, they seem to be able to outrun the drones, though the midsize crafts are keeping pace and picking off stragglers. There's just 1,000 miles to the force field—the race is on.

Anna sees, from the left corner of her eye, the transport destroyer group rapidly approaching. Hundreds of enemy ships will get through the force field before the control center has time to close it. Worse, the massive laser cannon is beginning to extend out from the front red sphere of the oncoming destroyer. She knows what she must do; they must protect Earth, no matter the cost.

She shouts into her transponder, "ABORT. ABORT. REENGAGE WITH ENEMY FLEET. NO ONE GETS PAST US."

She pulls her ship up, turning away from the Earth to take down as many enemy crafts as she can, and her group instinctively follows her lead, knowing full well this is to be their last stand.

Robert's voice crackles through her headset, "Commander Small, your order is to return to Earth!"

She grits her teeth. "No, Commander Wilson. I can't let enemy ships or a laser blast into Earth's atmosphere. Close the force field," she calmly but firmly replies.

"But Commander Small—"

"Do it now, before it's too late, sir!" she interrupts. As she fires on the incoming ships, she thinks of her three brothers. Knowing that they will grow up to have families of their own, safely on Earth, she feels at peace. Her sacrifice is worth it.

Seeing the solemnity of Thornhill's face and the destroyer's cannon now fully extended, Robert hits the red button once more, turning the force field back on.

No sooner does he do this than a great blast is shot from the destroyer, wiping out half of the remaining SF-01's fleet. Commander Small's camera on the screen goes to black. Had she not forced the force field closed, irreparable damage to the planet may have been done. One-by-one the remaining SF-01s go offline, having been outnumbered twenty to one.

900 pilots lost in a catastrophic miscalculation by Robert Wilson. Thanks only to the bravery of a twenty-two-year-old woman and the extraordinary loyalty she had built up in her group of pilots, mostly civilians who had never flown a military mission before today, that is all that was lost.

Disgusted by his failure, Robert walks silently out of the command center and into his office, takes a seat in his chair, and buries his head in his hands, shedding more than one tear. He had only just met with Anna Small a few weeks ago. She was a charming, motivated, and inspiring young woman with her entire life ahead of her. For her to be one of the casualties of the attack makes the loss all the more personal for Robert. He feels like a fool, a man who let his arrogance and zeal for victory blind him to the fact that Tiberius and Frozos were trained and skilled conquerors. He should have known that there was a trap.

More troublingly, he can't help himself but wonder that if he had provided a more fulsome briefing to the national military representatives, maybe someone would have asked a question that caused him to rethink and avert this entire disaster. While training in Killjorn, Robert had excelled in schoolwork and technology while his military strategy skills were deemed "mediocre." Did he overestimate himself in taking this role to lead the military resistance to Frozos? Were his successes to this point merely good luck? These thoughts race through his head as he replays the briefings he attended and intelligence reports he had read. Was there some clue he had overlooked?

While beating himself up, a paper that had been half-leaning over the edge of his desk falls to the ground. There was no perceptible gust of wind in his office, nor did he touch it. Rather, it finally ceased to fight gravity and fell to the ground, folded in two. Robert looks over at it and picks it up. Unfolding it, he recognizes it immediately as the paper he wrote on the very day that he met Frozos and was given the assignment to come to Earth. At first, as was often the case in these little moments when fate collides with reality, he thinks of his mother whom he did believe to this day was watching over him.

He likes to think that in some little way, she pushed the paper over at this very moment to provide a gentle reminder. As he stares over the phrase "REMEMBER THE MINE" over and over again in this hour of mourning, defeatism, and self-doubt, he is reminded of the most perseverant man he ever knew.

CHAPTER 24

Nayan
Earth Year 2011

At fourteen years old, Marcus is now nearly fully grown, standing at five foot eight inches, and hardened by years of hard work. His messy black hair has been replaced by a crew cut—the mandatory style for all workers. He and his father, Jesse, have been slaves for three years now, with Marcus still working in the raptium mine as a member of crew #1949. As he has grown older, stronger, and more experienced, his responsibilities on the team have grown. Originally, Marcus did mostly menial, lightweight tasks—bringing water to the miners, moving small debris off the mine cart tracks—but as he has grown, he now moves heavier material and loads carts with mined raptium ore for processing.

Crew #1949 is comprised of thirty-six workers, twenty-eight of whom have been working together for well over a decade now. Marcus has found them to be an amiable group of men, just looking to do their work, keep their heads down, and stay in the good graces of the guards. They consistently are more productive than about 67 to 75 percent of the crews and less productive than 25 to 33 percent. This is exactly where the crew chief, a bearded fellow named Cornelius but who's official mine number is RR964, tries to place crew #1949. Productivity in the bottom half of mine crews can lead to curtailed meals, harsher assignments, and beatings from the more brutal prison guards. By the same token, he has seen the top performing crews literally work themselves to death when there really is no reward for being the best. His years working the mine and fostering an understanding of what the guards really need to see crews produce have led Cornelius to aim for this level of productivity. Productive enough to stay in their masters' good graces but not so productive as to cause undue fatigue, or so he told Marcus once.

Marcus has become a popular member of the team. At fourteen, he is still too young to be a lead miner, but his official responsibilities are in assisting the trained miners and in loading carts with ore. From their first night in the mine camp, Jesse emphasized to his son the importance of being a helper, doing all that was asked, and going above and beyond what is needed. Jesse realized that a child could be seen as an unreliable liability by a crew, but if the child worked hard, never complained, and did what was asked, he could potentially be quite popular. At the end of each day for the past three years, Jesse has asked Marcus to name one unassigned task he did. If he couldn't name one, Jesse asked him to think of one task he could have done and didn't and to be sure to find a way to help that worker the next day. This attitude has boosted Marcus's popularity, and he has even begun to do some mining, giving the primary miners who are getting older a half an hour break every now and then to catch their breath. The guards have been turning a blind eye to this behavior, uninterested in upsetting the apple cart of the steadiest producing raptium crew. In exchange for his going the extra mile, senior members of the crew often share extra rations or their leftovers with Marcus, who is after all a growing boy with a teenager's appetite.

While all of the crew is friendly and polite to Marcus, he has noticed the fealty they show towards the guards. Cornelius told him on his fourteenth birthday, "In this mine, there is no living. Just surviving." This mindset pervades the group; hope for freedom is all but lost. These workers have seen too many of their friends try to escape or rebel, only to die. Marcus is seeing firsthand the soul-crushing nature of servitude. These men have spent over seven years working under the League of Planets's military rule and have given up hope of ever having control over their lives again. They have managed a way to operate within the system and lead a tolerable existence, but no longer push back against the system itself—a point Jesse frequently drives home.

While Marcus has been lucky to work with a decent, cohesive group of men, he knows Jesse's work has been much more grueling. This is evident just based on their physical appearance. While Marcus has grown and filled out due to the rigors of his daily work, his father has been fading away. He barely weighs 120 pounds and has the complexion of a ghost—the physical effects of his three years in the refinery of Block C, melding nayanite with carbon. The average worker only lasts about fifteen months in these conditions. Jesse is entering his thirty-seventh month, making him the longest serving worker in this facility by over a year.

Marcus knows his father has seen at least two people die in each job in the factory, while some of the higher risk jobs have had six or seven deaths. While all are labelled as accidents, Jesse can tell those that are intentional from people who can no longer tolerate the cruel conditions and weight of slavery. He has come to recognize a certain look in the eyes of those prepared to commit suicide by industrial accident—the look of hopelessness and despair that can send chills down a grown man's spine. Unlike Marcus, who has been able to develop a working relationship, if not outright friendship, with his crew, Jesse keeps to himself. Due to the high mortality rate, his crew is effectively a revolving door. Developing friendships only makes the deaths more painful, so everyone in the refinery keeps to themselves.

Jesse's tenure has become the stuff of legend among both the guards and fellow workers. To some, the very fact that he refuses to die is itself seen as an act of defiance. He has worked the easiest and the harshest shifts throughout the refinery, operating heavy machinery, carrying material, and melding the hot metals, all in temperatures near 100 degrees. The work has tormented his body, weakening him greatly, but he has persevered. Marcus worries about him constantly, but he's fairly sure the reason he's still on his feet is that he is the only worker with a child at the mining facility. Every evening as he walks to Barrack 47, he knows that he will be spending time with Marcus. Not a day goes by when he doesn't manage to put on a smile before walking through the doors and to their shared bunk bed. It's usually a twenty- to thirty-minute walk between the barracks and the plant, depending on how grueling the day has been.

Arriving home at 7:00 PM, Marcus and Jesse have developed a consistent routine of cleaning up in the showers and then heading over to the cafeteria hall for dinner at 7:30. They always sit at the same section of one of the long tables next to other members of crew #1949. Conversation is usually reserved to the events of the day and the occasional random thought. After about thirty minutes, they leave to go back to their barracks, before most of the others have left. Back "home," they crack on with schoolwork.

Without any of his textbooks, it is quite difficult for Marcus's dad to teach him. This challenge is further compounded by the lack of paper and pencils, so they use a stick to write on the dirt floor. Jesse tries to recall the syllabuses and lesson schedule from his years as a college professor, and they do the best they can continuing to develop Marcus's knowledge of mathematics and science. Each night they try to work for about three hours, until between 11:00 and 11:30 PM. Most of the men in the barracks don't understand why Jesse bothers teaching Marcus these things, which will never get used.

Jesse, though, sees knowledge as the only way out of this mine, one way or another. The vast majority of the time they spend on math and science, but Jesse tries to spend a bit of time reminding Marcus of history and their values, generally at the beginning of the night's lesson when most of the other workers were still eating dinner. They discuss how the factory guards prey on the hopelessness of the situation, how once free, strong men have their spirits broken by long-term enslavement. Jesse ensures that Marcus understands the corrosiveness of totalitarian rule so that he instinctively hates it. He reminds Marcus of his mother frequently. If she was willing to sacrifice her life, they should be able to sacrifice several years of their lives if necessary.

One distraction from their lessons has often been the arrival of newly captured men to their barracks. With Nayan's population almost entirely subdued by now, most new workers come from other planets. They provide new information about the developments of the galaxy. Aside from these tidbits, the only information that the workers can glean is from the weekly thirty-minute news brief, which is little more than a propaganda session, reporting Frozos's exploits, both real and imagined. Admittedly, some of the stories shared by the newly enslaved are also probably imagined or exaggerated, but it can be refreshing to hear these stories. Unfortunately, the news is rarely explicitly positive. Frozos remains clearly in control of the League of Planets. His military's size and power continue to grow, aided by the raptium supplies from Nayan's mine, and the planet count has steadily increased by nearly one hundred during the three Earth years Marcus and Jesse have been enslaved.

That said, there are signs that resistance and rebellion continue to fester. The size and strength of this resistance as well as where it operates from are unknown, and estimates have ranged from tens of thousands of fighters to tens of millions. In reality, the truth likely lies somewhere in the middle. There are likely a few hundred thousand fighters who are supported by the helping hand of millions of merchants who let some supplies go missing, leak the location of supertanker transporters, or provide shelter just as Marcus's parents once had.

Cobbling together what he has heard from all the various stories over the years, Jesse is convinced that the resistance to Frozos is real, and this fact is enough to inspire some hope in Marcus and among the workers, though it does fade the longer workers spend in the facility. But it seems like the rebels avoid direct military conflict with the bulk of Frozos's forces, likely in recognition that they lack the numbers or equipment to challenge his military supremacy. Instead, they pick off the stray destroyer group or pilfer supplies to disrupt life in the League, create discontent, and slowly but steadily build their own military readiness.

This is a sound strategy, but it also is a patient one. It could take years to sow enough discontent or build enough firepower to challenge Frozos, whose own military power is also steadily on the rise. This patience is in keeping with the one consistent tidbit in all the rebel stories, that the leader of the movement is indeed the former ruler of that aquatic planet that held out like none other, Aquine. Jesse has yet to come across one who has seen him in person, but references to this "King Hammerhead" are ever-present and intertwined with the mystique of the resistance. This figure, given his name, is of great inspiration to Marcus who imagines what he must look like and asks newcomers for any and all stories they know of him. Jesse is certain some of these stories are invented, but he is happy for hope to be preserved in Marcus's spirit.

There is no proof that King Hammerhead is alive or a myth. However, Jesse does remember as a student many years ago studying the aquatic worlds, which largely were a mystery to the known universe. In particular, he remembers reading that the lifespan among these species is exceptionally long. Indeed, some were said to live nearly 250 Nayan years (about 300 to 400 Earth years), if not longer. The perspective of a life that long could explain why the resistance's strategy is defined by its apparent patience. What seems patient to a man with a lifespan of eighty to one hundred years would seem totally normal to that of a being who lives four times as long. Jesse isn't certain that King Hammerhead exists, but he does believe that someone like him is running a rebellion effort.

And so it was for three years in the mine. Marcus and Jesse worked long nights studying and hard days at work to satiate the demands of the guards. Finally, these efforts are set to pay off, or so Marcus and Jesse hope. Each year, the League runs a "test" at all of its labor camps. The test is open to all individuals from fourteen to twenty-five who have received approval from the supervisory officer that they have the physical strength, loyalty, and mental discipline to serve in Frozos's army. It is through this program that the officer who captured Jesse and Marcus three years ago graduated. The contents of the test are unknown but it said to focus on critical reasoning. Applicants have two hours to complete it in the morning, and those that are accepted know by the day's end. Most of the graduates, after training, work as guards in a mine, though some do go to the frontlines. The acceptance rate is about 5 percent. Marcus's dad noticed that the workers who report on others tend to "pass the test," which has led him to believe the test is really a sham—a tool to create hope among workers and to keep young ones loyal during years they would otherwise be most restless.

Marcus had received approval from the guard overseeing crew #1949 to take the test, thanks to lobbying by Cornelius. Test day is a holiday for all workers, complete with better meals, and often visits by higher-ups in the League. This year, an up-and-comer, Vice Admiral Tyrone Tiberius, is attending ceremonies at the Nayan mine.

Marcus is sitting at the long table in the cafeteria, alongside all the other test-takers. He hasn't written with a pencil in years; he hopes he remembers how. His father had given him clear advice—the goal is not to do well on the test; the best he could do by doing well would be a life as a low-level guard, a cog in Frozos's machine of death. Jesse has told Marcus that his only chance to get off this planet and achieve true success is to show-off his actual genius in the sciences. The game plan is simple: answer every question that pertains to Frozos's rule, if there are any, by responding the way a loyal soldier would. Ignore the other questions, and instead write down every complex mathematical proof and scientific formula he could think of. Show off his knowledge base.

At 10:00 AM, a guard in the front yells, "Begin." The several hundred applicants seated at every other seat to avoid cheating open the booklet and begin. Marcus takes a cursory look through the ten-page booklet, scanning for questions that would test loyalty. He sees none—most are straight forward math and reading comprehension questions that he could do in under thirty minutes. Contrary to his father's advice, he answers all the questions. That leave him ninety minutes to start writing out every proof and formula he can, touching on everything from physics to engineering and linear algebra. Some of the applicants near Marcus notice that he is writing furiously, far more than they are, leading many looking back through their tests to see if they missed something. Confused but satisfied that they answered the questions, the other applicants hand in their test well ahead of the two-hour mark while Marcus continues writing until the guard calls time with just a handful of people still working—most of whom probably won't be passing.

Marcus drops his pencil, closes his booklet, and hands it to a guard, walking nearby to collect tests. He heads back to the barracks by himself. It's a beautiful day outside, and most workers are hanging outside the barracks. As he nears Barrack 47, he passes his crewmates, lounging on the grass. They cheer and hoot, asking how it went. Marcus shrugs his shoulders and offers up, "Pretty well, I think. Fingers crossed!"

Returning home, Marcus walks inside to see his father pacing back and forth by their bunk, the footprints all over the dirt floor betray the fact that he has been doing this for much of the past two hours.

"Hi Dad!"

Jesse looks up from his pacing; he was so deep in thought that he didn't even notice Marcus walk in. Smiling, he asks, "Well, how did it go?"

"Pretty good. The questions were super basic. I answered them all in less than twenty-five minutes, and like you said, put down as much of what I know as possible."

"Fine, fine. I'm sure it went well. Let's go outside and enjoy the rest of the day. No use just sitting here and worrying!" Before they walk out, Jesse gives Marcus a big, long hug and says, "I love you very much, Marcus. Your mother would be so very proud of you, and so am I."

"I know, Dad. I love you, too."

"Promise me, Marcus, you'll never forget all you learned here. Never be consumed by hatred or revenge; be inspired by love."

"I promise, Dad."

"Good," Jesse says as he puts his arm around Marcus's shoulders, and they walk outside together. "Remember, don't let them embitter you or drive you to hate. Let them hate. Act out of love, and they can never beat you."

Marcus brushes a tear from his face, trying to hide it from Jesse. He feels a pit in his stomach as he processes this fatherly advice, sensing their time together is near its end.

After about two hours, a guard rushes over to where Marcus, his father, and many of the residents of Barrack 47 are lounging. "NJ273? Your attendance has been requested."

Marcus gets up to follow the guard, with a smile and a nod from his dad, while the group cheers and congratulates him. They all assume he must have passed and been drafted into the army. Why else would he be called in for a meeting?

Marcus silently walks alongside the guard. They walk past the barracks and the cafeteria hall to the officers' headquarters, a large brick building he has not entered since the day he and his father were captured. They then proceed upstairs and into the office of the head soldier of the mine.

"This is NJ273 sir," the guard says before walking out and closing the door behind him.

Sitting in the chair is Vice Admiral Tiberius. He has the same reptilian face and fast-moving yellow eyes, though he is perhaps twenty-five pounds lighter than he will be when laying siege to Earth. "Sit down, Marcus, I believe it is, if these records are right? I don't deal in worker numbers."

"Yes, that's right, sir," Marcus says politely as he takes a seat.

"Tell me, do you know who I am?"

"I believe you are Vice Admiral Tyrone Tiberius, one of the top commanders in the League of Planets's space fleet."

"Yes. I carry a lot of weight, and my endorsement or criticism can permanently alter a career path, which brings me to your test," Tiberius says.

"Yes, sir. I can explain," Marcus interjects nervously.

"No need, son. Let me talk my piece first. The grader was dumbfounded by the scribbles but smartly passed the test on. These are extraordinarily complex proofs. I take it you didn't take this test because you want to be a mine guard some day?"

"No, sir. Updates we hear about Supreme General Frozos's conquests are so exciting to me, and I want to participate in them."

"Good. So I take it you have always studied the sciences. Reports from your file indicate you spend nights working with your father on these problems?"

"Yes. He is an academic. I appreciate his knowledge and what he has taught me, but like many academics, he doesn't appreciate the reality of daily life." It pains Marcus to say this, but he has run through a conversation like this with his father many times to ensure he passes the loyalty test. He must lie and do so convincingly.

"Why do you say that?"

"He has spent his life in a classroom. I've spent mine here. I've seen that some are happier being ruled, just working and being fed. Power is meant to be held by those willing to wield it. The Supreme General and yourself seem like people who understand this. That's why I want to learn from you."

"And learn you shall. But first, I need evidence that you actually understand what you wrote down rather than mindlessly memorized the material. So solve this problem. It shouldn't take more than a minute or two and is simpler than much of what you wrote." Tiberius pushes over a piece of paper with a pencil.

Marcus looks over the problem—a physics problem about gravitational forces and planetary rotations in a multi-solar universe. He immediately smiles. These problems had long been a nuisance for him, but he remembers clearly that his final test in the cave before being captured was on this very topic. He can't help but believe that his mother's helping hand has played a role in turning destiny in his favor. Having subsequently done countless problems like this with his father, he bangs out the problem in less than a minute, calmly pushing the paper back to Tiberius.

Tiberius reviews it against another paper. "Well, you couldn't have bluffed your way through that one. I've called you here because you have different skills than most of our recruits from these mines, and you seem to have the ambition to match it. We are running a special program for young folks like yourself. You'll be dealing with long-term missions that are critical to the League. Interested?"

"Very much, sir," Marcus replies.

"I should tell you that the punishment should you fail training will be very harsh. Great rewards always come with serious risk. You understand what I'm saying?"

"I do. And I will take great risk to give me a future off of this planet."

"Good. The officer outside will take you to my personal ship right away; this assignment is of the utmost secrecy."

Marcus hesitates, realizing this means he won't say goodbye to his father, leading Tiberius to spell it out bluntly.

"Your assignment will be extremely secret. Don't worry, I will make sure your father and coworkers know you passed the test and are getting a strong assignment. You won't be able to say goodbye to them yourself, but based on what you said about them, I assume that's fine?"

Marcus keeps his composure and says, "Yes, of course sir. Thank you for this tremendous opportunity."

With that, he gets up, Tiberius leads him to the door and tells the guard to bring Marcus to his ship. Marcus, holding back tears, realizes that the final question was the true loyalty test. He also now understands why his father hugged him so dearly. He only wishes he had hugged him back for even just one more second. The realization that he will never see his father again comes over him as he walks aboard Tiberius's ship, though he can't show sadness without risking that he would expose where his true loyalties lie.

Three days later, with Tiberius's backing, he is on Planet Killjorn, where he will spend the next three years of his life. About two months later, word is passed to him that his father has died. He was killed in an accident from falling nayanite. He pushed another worker out of the way, and the debris crushed him. Marcus knows he was only told this as one final test, and so again, he is forced to hide all outward emotions. In the days that followed, he comes to understand why his father had outlived any other worker on that job: he had a reason to live. Jesse was motivated by giving his son a better life at any and all cost, persevering under conditions that would have killed any ordinary person.

As Marcus grows older, he appreciates that his father sacrificed as much to protect him as his mother. While his mother sacrificed her life to save him, his father endured a living hell to save him. More than anything, he wants to avenge their deaths, but he constantly reminds himself of his father's plea: be inspired by love, not consumed by hate. That is the only way to truly beat the League and to honor the legacy of his parents.

CHAPTER 25

Jersey City
June 2, 2029

Robert Wilson stands up from his chair and puts the paper of his childhood back onto his desk. His confidence in himself remains unsteady, but his determination to push forward has been renewed. He will honor the legacies of his father and mother, no matter the personal cost. There is a knock at his side-door from the command center.

"Come in."

The aide who several weeks ago told Robert that he was sure of victory walks in. "You should come over, Commander. Tiberius has hijacked the airwaves."

Robert quickly walks into the command center, where Tiberius's reptilian face is on the screens, interrupted only by footage from the battle showing SF-01s getting blown to smithereens. The Admiral is standing in his conn with the giant window to his back. Outside the window, the moon and the patrolling transport destroyer are visible.

"Turn the volume up," Robert says to the front row.

"Supreme General Frozos and I warned you that resistance would be futile; that your planet was centuries behind us in technology. But you followed the empty promises of a man who had a mere three years of formal education. Yes, that's right. Your Robert Wilson was merely a mineworker; he has no military experience. Now your sons and daughters are dying because of his incompetence and personal, irrational hostility. His are the only hands with blood on them.

"Just now out in the distance," Tiberius continues as he turns and points out the window to four fast approaching white dots, "you can see four more spacecrafts arriving. Two are the supertanker transporters escorted by two additional transport destroyers. We now have seven destroyer groups outside your force field. Your military is not the only one who has been using recent weeks to gain strength. This is the most potent fighting force we have ever dedicated to one planet.

"Your best choice is to surrender now. The two supertankers are carrying more sunsheet fiber. Within three weeks, nearly thirty percent of your planet will be covered, creating catastrophic and irreversible loss of plant life as global temperatures plummet into a new ice age. Surrender now or freeze and starve to death. It's really that simple."

As Robert turns around to tell the staff to reduce the volume, he's surprised to see Mark Morrison and Chris Bailey proceeding down the stairs at the back of the room.

"I know, I know," Chris says loudly to the gawking room of staff, "We're breaking the rules. But honestly, who really cares? I say, the heck with it, it's time we just win this damn thing!" Quite the about-face from Chris's usual reserved style, Robert thinks to himself.

From the corner of his eye, Robert sees Jake Thornhill smile to himself and nod along before saying, "Commander Wilson, we are going to be very busy over here. I suspect you take our landlords into your office."

"You read my mind, General," Robert parries back, smiling. He leads Mark and Chris into his office. He pulls two folding chairs to his and the three friends sit.

"Sorry about the sparse setup—not as nice as my office upstairs, I know."

"So, tell us, Robert, really, how are *you* doing," Mark asks.

"Well I screwed up royally. This one is all on me."

"Actually, congratulations are in order," Mark says.

"I'm sorry, I'm confused."

"You can now be a great military hero. General Douglas MacArthur got his ass kicked out of the Philippines in World War II before turning the tide in the Pacific. He didn't respond by rolling up into a ball. No, he promised, 'I shall return,' and he did."

"And don't forget Winston Churchill," Chris adds. "In World War I, he attempted a disastrous landing in the Dardanelles, destroying his reputation for a time. Yet, he was the man who rallied the British people and the world to 'never surrender' to tyranny."

"You see," Mark says, "the true measure of a man is realized in life's valleys, not at its pinnacles. And if we didn't believe in you, well, there's no way Chris would've signed on to this insane plan seven months ago. I of course still would have," he jokes, desperately trying to add some levity to the grim setting.

Robert smiles. "I appreciate that. A wonderful man once told me something very similar, but I'm grateful to be reminded of it."

"Let me ask you something," Chris says. "You failed, by all accounts, spectacularly. I mean a disaster that will be infamous. It was an ill-conceived plan from the get-go. When the failure became evident, how did the pilots respond?"

"Heroically. True heroism. The commanding officer saved the planet, frankly," Robert says.

"And the officer was an Arbor Ridge intern, right? Anna Small, I heard?"

"Yep, that's right."

"Just a plain-old, ordinary civilian," Chris says. "Tell me, has there been a time this entire battle, from when you told Mark and myself, brought aboard workers here, had their families come, challenged Neverian, or with these pilots, when you've overestimated us, us being ordinary civilians?"

Robert leans back in his chair, pondering. "Nope. Can't think of one."

"So then," Mark interjects, "why in God's name are you going along with these government leaders desperately trying to keep us out of the fight? I mean, for heaven's sake, it's our planet. And I'll be damned if we don't want to protect it as much as anyone. Stop telling us to be calm and ignore the threat!"

"That's right," Chris adds on, "so buck up and don't take this beating lying down."

Robert nods his head strongly in agreement. "I've missed talking to you guys so much the last two months. I needed this advice. If we win this thing, it really is due to you—I mean it. But don't worry, I'll take all the credit." Robert cracks a much-needed smile.

"Hey, what else is new?" Mark jokes.

It is now 6:00 PM in Jersey City. Robert, wearing the same suit but a different red tie, is standing behind a metal lectern in the lobby of the Arbor Ridge tower, its great oak tree behind him. He didn't want to let cameras into the top secret facility and was no longer as worried about showing a separation between PEACE and Arbor Ridge; there are more important matters. Several feet in front of him are half a dozen television cameras with the crews of the major networks. Robert hasn't even called world leaders, not even President Victoria Larom, since the battle. He is going directly to the people.

"Good evening. I have promised never to lie to you, and so I will offer nothing but the unsparing truth tonight. As the Commander of PEACE, I am solely responsible for today's defeat and the loss of 900 lives. We lost not because we lack the technology or skill to win battles in space, but because I made a strategic blunder, not considering the potential of a decoy ship, and approved a fundamentally flawed battle plan.

I will carry the burden of the unnecessary loss of human life due to my error for the rest of my life.

"I agree with Admiral Tiberius that today represents a turning point in this, our first space war. We will rise from this defeat stronger with greater resolve and smarter strategy. This planet can't be knocked out with one punch, and because you can't be, I won't be. While I will carry with me deep grief, particularly for Group Commander Anna Small who was only twenty-two years old, I will also take inspiration from what they did today. Commander Small ordered me to close the force field, sentencing herself and her group to death because she saw a laser cannon set to fire through the opening. Her sacrifice literally saved this planet.

"Remember, this was the action not of a twenty-year veteran of our military but of a civilian just old enough to graduate college. If we can't each strive to be as mature and committed as she was, then maybe this planet isn't worth saving. But I believe we can and will be.

"Yes, as I told you on April fourth, I worked alongside my father as a slave on a mine. He worked every night to give me an education, so that I could leave the mine. I did. Thanks actually to the support of then Vice Admiral Tiberius, unaware of my true motives, I got into a spy training program and am here today as a result. What I love about this planet is that humans aren't judged by their parents' accomplishments or what degrees you have. You are judged based on what you accomplish in your life. It doesn't matter if I had three or thirty years of 'formal' education, I am happy to be judged by what I have done here on Earth.

"That's why I am speaking to you from the Arbor Ridge lobby because this is where I've accomplished things in my life, and I was reminded today by two dear friends of what that is. I'm proud of what this company is, but I've accomplished so much because I've relied so heavily on the work-ethic, ingenuity, and honesty of humanity. Arbor Ridge received twenty-five percent of America's patents last year; I was responsible for fewer than one percent of those. You, the people of this planet, power the drive and innovation of our daily life.

"Sadly, in my effort to keep calm among you, the public, I've been selling you short and leaving our greatest weapon off the battlefield, losing sight of why I was so confident we'd win in the first place. I believe we should be calm, and that no one should be panicked, but we should be fighting calmly together not calm because we are detached from the fight.

"This war is to protect Earth, and we need to marshal all of Earth's resources if we are going to be successful. Relying on fifty thousand pilots and one supply chain simply isn't going to get the job done. Here is the reality: this war, or at least this phase of it, will be won or lost in the next two weeks. I am not going to turn the force field off and hand over the keys to Frozos. So, you have a choice. Panic, give up, and enjoy the last two weeks before we face an extinction-level ice age. Or, you, the public, can remind your governments that in a crisis you are the source of our strength, not a weakness.

"We have thirty-nine thousand SF-01s. I need more than sixty thousand, but can only build nine thousand in the next two weeks. That means I need manufacturing companies globally to retool and reroute supply chains. When the Battle

289

for Earth is fought, a harsh reality is that some of Frozos's ships will be let inside the force field as we open periodically to let our jets in and out and as a way to manage the flow of fighting. That means we need to mobilize all of our traditional military resources, fighter jets, aircraft carrier groups, and anti-aircraft weaponry to protect cities and population centers from these enemy planes.

"This rapid mobilization will require coordination of our governments with each other, with the private sector, and temporary enlistment from some citizens. I believe that true character comes out in times of crisis, not in times of calm. Humanity has never faced a crisis this grave before. As we discover the character of man, I think we will find it to be our greatest triumph. Thank you and God bless you."

Robert walks off camera, his address to the world complete. Mark, Chris, and Thornhill who were watching from behind the camera meet up with Robert, each offering the heartiest and most sincere congratulations on a job well done. As they are chatting, Chris notices a crowd is beginning to assemble outside of the mini-force field boundary around Arbor Ridge's Jersey City building. It's only been about ten minutes since Robert finished, but there must be at least 500 people outside, with the sum growing by the dozen.

One of the cameramen who is breaking down his equipment says to them, "We're interviewing them now if you want to watch the feed."

Like children on Christmas day, the four men rush over and scrunch around a small TV.

"Why are you here?" the reporter asks the crowd.

"I want to sign up to help. I didn't know where else to go."

"I want to show my support."

"I have a small trucking business and wanted to know if my trucks could be of use."

"I just want to show I'm ready to fight for my home."

The shouts from the crowd make it quite clear. The crowd is calm, clear, motivated, and growing.

"You know," the cameraman says, looking up from his phone, "this is going on everywhere. Outside the White House. Your other buildings. In Beijing, Paris, Moscow."

"Thank you," Robert smiles. "Let's head downstairs."

As the four men walk out of the elevator and onto the SF-01 assembly one, the briskness of the pace is immediately apparent. The crew is motivated to get production as high as safely possible without sacrificing quality. Everyone is working just a bit harder. They walk into the command center where screens show images of peaceful crowds assembling everywhere around the world.

Members of the command center are fielding a flurry of calls from manufacturing companies offering their plants, commercial airliners offering to use their planes to haul cargo, and more. Across the U.S. in the past hour, news networks are reporting that over forty million people have joined these "volunteer crowds," as they've been dubbed.

Robert's phone rings.

"Hello, Madam President.... Yes, I apologize for the lack of heads-up.... Yes, I am certain. Likely closer to one than two, but we need to keep some flexibility.... I look forward to it."

Robert hangs up, grinning to himself.

On the screen, an anchor says, "And we have breaking news. President Larom is about to address the American people from the Oval Office. To the White House."

The screen flips to Larom sitting behind her desk in the Oval Office, wearing a navy-blue suit.

"Good evening, my fellow Americans. Our nation is great because it is governed by we, the American people. Our system presupposes the innate heroism and cool-headedness of a determined, morally just citizenry. As Commander Robert Wilson outlined it, I see no sentiment more American than his that you the public are our greatest asset.

"Tonight, you are making yourself heard, and your government is very pleased that you have. I am also glad to report that governments across the world, democracies and dictatorship alike, are responding to the same righteous indignation of their citizenry. We are coordinating with allies and NATO forces to ensure none or our allies are left particularly vulnerable. No nation will be deploying any of its nuclear arsenal; I do wish to be clear on that.

"I have spoken with Commander Wilson who has confirmed the battle for Earth will commence inside of two weeks, and so all of Earth is going on a wartime footing like never before in our history. For the next fourteen days, everyone's job is to help prepare the planet. Global financial markets have been closed through June sixteenth to drive home the point that we are focusing on the one task at hand.

"What does this mean? We expect every manufacturing firm, and will order those who are noncompliant, to either produce material for SF-01s or to supplement our military's arsenal. Military shipments will get priority for trucking, rail, and cargo air companies. We are deploying the entire U.S. Navy to guard major port cities. I am federalizing the National Guard, calling up the Army Reserve, and we will be deploying them to key localities likely to face the gravest risk.

"I know you want to help. There are several ways you can. If you work in an industry that will be building out our war machine, directly or indirectly, go to work and work hard. If you don't, your town or city may be enlisting supplemental forces to help prepare key infrastructure for battle. If you are caring for children or the elderly, you may want to consider temporarily visiting family or friends in less urban settings.

"I agree with Commander Wilson. We should not panic nor be complacent. Rather, let's calmly work together to bolster our defense and end this war. Thank you and God bless America."

Robert, in PEACE's command center, is relieved to see such a strong, unequivocal statement from the President. Staff monitoring other nations' responses are reporting similar comments from other world leaders.

Up in space, Frozos and Tiberius are each looking out from their respective conns down at Earth. Both men are surprised at the response to today's developments. Frozos is disgusted at what he sees as the foolishness of the public, whereas Tiberius has a grudging respect and admiration for their perseverance through this ordeal. He hadn't seen a planet hold out this well since a single planet held out for over twelve months. That siege over twenty-five years ago catapulted Tiberius to Vice Admiral, as he finally conquered it after his predecessors had failed for over six months. His tactics had been brutal and there were no known survivors. He wondered if a similar outcome here was proving inevitable.

CHAPTER 26

Jersey City
June 13, 2029

The past eleven days have truly seen the best of humanity as the planet mounted a genuinely global response with an intensity the like of which has never been seen before. The speed at which manufacturing companies retooled factories and assembly lines to at least partially assist in the production of military goods globally has been extraordinary. Over these eleven days, 25,000 SF-01s have been produced for a global fleet of 64,000. With 68,000 trained pilots, Robert Wilson will be able to launch every plane. He can even change out some pilots if needed depending on the duration of the battle. Pilots have been training constantly on simulations based on the current military situation to determine the optimal group of 64,000 to send.

Carrier groups have assembled along the coast of the Americas, East Asia, the Middle East, Western Africa, the

Mediterranean, the Arctic, and the North Atlantic. Cities that house Arbor Ridge towers are anticipated to face the heaviest assaults, both because that will be the entry point of enemy ships and because they will want to try to take the towers down to permanently impair the force field. Given the mini force field structure around the towers—which can remain on even if the global force field is turned off—Robert is comfortable they will withstand a heavy assault but Admiral Tiberius doesn't know this. So, for the past seven days, the aircraft carrier USS *Gerald R. Ford* has been parked just outside New York harbor. Its presence has been a daily reminder to Robert that he is not fighting this war alone. All of mankind is as deeply invested in this war as he is.

Major cities are now half-empty as much of the population has moved out to more rural areas. Shorelines are filled with anti-aircraft artillery, tanks and trucks are being housed near major cities in the event there is an attempted landing and it goes from an aerial to a ground conflict. In addition to the active military and reserve forces, recent veterans have been brought back, and local police forces are being used as supplementary forces. Over seventy million people are now serving in a military role; this is about double the number from three months ago. Robert hopes that few of these people actually see action.

Over the past ten days, there has been active debate and study around the military plan. It has been agreed that the majority of the fighting should occur outside the force field. Periodically, they can turn off pieces of the force field for SF-01s to get a few dozen small and medium sized crafts inside the force field. The traditional human forces would destroy these planes as they entered lower altitudes. As long as the count of planes inside the force field numbered in the dozens and not hundreds, conventional forces should be able to handle them given the overwhelming numerical advantage. This activity would be moderated or increased based on the success rate, and it has been widely agreed that under no circumstance would a destroyer be allowed to enter the force field.

There has been some debate about the initial launch of the SF-01s into space. There will be nearly thirty minutes for the enemy to prepare to attack them as they exit the force field—the most dangerous part of the mission. Robert has strongly argued that they need to get as many planes out at the same time as possible to avoid a slaughter once in space, but there is a worry that the entire fleet could be wiped out, which argues for a more incremental approach. Behind the scenes, a group of nations has been working to build opposition to Robert's plan, and he is unaware just how much opposition there is.

Robert has committed to a strike date between June 9 and 16. They have now passed the 60,000-plane threshold, so they have been ready to go for three days now. There has been little military movement in space, other than the steady increase in sunsheet covering—now about 20 percent of the planet—and global temperatures have begun to dip the past few days. World leaders are beginning to get antsy, wondering when Robert will hold consultations to begin the strike. Since June 8, Robert has been spending more of his time looking at satellite imagery, what for, he hasn't said, but it has something to do with his decision not to begin the attack.

It is 11:00 AM on June 13 in Jersey City. Robert is sitting in his office, studying battle plans one more time. He hasn't left this building in eleven days, and he's feeling a bit ragged, hair unkempt, and a few days since he last shaved. There is a knock at his door.

"What is it?"

A young aide opens the door, sticks her head in and says, "There's unusual activity when you have a minute, sir." She then closes it.

Robert looks up, intrigued. Every day at around noon and again at midnight he asks for a rundown on the situation at each of the fifteen force field sites, including whether or not anything unusual has been reported. But, over the past eleven days, everything has been normal, consistently to his disappointment. He immediately jumps out of his chair, runs to the door, but stops himself before opening it, taking a breath to collect himself, opens it and calmly walks into the command center.

"What is it?" Robert asks to the entire room.

"Something unusual, take a look for yourself," Jake Thornhill replies, pointing up to the screen. "That's our force field projector in the South Atlantic."

Up on the screen are cameras from various angles on the decks of the supposed Arbor Ridge research facility, which like the Indian Ocean facility has been housing SF-01s as part of Project Ridley. It is a beautiful day, but the seas appear rather rough, that or there are some objects in the water, but the cameras aren't focused in enough.

"Is something in the water?" Robert asks.

"Zoom in," Thornhill tells the front row.

As the cameras focus in on the water, the picture becomes clearer. There are hundreds, probably thousands of sharks of all species and sizes circling the facility.

Thornhill notices that Robert doesn't seem surprised, instead he has an amused smile. He continues, "This has been going on for thirty minutes. Hundreds of sharks swimming in an orderly fashion. No attacks, no feeding frenzy, just making their presence known. We've been talking to the top marine scientists, and none have ever seen anything like it. The crew of the facility are nervous."

"Tell them not to worry," Robert says, mind elsewhere, as he continues to stare up at the screen. After a few more moments soaking in the visual, he turns to Thornhill, "We need to get the military representatives assembled. We strike today."

"Yes, sir. I will set a call for 11:30."

"Perfect."

It is now 11:30, and Robert has used the last twenty minutes to freshen up, shave, put on a suit with a dark blue tie, and his lapel pin. He is sitting in his office in front of his monitors as the supervisory video conference with the several dozen military representatives who can participate in but ultimately do not decide on PEACE matters is about to begin. At the start of the call, Robert defers to Thornhill to run through the situation up in space, technical details of the military plan, and so forth. Robert notices while Thornhill is speaking that several of the European military officials, from France, Italy, Spain, Belgium, Germany, Sweden, and a few other nations, are moving their lips without any sound coming out. It would seem they've placed themselves on mute and have engaged in their own sub-meeting to reach a European consensus.

About twenty minutes into the meeting, with the technical briefing ended and a question and answer session underway, the French Air Force chief speaks up. "All of our models suggest this is a suicide mission. Based on the limited knowledge of their technical capabilities and the number of forces, we're likely to get wiped out. Computer simulations show less than a five percent chance of victory. That's why I think a gradual strike is more prudent than sending every ship up at once as you propose."

Robert sits forward in his chair, entirely unperturbed, having expected this question to arise at some point. "I'd expect no less from the computers, but we don't fight battles via models."

"Maybe not," the general blusters, "but we can't launch a sixty-thousand-man suicide mission on your hunch."

"No, of course not," Robert calmly counters, "but your computers miss one thing, the most critical element of my entire strategy."

"And what's that?"

"The human element."

"Please, we're too experienced and battle-hardened to be swayed by your rah-rah spirit, Commander Wilson, give us more credit than that," the general says, his face growing red with agitation. Several of his fellow European leaders are also now nodding their heads visibly in agreement.

"You misunderstand me, General. I'm not waving the flag; I firmly believe in the power of the human element, and I am prepared to wager the future of this planet and this species on it. Why, you ask? I'll tell you." Invigorated with passion, Robert jumps out of his chair, knuckles pressed to the table, as he continues. "My whole career, making military equipment, I've wanted them to be human-operated. Why? Well, with the brainpower we possess, let alone Frozos, we can develop a computer model that will make every rational move. In that game, the better equipped military will win, nearly every time. That's what your computer simulation is capturing because it can't know what irrational decision or gut-feeling each pilot will have.

"Now when you have the strongest force, that human element can be suboptimal. But when you're the underdog, it's the human element that provides your chance for victory. We have nurtured this element and built our forces around it. When I recruited players from *Galactic Flyer*, we didn't just pick the highest scorers because we fight in squadrons. I needed flyers who would reflexively, without even realizing it, make the same decision. Each individual was chosen because his or her activity in the game unveiled a trend, and we needed that skill set to complete a team. We train as teams, not individuals, because a good organization is greater than the sum of its parts.

"So we have squadrons with character, those that are 'irrationally' cautious, those that are bold, those that turn right too

often or left too often. Left to their own devices, each irrational decision can result in chaos, but we are trying to capitalize
and harness the human element in a coordinating fashion to
create a symphony, not of music, but of war. We are built to
thrive off of the unexpected, and today, I assure you, we and
Frozos will face the unexpected.

"That, sir, your model did not account for. More importantly, that Frozos's computer-assisted flyers will not account
for. And that, sir, is why, today, we shall prevail." With that
rhetorical triumph, Robert sits back down.

The chastened French representative sits silently.

After a bit of uncomfortable quiet, the Taiwanese representative says, "I think you will find agreement from those
of us here that you have a sound plan. You have our support.
Good luck and Godspeed."

This is quickly followed by a chorus of well-wishes. The
final battle is set to begin.

It is now high noon over New York as Robert walks back
into the command center where Thornhill has also returned
to from his own office. "Okay, folks, this is it," Robert says,
"Operation Cooler King begins now. I expect all sixty-four
thousand of our birds off the ground, and there will be a
synchronized launch into space at exactly 1:00 PM. We do
this right, and we'll be having dinner tonight as a free and
secure people."

This announcement starts a flurry of activity. Orders are
being sent across all the PEACE and joint PEACE national
military bases to begin to get planes in the air. Getting every
plane off the runways is about a ten- to thirty-minute process,

depending upon the size of the facility. The plan is for the last plane to be off the ground by 12:50 PM New York time, allowing for ten minutes of delay before the 1:00 PM launch. In many parts of the world, pilots are being awoken from their sleep by the sound of alarms. Everywhere, pilots are dressing for combat, getting in a final meal, or saying a prayer.

Meanwhile, PEACE is also making contact with the leadership of each national military as to the 1:00 PM start time. Given most nations of the world were on the call, this should be no surprise. National militaries will be using the final hour to enter a state of battle readiness. Thornhill's command center will be the critical conduit between PEACE and national militaries with a hotline established. Coordination is critical to ensure no city is overwhelmed by enemy forces as PEACE turns the force field on and off. As of now, the force field will open for twenty seconds at 1:23 PM New York time globally. This should provide enough time for the fleet to get out without letting many ships in. The hope is to keep it closed for at least fifteen minutes to let the battle develop and then begin to use it like a release valve, relieving pressure on SF-01 forces where needed.

As this is going on in the command center, Robert has arranged for a crew to take down the outer wall of Robert's office, and are now moving the black spherical ship out of the room and to the entrance of one of the underground railway tunnels. He hasn't disclosed his reasoning with anyone but needs a backup plan should the battle not go as hoped.

It is now 12:40 PM—twenty minutes to launch. The exit from the force field is the most dangerous moment of this entire mission. There is simply no way to keep the attack secret. With seven transport destroyers, armed with heavy guns, and carrying thousands of drone attack vessels each, as well as hundreds of small manned-crafts, Tiberius will undoubtedly detect the launch and deploy resources to any and all parts of the globe to push off the attackers.

If they survive the first two minutes, Robert thinks they can win, but Thornhill is unconvinced that launching everyone at once is a worthy gamble.

"Twenty minutes to launch, sir," he says to Robert, "we still can adjust plans."

"No, Jake, it's full steam ahead. At one o'clock, I am going to broadcast to the world the commencement of the attack," Robert replies, matter of fact.

"But sir, that will tip off the enemy."

"I know. Trust me, I know exactly what I'm doing."

Thornhill walks right up to Robert. "Robert, I'm entitled to know before I send sixty-four thousand men and women out, possibly to their deaths."

"You are," Robert concedes. "Quick, let's go into your office."

A few minutes later, Thornhill walks back into the command center, satisfied. "Tell all pilots, the 1:00 PM launch is a *go*." Up on the screen, Thornhill can monitor events from satellite feeds, pilot cameras, and views of major cities. The command center staff has been assigned portions of this to monitor to bring trouble spots to Thornhill and Robert's attention.

As the command center makes last minute preparations, Robert ascends to the Arbor Ridge lobby where a lectern has been set up in the same spot as his remarks eleven days ago. Exactly at 1:00 PM as the PEACE fleet launches, Robert cuts into all regularly scheduled programming across all television stations.

"Good afternoon. I am speaking to you today to let you know that the battle for Earth has begun. As I speak, sixty-four thousand brave souls are launching into space to eliminate the enemy threat and preserve our way of life. Please stay calm and at home to allow PEACE forces and national militaries to act as needed. We are a wonderfully large and diverse planet filled with people of many creeds, beliefs, and religions. I ask those so inclined to join me in a moment of prayer."

Robert bows his head before continuing.

"Dear Father, today our planet is acting as one to ensure that freedom, equality, and liberty will be preserved. Thousands of your flock are running toward conflict to protect their loved ones, their neighbor, and their fellow man while millions more are manning our defenses to do the same. Please look over them, protect them, and guide them so that their motive and weapons are true.

"If our cause be just, as I believe it to be, aid us in our hour of great need, so that tomorrow we can begin life anew with our faith in you and ourselves replenished. Provide for us today with the courage, strength, and friendship to prevail. And please accept with open arms those of us who make the ultimate sacrifice to protect the sanctity of our world.

"Amen."

Televisions turn back to their regular programming. Robert looks up from the lectern, and he leaves the Arbor

Ridge lobby to head back into the command center. By the time he gets there, it is 1:07 PM.

Before he can even ask the question, Thornhill says, "The launch has gone smoothly. We're a third of the way up. The destroyer groups are now pushing in. Six destroyers themselves are within a thousand miles of the force field, and one remains pinned to the moon, where we aren't launching from as of now. Smaller crafts have moved within two hundred miles of the force field. Frozos's ship remains well back from the rest. I just hope you're right."

"So do I, so do I...Is—"

"Yes," Thornhill interrupts. "The unusual activity has continued."

CHAPTER 27

Jersey City
June 13, 2029

At 1:22 PM, the fleet of 64,000 SF-01s begins to reach the edge of the force field. In front of them, hundreds of ships can be seen across the horizon, an intimidating display of force. From his place in the command center, Robert just hopes that none lose their nerve and do indeed fly out as ordered.

At 1:22:50, there is a burst of light that consumes the entire planet, blinding everyone for several seconds, wearing off just as the force field opens. As pilots regain their vision and fly out, they are greeted by the sudden appearance of at least 20,000 ships, firing at Tiberius's army from behind, providing just enough cover for the SF-01s to get out into space, largely unharmed, and for the force field to close back down before any enemy ships are able to enter.

The crowd in the command center cheers as they see these new ships arrive. Someone shouts out, "63,857 SF-01s are operational. No enemy ships inside. Cooler King has launched successfully!"

Robert raises his right hand triumphantly. He always believed, unshakably, that a rebel cause against Frozos really did exist. His mother and father were associated with it many years ago, and today, he is partnering with it. He bet the entire planet's existence that they would arrive to help. The demonstration of sharks today convinced him. He always was fascinated with a "King Hammerhead" after all; what greater sign could be given? That's what convinced him to give the speech at 1:00 PM. He wanted to give the timeline to the resistance because he was certain that they would be listening. Now, he can only watch and hope that the combined forces are enough.

He is watching as the nearly 64,000 SF-01s and 20,000 to 25,000 rebel ships of all shapes and sizes engage in combat. Suddenly, the satellite cameras show the emergence of two gigantic ships, about 20 percent larger than the transport destroyers. They are a dark blue, almost blending in to the night sky. Their appearance leads to another roar of applause in the command center. Mark Morrison and Chris Bailey have just walked in and are watching in amazement as another alien force appears to be helping Earth. Mankind has gone from thinking it was alone in the universe three months ago to having alien allies in an apparent intergalactic war.

On the other side of the planet, above Tokyo where it's well past nightfall, the sky is lighting up from the heavy fire occurring up above. Residents in Asia are looking to the night sky wondering what is occurring. A government blackout has turned off all livestreams from the various space stations, lunar bases, and satellites. Families are gathering together, hoping for the best. Residents in Europe, Africa, and the Americas are noticing that the day is getting brighter as sunsheets are destroyed in the battle. While none of the SF-01s are targeting them, it is inevitable that stray laser fire would hit and damage the fiber networks. Television news stations have little to report from space, instead bouncing among live shots of major cities where Navies and Air Forces have been deployed but no enemy ships sighted.

At 11:15 AM, President Victoria Larom had taken a secret flight to the secure West Virginia bunker as a safety precaution in case Washington D.C. comes under attack. Now, she sits at the head of the table in the Situation Room in the bunker. On her screen, she is watching the live feed from PEACE, alongside her military and security advisors. At the moment, there is little to do but watch, though the generals are in constant contact with commanders stationed in each of the major cities. A sense of shock hit the room when the alien ships arrived, and while she did not expect it, she is a bit less surprised, having felt that Robert has been keeping some elements of his plans secret, perhaps from everyone.

Aboard his ship, Tiberius is frantically barking orders. Looking out from the conn, he sees thousands of ships battling it out. Thus far, the fighting is almost exclusively occurring in the thousand-mile stretch between the force field and the six transport destroyers, which have yet to get directly involved in the struggle. They could use their large laser cannons, but given the magnitude of the blast, they would eradicate thousands of their own ships too. Tiberius has sent out virtually all of the small and drone crafts that the transport destroyers carry.

"What are our losses?" he shouts.

"Six percent of our manned crafts and nine percent of our drone crafts are now unresponsive, sir."

"And theirs?"

"Three percent of Earth crafts and two percent of unidentified crafts."

Tiberius is relieved. He believes he has two to three times as many ships, so at this loss rate, it will be a brutal battle but one in which he should be triumphant. That said, the first two minutes were supposed to be the most dangerous for Earth's forces, and instead, they have exited it mostly unscathed. Both sides have reasons for optimism.

Just as Tiberius is feeling relieved, a junior officer from the radar division shouts, "Two large ships have just entered the battlefield. They are larger than a transport destroyer, sir!"

"Get me a visual!" Tiberius demands. His ship pivots and from the great window of his conn, he sees the two dark blue rebel carriers.

One of these ships hovers about 40,000 miles away from the battlefield, similar to *Magnus*. The other steams towards the transport destroyer guarding the moon.

"Let it engage," Tiberius says. "I want to understand what it is capable of."

The rebel carrier moves in within hundreds of miles of the transport destroyer guarding the moon. The two ships fire laser cannons upon each other as they pass by, with the blows seemingly absorbed by their shield systems. As the ships turn to face each other again, several hundred small crafts exit through the great bay doors of the carrier while the large laser cannon extends from the red semi-sphere of the destroyer. The drone ships swarm the sphere area, firing laser shots. A great explosion occurs, sending shockwaves all the way through the battlefield as the red semi-sphere explodes from the onslaught of attack, seeming to cripple the entire ship.

The rebel carrier makes another passing at the now limp transport destroyer, firing all of its cannons across the hull of the destroyer as they pass, causing a series of fatal explosions. The carrier turns and heads toward the primary battlefield in the ring around Earth, tailed by several hundred surviving small crafts.

Robert is watching from the command center, his two friends by his side, as the first transport destroyer is eliminated. Sensing the opportunity, he says to Thornhill, "Send out the lunar forces."

Within moments, the lunar contingent, over 500 of the most experienced PEACE pilots are in the fight, hot on the heels of the rebel carrier group. Soon, they are in the action in the Asian sector.

It is now 2:06 PM in New York. Fighting has been going on for nearly forty minutes. 2,500 SF-01s have been lost in the battle, but they appear to be inflicting a heavy toll on the League of Planets's forces. There is, however, a clear difference in losses by sector. The battle is going much better over Asia. Thanks to the presence of the rebel carrier and the lunar forces coming from behind the front line, they have encircled much of the League's forces with tens of thousands of small crafts and two transport destroyers surrounded by SF-01s on their Earth side and resistance ships to their spaceward side. In the last five minutes, they have been destroying at least ten ships for every ship they've lost, and some squadrons are even making bombing runs on the transport destroyers themselves.

The American quadrant is proving to be more difficult. Here, there is no help from the spaceward side of the lines, and the SF-01s and rebel ships are fighting with the force fields to their back unable to break through the enemy line 1,000 miles above. They are losing nearly one ship for every one that they destroy—an unsustainable loss rate given the difference in force size.

Thornhill turns to Robert. "We need to relieve pressure over the U.S."

"Agreed. Send the three closest squadrons inside the force field, and let's see how the military handles it."

Thornhill passes on the order. Robert hits the red button on the black remote, shutting the Jersey City tower down. Seventy-two SF-01s dip inside the force field. As the ensuing drones follow them down, they turn up above the force field line. Robert clicks the remote, turning the tower back on. Seven enemy spacecrafts are destroyed as they ram into the force field on their attempted exit. He then hands the remote to Chris and Mark. "I trust you more than anyone else to operate this judiciously," he says, before leaving the room. That leaves forty-seven enemy ships inside the shield. They begin a descent down toward New York City.

Fighter jets begin taking off from the aircraft carrier patrolling the New York harbor. Jets are also scrambled from nearby bases in New Jersey and Pennsylvania. The U.S. Air Force will be the first national military to interact with the alien craft, and they are motivated to prove their mettle.

About five miles above the Manhattan skyline, fighter jets begin firing upon and tailing the alien crafts. However, they struggle to keep pace, and the cloaking technology on the League's ships makes accurate firing extremely difficult. Only eight crafts are destroyed at the cost of fifteen fighter jets as they near the one mile above sea level mark.

Anti-aircraft missiles are fired from the ground forces and from the Naval ships to slow the advance. About seventy rounds are fired, and there are thirty hits. Meanwhile, the pursuing fighter jets are able to hit another three while suffering six more losses.

Now just 3,000 feet above Manhattan, six alien crafts are left. They begin firing upon the naval forces, critically wounding two cruisers, while the carrier group desperately continues to fire.

Suddenly, from the west, there are laser shots fired, hitting each of the six remaining enemy crafts. There, next to the Jersey City headquarters, Robert's black spherical ship is hovering, having fired some of its emergency ammunition for the journey from Planet Killjorn back in 2014. New York City has been spared, but the cost was steep. It would appear that thirty to fifty enemy crafts will be the most that major cities will be able to handle, far less than hoped to be an effective safety valve.

Robert radios in to Thornhill: "How are we doing, Jake?"

"Asian Front remains strong, but our losses in the Americas are steep, and I'm hesitant to send many more through the force field."

"Okay, can we divert resources from the Asian fleet?"

While Robert is talking to the command center, the second rebel carrier opens its bay doors, releasing several thousand drone crafts, which head full speed toward the American front. They immediately begin firing upon the morass of SF-01 and League plans, levelling a heavy toll as—like in Asia—they try to encircle the League's planes.

Tiberius's ship is directly above the Eastern Seaboard of the United States, so he has a direct view of what the rebel forces are trying to do. Being encircled here would be a catastrophic blow to the war effort.

"Extend the laser cannon," he orders.

"But sir, we have many ships and men down there."

"I know, but we'll take out more of theirs. And the loss ratio will be inside our tolerance band," Tiberius callously responds. He realizes this is a battle of attrition, and the numbers are on his side. He will be ready to strike within two minutes.

In the Jersey City command center, staff rush to Thornhill to show him the extension of the laser cannon. If they do nothing, they will suffer a crippling loss of ships on this front. Even if they win over Asia, the residual strength may not be enough to deal with the remnant League forces. But if they open the force field to escape from the blast, they risk letting in thousands of enemy ships.

He turns to Mark and Chris who have the remote to the force field. "Robert delegated to you. What do you decide?"

Just then a voice booms over the secure communications feed, "Open the force field. We will help protect you."

"Where'd that come from?" Thornhill demands.

"I don't know," someone from the communications team shouts, "but it originated from the South Atlantic, not space."

Thornhill tells Mark and Chris, "The sharks in the South Atlantic are why Robert picked today to fight."

"Then let's open it now," Chris says as Mark nods in agreement. Together, they open the London, Bogota, Sao Paulo,

Jersey City, South Atlantic, and Los Angeles force fields while Thornhill orders a full-scale retreat inside the force field. The SF-01s will then fly into the Asian quadrant to see if they can deliver a knockout blow to the League's forces there.

Suddenly as the force fields open and the retreat begins, an aide yells, "Put the South Atlantic on the screen."

The water about 500 yards past the Arbor Ridge research facility has grown tempestuous, bubbling white hot. The sharks that had been circling the facility have disappeared in the past few minutes. From the raging waters, a ship begins to rise. It has the same navy-blue and submarine-like shape of the carriers that arrived just two hours ago. It is covered in sea moss and coral, betraying an existence on Earth's seabed that must be in excess of fifty if not one hundred years. This ancient ship rumbles northward.

16,000 SF-01s were sent from the force field zones that Mark and Chris opened. Just 8,000 returned alongside 5,500 drone-operated rebel forces. Behind them, 15,000 enemy ships have entered the force field. Mark and Chris closed the force field mere moments before Tiberius was able to fire off a large laser cannon shot, which was absorbed easily by the force field. The 8,000 SF-01s head toward Moscow or Bangkok with each location where half of the fleet will re-enter space to complete the fighting on the eastern front. 3,500 of the rebel fleet stay behind to engage with the earthbound enemy forces while 2,000 follow the SF-01s.

The militaries of the United States, Europe, South America, and Africa have begun to deploy in anticipation of the arrival of thousands of enemy crafts. However about four minutes after the force field closes, the alien craft that had been hiding under Earth's oceans for decades arrives next to Manhattan. News networks around the world cut to live shots of Manhattan. There has been no reporting to the fact that friendly alien forces have arrived, so as far as the audience knows, this is an enemy ship. However, no U.S. military personnel engage.

Rather than aim at the city, the ship begins firing massive laser blasts up into the sky. The sound of the blast can be felt inside the PEACE command center, 150 feet underground in Jersey City. To those in New York City, it must sound and feel as though they are being attacked, not being saved from attack.

The laser blasts, one after another for ten minutes, eradicate the approaching enemy ships, all 16,000 of them, who were being contained by the residual force of 3,500. All of these ships were also destroyed. In effect, this rebel ally sacrificed all of their unmanned ships to help save Earth. This mission complete, the carrier begins its launch skyward to take part in the battle.

Tiberius stands at the conn, dumbfounded by the utter devastation of his earthbound fleet.

"Where did that ship come from? How did our surveillance not detect it for the past two *months?*"

"Sir," the senior officer on the surveillance team sheepishly says, "it appears to have arisen from the sea floor. Our surveillance scans focused on land masses and near shorelines due to your orders."

Tiberius is aghast at this detail. The persistent rumors of the past twenty years must be true. His mind briefly flashes back to the battle for Aquine that led to his promotion to Vice Admiral and made him Frozos's top military advisor—the siege of an aquatic planet. That battle made his career, and he is determined not to let this one unmake him.

He has lost nearly 60 percent of his small crafts now, compared to about 20 percent of the combined Earth-rebel fleet. More troublingly, he has lost three of his transport destroyers, one over the moon and two over the Asian front. He is watching footage of the final minutes before the second Asian transport destroyer was destroyed. The Earth and rebel forces have formed a symbiotic relationship. Earth's ships are faster and more agile while the rebel fleet has larger, more powerful artillery and bombing capacity. As a consequence, the SF-01s lead the runs, back and forth over the transport destroyers, clearing the path for the rebel fleet to drop their loads, gradually breaking through the shield and leaving the ship dead in space, a giant helpless target. Their burning carcasses have lit the night sky over Asia.

"Send the remaining four transport destroyers to the Asian front. That is where this battle will end," Tiberius orders. The rumble of his craft's engine vibrates the conn as his ship begins to move towards the heart of the battle.

The League's forces have been decimated in Asia, because they have been pigeonholed, surrounded by the small crafts on the Earth side and the carrier and rebel forces on the space side. The second rebel carrier has already begun to move and join the first on the space side of the conflict to firm up the front line. Now, Tiberius plans to reset the rules of engagement.

He will be positioning the four transport destroyers to the boundary of the conflict. By surrounding the forces surrounding his fleet, he can entrap them and relieve pressure on his beleaguered pilots. This will hopefully be the final blow and put an end, finally, to this exasperating siege.

Thornhill notices in the images of New York City that Robert's spherical spacecraft is no longer hovering next to the Jersey City tower. "Where did Robert's ship go?" he asks.

There is a scramble on the radar team before someone says, "When Mark and Chris opened the force field to let our fleet back in, one ship left."

Another chimes in, "Our satellites are picking up a black spherical alien ship headed towards Frozos's ship. Frozos's ship is now advancing toward the Asian front."

Desperate, Thornhill radios, "Robert, are you in space? Get back. We need you here more…Robert?!"

After a pause that could be counted in seconds but felt like hours, Robert responds, "You're in good hands. I'm doing what needs to be done. Over and out."

Standing at the helm of his ship, Supreme General Frozos has a direct view of the fighting occurring over Asia. The battlefield stretches for several thousand miles. Small crafts are flying everywhere, bounded by the four remaining transport destroyers and the three rebel carriers, which are engaging each other in conflict. It is now 5:30 PM in New York; the fighting having gone on for over four hours. Each side has been weakened heavily.

Just now, there are twin giant explosions, from a rebel carrier and transport destroyer. They had been parrying laser shots for the past thirty minutes, with shield strength reaching critical depths. Their final volley at each other proves to be their last. With only three remaining functioning transport destroyers, the ability to contain Earth's forces inside the Asian zone would be severely diminished.

Frozos now realizes this battle of attrition will be merely a question of who is the last man standing. He barks to the weapons crew, "Prepare the planetary cannon."

"But sir, Admiral Tiberius is there."

"I am aware."

Magnus is equipped with the most powerful arsenal of laser cannons in the entire League of Planets. With one shot, he can eradicate a planet triple the size of Jupiter. *Magnus* will move into range of the battlefield and eradicate every single ship, in his fleet, Earth's, and the rebel forces. He will leave Earth weakened, but at least he will be taking out the meddlesome resistance fighters in the process.

Frozos sits down in his chair at the conn, waiting for the cannons to charge up.

"Sir, we are getting warnings that someone is in your personal chambers. Shall we send security?" A communications officer shouts to him.

"No. I will go."

Frozos walks out of the conn and into his private office, a Spartan room, more befitting a field general than the leader of the universe's largest empire. When he arrives, he's surprised to see Robert Wilson sitting in his chair.

CHAPTER 28

Magnus
June 13, 2029

Frozos closes the door behind him, warily. Robert has a laser pistol in his hand, pointed right at Frozos, who is unarmed.

"How did you get aboard?"

"Did you forget? I was valedictorian on Killjorn. One of the perks was flying to Earth in an officer-level sphere. I've kept the ship, and so as I approached your ship in it, I was welcomed aboard. Go ahead. Call below and ask if a black spherical ship is in your landing bay." Robert gestures with the pistol to the phone on top of his desk.

Frozos slowly walks over to the desk and picks up the phone, hits a few buttons to call the landing bay directly. "Landing bay?... This is Supreme General Frozos. Have you accepted any ships in the last thirty minutes?... Thank you.... Cease all activity immediately." His calm voice hides his immense alarm. Several individuals will undoubtedly be spending the rest of their lives in prison camps because of this error.

"Well, Robert, or do you prefer Marcus?"

"Robert will do just fine. Why don't you have a seat, Anton?"

Frozos takes a seat across from Robert. "Well, I must congratulate you. You've taken complete control over Earth. I tell you what, why don't I let you be dictator over Earth? You practically already are! If you merge into the League of Planets, I will need a successor someday."

"No deal. You don't need a successor. You need to be wiped away from the face of the universe."

"Then why haven't you pulled the trigger? I've been reading through your files again. You and I are very alike—we've risen from nothing to take control of planets."

"But I didn't rise from nothing. I had a good life. Until you took Nayan, murdered my mother, and enslaved my father and me."

"Is this what it's all about? Some petty personal squabble? Your mother was no one to me, nor the millions of others who have resisted. Don't assign personal meaning or weight where this is none."

"You see, that is where you and I differ. I will never allow myself to look at lives like mere numbers and statistics. I will recognize behind every face, there is love, dreams, and ambitions."

"You think that makes you strong? That makes you weak!" Frozos says, increasingly agitated. "Within moments, I will have the ability to wipe out every ship on the battlefield. And

I will. I am prepared to sacrifice my men to win this planet. And because of that, I will fire my laser cannon and end this conflict once and for all, eliminating every ship, League, Earth, and Rebel alike."

"I'm glad to hear you say that, Supreme General. You see," Robert points to a flashing red light on Frozos's desks. "We've been broadcasting directly to your entire fleet. I wonder if they share your zeal for their martyrdom."

Frozos lunges at Robert. As his hand attempts to grab the laser pistol out of Robert's hand, it goes right through it as if through air.

"I see you forgot that your entire office is equipped with the finest in hologram technology. It really is very life-like," Robert says as he "stands up" from the chair.

"I will not rest until I have control over your puny little planet and have sent you back to that horrible, insignificant mine at Nayan."

"Well, Earth is not *my* planet. I am but one of seven billion residents. You may try again in the future; I have no doubt. But not today. I know you are motivated by hate and revenge, that's why you believed I would have come all this way to kill you. Your hate blinds you. We are motivated by love, love for each other and for our freedom. That's what makes you weak and us strong. Go ahead and call up to the conn. I think you'll find that we are holding our ground, even though your attack is coming while your fleet is in panic and disarray."

Frozos takes the phone and calls up to the conn. "Status alert? Two more transport destroyers destroyed?… Tiberius in retreat?… Fire the laser cannon now!"

Frozos turns to Robert. "No matter. In fifteen seconds, your precious fleet will be gone."

"Funny," Robert says. "You never asked what my ship was carrying, since I wasn't on it."

Robert smiles as Frozos's face drops. There is suddenly a loud explosion that shakes *Magnus*, nearly knocking Frozos to the ground. Robert's sphere was filled to the brim with Earth's most powerful explosives. Combined with a few remaining laser charges, this explosion rocks the loading bay with a fire spreading across much of the ship's lower level. With the loading bay sitting atop the laser cannon, the explosion has taken it offline.

Frozos rushes out of the office and to the conn.

"Sir," the head weapons officer says, "it will take us at least thirty minutes to get the cannon online and our shields are not fully functioning. Tiberius and the remaining 250 crafts are headed this way. There are still thirty-four thousand SF-01s, thirteen thousand rebel ships, and two of their carriers. I cannot guarantee the ship's safety if we do not retreat immediately."

"Very well. Set course for Centurem. Tell Admiral Tiberius I expect his resignation and a statement accepting full responsibility when we arrive."

In the command center, there are cheers all around. The losses have been severe, about 45 percent of pilots who took off to protect the Earth will never return, but they have won the day. Frozos's ship is limping off into the distance, followed by the remnants of his once extraordinary armada. While the room cheers, Thornhill, Mark, and Chris look at each other solemnly. The explosion on Frozos's ship must have something to do with Robert's spacecraft. Their eyes connect—there is no need to say what the three men are thinking. Suddenly, there is another, louder cheer in the room. Standing at the door in the back of the room and walking down the stairs is Robert.

"But how?" Mark asks.

"I'll save the details for later. I just needed to be sure Frozos believed I was on his ship, so I felt it necessary to make PEACE believe it too, just in case he could hear our communications. I'm sorry I didn't have time to tell you."

The four men share hugs, handshakes, and pats on the back.

"Well," Robert says to Mark and Chris, "shouldn't we let our pilots back in?"

"Oh, my goodness, I completely forgot!" Chris says. He and Mark press the button, opening the force field over Asia.

Thornhill turns to the communications staff. "Tell them to buzz and flyover the major cities if they want. They deserve some fun after one hell of an effort."

While the SF-01s re-enter Earth's atmosphere, the rebel ships stay in place. When the force field closes again, they turn and shoot off, deep into space, as silently as when they came.

"Who were they?" Chris asks.

"Friends," Robert responds. "Just friends."

"Well to be honest, I kind of hope we never have to see them again," Chris deadpans.

Over the next ninety minutes, the fleet of surviving SF-01s fly over major cities, signaling to an anxious world that the war has been won. Earth has been saved. Robert communicates the same message to world leaders who began withdrawing military forces from major cities.

At about 8:00 PM, Robert is once again in front of the Arbor Ridge oak tree and behind the cameras.

"Good evening. It is with profound joy that I announce that the battle for Earth is over, and that we have been victorious. In the hours and days to come, I am sure that footage from the battle in space will be released. Let me just say this. We nearly wiped out the entire fleet with just one transport destroyer, a few dozen small crafts, and Frozos's personal ship surviving and retreating.

"This victory came at heavy cost. We lost 30,102 pilots, out of 64,492. Each of these pilots had a face, a name, and people whom they loved. I wish I could list off every name to you. Most of these men and women were civilians two months ago, and they chose to lay down their lives to protect ours. They are true heroes. May we live out our own lives to justify their sacrifice.

"As you saw outside New York City today, we were aided in our struggle against tyranny by another alien force. I do not know who they are, but they provided three carriers and over twenty thousand pilots to the fight. At the conclusion of the battle, they left as unannounced as they came. We owe them deep gratitude. Their presence is proof that the thirst for freedom is truly universal.

"Based on the outcome of this battle, I do believe the state of emergency we have lived under is over. I have communicated this to global political leaders. We of course will be monitoring space for signs Frozos attempts to return, but this is unlikely anytime soon. Barring their return in the next few weeks, which again I do not foresee, we will be thinking about the future of PEACE, if there is any, and presenting those plans in a month or so.

"Thank you. God bless you, and most of all, God bless the men, women, and aliens who put down their lives to protect us today."

CHAPTER 29

Washington, D.C.
July 12, 2029

One month has passed since Frozos's remaining ships limped into space. With each passing day, hope grew that they wouldn't be returning, some hoped forever. In reality, most accept that they are now living in a different world where interaction with alien intelligent life, both hostile and peace-seeking, is inevitable. The force field system that kept Earth safe in its hour of greatest need is unlikely to ever be removed, even if it no longer remains turned on 24/7. But with this battle with the League of Planets now over, life on Earth is returning to normal.

Commercial and government flights to the International Space Station and moon base have resumed. Governments globally have begun to ease policies implemented since April 2, rescinding states of emergency and removing military presences from major cities. On June 18, financial markets reopened, and nonessential work resumed. Cities that had been emptied are filling back up.

The global supply chain that Robert Wilson had built to manufacture the SF-01 for PEACE has been shuttered. Companies that retooled factories and assembly lines reverted to their standard production. For a time, rival businesses had put aside their differences to coordinate activity on a global scale, but the competition that defines the economic system has recommenced. Workers have resumed normal activity, and vacation activities have boomed with hotels globally reporting record occupancies as millions look for the mental breather that a vacation offers.

In the United States, President Larom has worked to restore a degree of normalcy to the political system. Her choice for Vice President had been delayed by the imminent threat posed by Frozos. Three weeks ago, she chose from the slate of three candidates proposed by the opposition party, choosing the senior Senator from Arizona, William Whitestone. The Senate confirmed him four days ago, and he has been sworn in as Vice President. She is now focusing on an agenda of anti-corruption and restoring intelligence agencies to ensure that there can never be another instance of infiltration into the upper echelons of the government as happened with the election of Nick Neverian as President. Next week, Neverian is set to appear in criminal court on charges of election and immigration fraud.

Robert Wilson has continued to oversee the operations of PEACE as its Commander. In the days after the battle, operations continued as normal with the supply chain rebuilding the

SF-01 fleet to fifty thousand units. Over the past two weeks, he has been meeting with government officials around the world to solicit their opinion about the future of PEACE and the force field, which he retains control over. During his meeting with President Larom to solicit her views, she announced that the U.S. Citizenship and Immigration Services had at her behest processed an application to make Robert Wilson officially an American citizen. There in the Oval Office, Robert swore the oath of citizenship. After years of pretending, he now truly is an American citizen.

The more than 30,000 pilots who died to save Earth have been offered ceremonial burials at each nation's military cemetery, an unprecedented honor. Robert was there personally for Anna Small's burial service. Only four of the Arbor Ridge interns who were critical to this project are still alive: Jerome Smith of America, Dmitry Ivanov of Russia, Samantha Sharp of Australia, and Kim Ji-Yoo of South Korea. They each have asked to remain at PEACE if possible.

It is nearly 8:00 PM in Washington, D.C. on Thursday, July 12. Robert is sitting in an office on Capitol Hill, just outside the floor of the House of Representatives. This is the same office he had sat in with Chris Bailey on April 6 before addressing Congress and the American people to outline his vision for PEACE and defeating Frozos. Tonight, he will be outlining his vision for PEACE in the "post-Frozos" world. Would he remain as Commander? Would he resign and return to Arbor Ridge? He has not told anyone of his proposal, working on this speech alone, and so speculation has reached a fever pitch. His personal approval rating is near 90 percent, higher than any government, affording him significant power and political capital. Sitting with Robert are Mark and Chris.

There is a knock on the door, and a man walks in. "It's time, Commander Wilson."

"Thank you." Robert gets out his chair. He puts on the suit jacket hung over the chair. The black suit is paired today with a red-and-blue patterned tie; as always, he has an American flag lapel pin on.

As he gets to the door, Mark puts his hand on Robert's shoulder. "Robert, I don't know what you are going to say tonight. Just know this. You have done something truly remarkable. As you speak tonight, remember why you did it in the first place."

Robert nods knowingly. As they walk out of the office, Mark and Chris are escorted to the balcony to watch the speech while Robert follows the man down the marble hallway. At the door of the House Chamber, he waits as the man shouts, "Commander Robert Wilson."

Ahead of his previous remarks, Robert was met with polite if tepid applause. Tonight, the roar is deafening as Robert is given a hero's welcome. All the Senators and members of the House on the center aisle are reaching for a handshake, and it takes Robert several minutes to reach the front of the room.

Upon reaching the lectern, Robert hands two copies of the speech, which have been sitting atop it, to the Speaker of the House and President Pro Tempore of the Senate. After another two minutes, and Robert's insistence for quiet, the audience takes its seat. Robert is set to begin a speech that will be watched by over one hundred million Americans and billions globally, outlining PEACE's future as well as his own. Would he voluntarily relinquish the tremendous power he had assumed two months ago?

"Mister Speaker, Mister President, and esteemed members of Congress, thank you for inviting me to address you and the American people tonight. It has been two months since I spoke in this chamber last. During that time, I have acquired two new titles. The first being Commander of Protecting Earth against Alien Conquest and Exploitation, PEACE. The second is a title that I will hold dear for the rest of my days, that of citizen of the United States of America."

That line spurs another massive round of applause. As the crowd settles down, Robert looks up to the balcony and makes eye contact with Mark and Chris.

"Tonight, I will discuss what I believe the future holds for PEACE and for myself…"

ABOUT THE AUTHOR

 Scott Ruesterholz lives in New York where he works in financial services. His political commentary has been featured in numerous outlets like Townhall and *The Federalist*. This is his debut novel.